NATIVES OF THE NIGHT

Eric Neher

I dedicate this book to my son, Wyatt Neher.

CHAPTER ONE

A Bully Falls

On the morning that the body was found, I was already late. It wasn't my fault; an early April storm had come through the night before and had taken out the entire town's electricity, including my alarm clock. There was nothing extraordinary about that. It was a part of the excitement; the allure, if you will, of living in Oklahoma. At the tender age of eighteen, I had already witnessed three tornadoes. One had ripped through the small center of our quaint little town of Blanchard, placing the roof of Harold's Meat Market through the front window of the local Subway sandwich shop. Thankfully, no one had died, but it was quite a while before we could eat fresh.

What had finally roused me from my less than honorable teenage dream was the sound of my cell phone blaring Carry On, by Kansas.

"Hey, man." It was Devon.

Devon Craig and I met each other in the first grade when his family had relocated from Oklahoma City. His father had grown tired of the city life and thought that uprooting his less-than-inspired family would somehow bring them closer together. This city has a way of stealing the years. At least, that was what he told them. It wasn't until after Devon and his mother had come home from a trip to the store that they learned the truth. While she was helping Devon into his chair, a loud crack from inside of the house startled his mother into dropping a dozen eggs onto his lap. She rushed in and found

Devon's father lying on their bed, the .45 still held in his hand. It turns out that his father's construction company was on the verge of bankruptcy, and their house was four months behind on the mortgage. But I think there was more. Devon had been born with muscular dystrophy, devastating his body from the waist down. My best friend had been confined to a wheelchair since he was five. For his father, it was an unspoken embarrassment. While other men sat around reliving last night's football game, talking about the exploits of their boys as if they were all prospects for the NFL he stayed within the shadows, an outsider looking in. It was just another reminder of the failures in his life.

Now, I hate football and always have, and much like my love for classic rock, I make no apologies for it. Perhaps this loathing for the sport was passed down by my mother, for which I'm thankful. My passion falls within the dying realm of literature, music, and girls. The latter seems to be a bit allusive, but I'm trying.

Devon, by nature, is normally a calm soul who usually takes an excruciatingly long time to act, be it during a chess game, or deciding on what movie he would like to watch. But this morning it was like something had possessed him. His voice had flown up an octave and his words were barely spaced.

"Did you hear the news?" he said.

"I just woke up," I said.

"Holy Shit," he said. "You're not at school?"

"Nope," I said, sitting up in my bed. From my window, I could see a tapestry of gray filling the sky. A distant roll of thunder split the air. The storm had passed but was still managing to throw out a few last-minute threats.

"Joe Clark's dead."

I clutched the phone and forced my fingers to relax. Let me be clear: Joe Clark was an asshole of the first order. He and his small band of Third Reich wannabes had been making Devon's life a living hell for years, and not just him. The town of Blanchard might be a small spot on the dark side of the moon, but it did have one thing that no other school in the country could claim; it was the number one place for handicapped children. This was because of Ms. Darlene Lighthorse. She had come into the school system at the start of our eighth grade and had quickly molded a once defunct program into something special. She was Chickasaw and had returned to her nation after completing a doctorate from some east coast school. It didn't take long for her to zero in on the small group of terrorists, and soon they were forced to withdraw, their wounds a conglomerate of suspensions and in-school incarceration. But they still managed to cause misery for Devon and the less fortunate. Cutting and replacing locks, tossing books into trash cans. There was, after all, only so much one woman could do when outnumbered. But now it seemed as though the Reich was down a man.

"What happened?"

"They found him at Lion's Park. He was stripped."

"Like raped?" I said. That was one image I didn't need first thing in the morning.

"No," said Devon. "I mean he had no skin."

I took the phone away from my ear, looking at the screen as if maybe the device was malfunctioning. After a moment I lifted it back up and said, "Are you bullshitting me?"

"I swear it's true," he said. "They found him sitting on a bench."

I closed my eyes and could see the gable-covered slab near the center of the park.   Rusted outdoor grills lined each side and at the concrete edge sat a row of picnic tables and benches. What I couldn't quite grasp was Joe Clark perched at one without skin.

"How is that possible?"

"I have no idea," he said. "Check and see what you can find out."

My father was going on his twelfth year as a local constable. He would have been one of the first to arrive at the scene. For a moment I considered logging onto my laptop and breaking into the Blanchard PD. system. It wasn't really breaking in, I had stolen the password years ago, so it was more like capitalizing on a past bad deed. Devon knew I had the password and wanted me to use it, but I decided against it. I was already going to miss first hour, which was History, and was determined not to be late for my second class; Algebra II.

"I'll look into it after school," I said.

"Not without me, you won't," said Devon, his tone was beginning to give me a headache.

"Okay," I said. "We'll look into it after school. Now, I've got to get ready."

I ended the call and rushed myself through all of the necessities required. By the time I pulled up in my sputtering Chevy Corsica (or as I like to call it; the ol' black and white) the bell had begun to ring. I rushed through the front doors, turned left, and flew by my locker without giving it a second glance. I burst through the classroom door, causing Mr. Floyd to drop his marker.

"Slow it down, Daniel," he said as I flopped into the front row.

"Is it true?" Sharon Brown asked.

This was a girl who spent most of her time immersed in celebrity gossip. She was sitting to my left and struggling to keep her voice low as Mr. Floyd began writing on the board.

"I don't know," I said.

"Your dad's a cop," said R.J. Smith, from behind me. "How could you not know?"

I guess they thought I carried a police radio at all times.

"I haven't heard any more than you have," I said.

"Mr. Lee," said Mr. Floyd. I was busted.

"Sorry, sir," I said.

"Is there something you would like to share with the class?"

I gazed up and saw that he was looking at me with an almost hopeful expression. Maybe he had a few questions of his own.

"No sir," I said.

"Then may I continue?"

"Please," I said.

"Thank you." A low rumble of laughter came at me from all sides. The weak one had been caught leaving the others free to gloat; such was high school.

After the bell rang, I made my way to my locker, quickly spinning the combination of my trusty Puroma. I placed my bag in just as Devon rolled around a corner.

"Have you heard anything else?" he said.

"Man, I've barely had time to breathe," I answered.

The hall was filled with students, all of them blabbing away in garbled voices, too meshed together to make any sense. They were no doubt talking about the skinned body of Joe Clark.

"I know I shouldn't be happy about it," said Devon, his eyes following the crowd. "But the guy was like a torture device for me."

He was right, of course.

"Do you think the others will stop now?" I said.

The others included Kyle Bentley; a missing link sort, with lumbering shoulders and greasy black hair that had missed the mullet is out memo. There were also Steve Kemp and Larry Jones. They both wore their hair with Marine Corp. gusto and struggled with anything over three syllables. I know I sound mean, but you must understand the precarious situation that all of us Blanchard Tigers had been placed in. There was a no-bullying policy, but it came with a catch. Or perhaps it was more like a brand. No one wanted to be the kid who ratted. The label guaranteed abuse and ostracism. I had seen it happen many times before, usually instigated by an angry parent who had seen enough. So, much like an oppressed country, we were forced into silence, relishing whatever victories we could find. The death of Joe Clark, as cruel as it sounds, was one such victory.

"I doubt they will stop," said Devon. "Probably restructure."

I hoped that he was wrong. But as it turns out, the worst was yet to come.

CHAPTER TWO

Police Report

After the final bell signaled our release I found Devon in Ms. Lighthorse's classroom. She was sitting at her desk, leaning towards him. They were speaking in hushed voices but I was sure that I heard Joe Clark's name. She looked up with a smile and waved me in. I entered the room and grabbed a chair near her desk. Her dark eyes locked onto mine and I couldn't help but look down at the desk. The woman was beautiful. Her face was like a portrait framed within waves of hair so black that it often looked blue. She had an exotic air emanating like constant light. And yet, she presented herself as one who was unaware of her beauty. Or, if not unaware, could care less.

"I'm sure you've heard the news," she said.

"He has," said Devon, with a grin that kind of creeped me out.

"What do you think happened?" I said, daring a look into her midnight eyes.

'I'm not sure," she said. "But you boys need to be careful."

She then stood and Devon rolled his chair back.

"Are you giving him a ride?" she said, coming around her desk.

"He is," said Devon. "We're going to be stopping at his house to do a little research."

Ms. Lighthorse grabbed her purse out of a cabinet by the door.

"Good," she said, and then looked over at Devon. "I'll see you first thing tomorrow."

* * *

****

My room was like a set to an apocalypse movie. Dirty clothes were strewn across the floor, sheets lay partially off of the mattress and my computer desk was in the process of buckling under the weight of scratched CDs and irrelevant idols of fancy. I could say that since my mother's accident I have found it hard to focus on such trivial things such as cleaning, but at some point even I would have to admit that it was a lie. The accident had happened eight years before, while she was driving home from work on the I-40 freeway out of Oklahoma City. It wasn't from anything so sinister as a drunk driver, or some idiot trucker who had fallen asleep. No, she had been texting with my father and didn't realize that the traffic in front of her had come to a stop.

For the first year after the wreck, she remained in a coma and it was only after the word terminate had been thrown around did she open her eyes with total recall. But after a couple of weeks, her memory began to fade. And two months later, she fell back into the darkness, her mind retreating into some hidden away space that neither my father nor I could reach. She had been placed in Cimarron Care Center; a place that tended to the hopeless. At first, my father and I visited her daily. I'm sure that he still clung to the hope that she might again step out of the mist, like in that movie with Robin Williams and Robert De Niro. It didn't happen and soon our visits went from once a day to once a week until finally settling on once a month. As I stated before, this had little to do with the condition of my room: I'm just lazy.

"Jesus," said Devon. "When's the maid coming back?"

"I wish I knew," I said, kicking a path through the unlaundered disaster.

Devon was finally able to make his way over to where my monitor stood with one sock draped over the screen. I quickly tossed it away and turned on the computer. Within seconds it lit up and I clicked on the Blanchard Police Department's site.

"After all this time, your dad still doesn't know you have the password?"

"As far as I know he doesn't," I said. "Maybe he doesn't care."

"Well let's see what we can find out," said Devon.

I typed in COPS4U and watched as the welcome page peeled away, revealing a much less friendly screen. Categories marked name, case number, date, and time filled the monitor. I didn't have the case number, and I wasn't sure of the time, but I did know the date, and I certainly knew the name. That would be enough. Within moments a one-page report popped up.

"Holy shit," said Devon, leaning forward. "Here it is." He then took out his cell phone and took a picture.

"If you get caught with that it's my ass," I said.

"I won't get caught," he said, placing the phone into his shirt pocket. I considered pressing the issue. Maybe my father knew I could get on the site and maybe he didn't, but I was sure that he would explode if he found out the PD's records were being passed around, especially in this digital age.

"Why do you want it?" I said.

"Just a reminder."

Yes, a trophy for the oppressed. I decided to let it go.

I turned back to the screen. The report was a grotesque testament of brutality and confusion. The details were straight out of an eighties slasher film. Joe Clark had indeed been skinned and what was even more bizarre was that the skin had been taken. The park where he was found sat in a valley surrounded by oak trees, pines, and cottonwoods. The local library stood a block away to the east but was hidden by the surrounding foliage. The police station was less than a mile away and yet during the growth of spring, the park might as well have been an island.

Joe had been propped up on a bench, his head tilted back as if gazing at the sky. He had been found by a group of junior-high kids cutting through the park on their way to school. They thought that it was a joke at first (one of them had approached the body for a selfie) and that was when they noticed the swarming flies and they called 911.

My father was the first on the scene, and it was his report that Devon and I were now reading. The page included a picture, which I enhanced.

"He looks like that dummy in Johnson's biology class," said Devon, absently.

I had seen enough and quickly scrolled back to the report and continued to read. The identity of the victim was still officially inconclusive, as there was nothing but eye color left to compare. It was the pile of clothes that they had found a few feet away that gave them the possible name. A ripped t-shirt with a picture of Manson lay across a weathered pair of jeans. There was a wallet with a driver's license and a phone in the pocket. Both belonged to Joe Clark.

The report went on to describe how my father had gone to Joe's house and learned that he hadn't come home the night before. I sat back and let out a shuddering sigh. Joe Clark was a nasty guy. I had seen him strike my friend on the back of the head as he walked past him in the hall at school on numerous occasions, and had even had a couple of altercations with him myself while trying to protect Devon. But to see that picture of him sitting there, stripped of both skin and dignity, simmered my hatred into an odd sort of sorrow. Should it have? Even now I'm not sure. And it wasn't only him that had my heart-wrenching. My father had begun his day by confronting a horror that went beyond words and was then forced to put that horror into words.

"He wasn't a nice person," said Devon. I looked over at him. His face held a remorseless expression; frigid and merciless. I could see something else swimming in his eyes. Was it anger? Could he be mad at me because of my compassion towards the kid that had made his life a living hell? He was skinned! I wanted to say, but instead reached over and exited out of the site.

"Would you rather he was still around giving me shit?" he said.

"Devon, he was murdered."

"And I think it would have only been a matter of time until he killed someone," said   Devon, spinning his wheelchair around and making his way towards the door. "Whoever did this did the world a favor."

He might have been right, but then again, I guess we would never know.

"Take me home," he said.

CHAPTER THREE

Breakdown At Breakfast

I pulled into Devon's driveway, removed myself from the stuttering vehicle, and lifted his folded chair out of my trunk. Normally we kidded around with each other during the process but not today. Devon just sat there with his twisted legs hanging out of the passenger side until I was able to adjust the chair and roll it over. He then braked the wheels and slid in.

"You want me to pick you up in the morning?" I said, trying to crack this wall of ice that had come between us.

"I have a ride," he answered, and without another word, he maneuvered to the ramp that led to the porch. I watched him for a moment, trying to think of something to say. In the end, I waited until he was opening the front door then turned back to my car. I can count on one hand how many fights me and my best friend had been in over the years. Superficial disputes that we later laughed about. But this was different. It was as if an ominous split had appeared, like a treacherous fork in the road. Joe's death was something that Devon thought should be celebrated; the fall of an enemy. I think this is what startled me the most. A murderer was loose in our small town and Devon didn't seem to care. Why would that be? Because they killed Devon's number one enemy? What if I was next? Or Ms. Lighthorse?

*****

That night I lay in my bed listening to the southern breeze brushing against my window. My father had yet to return, although he did call me. His voice sounded haggard and concerned. I promised to stay home and lock the doors. It was still early, barely past eight, but I had no desire to bubble my brain with television or anything else for that matter. I gazed up at my textured ceiling and watched the slow crawling shadows come to life. At some point, I must have dozed off, because I vaguely remember a shape filling my doorway. It hovered for only a moment and then turned away.

The next morning I wandered into the dining area and was greeted by my father.

He was in uniform, his shirt ironed and his pants pressed. But his face struck out at me with a contrast that caused me to pause. Wrinkles seemed to have formed where just two days before there had been none. Small discolored bags hung below each eye and his head sagged. He looked up as I entered the room, a smile forming on his face.

"I made you some eggs."

I admit this now because to withhold it would be unfair to both him and me. I understand that seeing the image of Joe the day before terrified me, but it wasn't until I walked into that room and saw my father sitting at our small table did I realize just how stricken with fear I really was. He seemed to have sensed this, or perhaps he was struggling with it himself. By the time his arms were around me, my tears were flowing. A sob escaped and I was surprised: It had not come from me. We led each other back to the table, each of us easing ourselves onto a chair. We sat there, both trying to regain our composure. Finally, as if synchronized, we were able to look at each other.

"Well," he said, wiping his face with a napkin. "Let's keep that between us men."

I burst out laughing. Within seconds he followed and it was wonderful to hear. It also produced a twinge of guilt.

"I'm sorry dad,' I said.

He jolted his head back in shock.

"For what?"

Yes, indeed. For what? The woman he loved had been gone for years, and he was still alone. Had this been by choice? Was it for me?

Shit, there was so much I needed to know about this man and all it took was one brutal murder for my eyes to be opened. But this wasn't the time to stack his already full plate.

So I said, "That you had to see that."

He reached out his hand, patting mine.

"It's part of the job," he said. "Though not exactly what I signed up for."

"Do you have any idea who might have done it?"

"I'm not even sure it was a person," he said.

"You think it might have been an animal?" This possibility hadn't occurred to me. What the hell could be roaming around Blanchard that could strip off a kid's skin?

"I don't know," he said, standing up. "I've got to get to the station." He made it to the doorway before stopping.

"Danny, I don't want you running around after school. You go there and come straight home."

Normally I might have tried to argue, but his fear-stricken expression expunged any debate. Plus, the image of Joe on that bench still lingered like a slow healing wound.

"I'll come straight home," I said.

"And lock the door behind you." With that, he left. I tried to eat but found that my stomach was closed. I trashed the remaining food and left for school, making sure to lock the door behind me.

CHAPTER FOUR

Back At School

The questions kept coming. Only this time they came with a more demanding tone. I had eighteen hours, plenty of time to grill my dad about what the police knew. My answers were met with angered disbelief and contempt. But I wasn't lying; I knew nothing more than I did the day before.

"You're full of shit," said R.J. Smith, as we funneled our way through the hall in between classes. "You mean to tell me your dad didn't say anything?"

"It just happened yesterday, RJ," I said.

"Right," he said, his eyes narrowing.

I patted him on the back and said, "I promise, you'll be the first to know."

From then on it got worse. Rumors were thrown out like burning chairs, each one more bizarre than the last. One such fabricated gem consisted of alien abduction. They had taken Joe and, after spending a few hours with him and realizing their mistake, had decided to put him back. But not before removing his skin. This theory had been formulated by Jim Eberly. And when asked why they would choose to keep his skin all he could say was; maybe for a curtain. Another jewel of deception had to do with Joe's father. It was well known that he had done a three-year stay in McAllister for his love of methamphetamine. Supposedly, he had been clean since, but everyone knows, according to Sharon Brown, that once you are a junkie you're always a junkie. This theory was by far the most sinister, as it dealt with filicide and insurance.

Then there were the less creative conclusions; a bear, a wild pack of dogs, and, of course, a serial killer. I went along with these conversations for no other reason than it took the heat off of me, feigning interest as our school spiraled into a QAnon outpost. Through all of this I kept my eye out for Devon, but he seemed to be hiding away.

By the time the lunch bell sounded my head was spinning. The rumors continued to flood through the school like a runaway aqueduct. I entered the lunchroom with an opened book in my hand, hoping it would be enough to ensure that I was left alone. I glanced over at the table designated for Ms. Lighthorse and her class. She was sitting with three of her students but there was no sign of Devon. Ms. Lighthorse waved me over.

"Hi, Daniel," she said, and I felt my face begin to warm. I wouldn't say that I had a crush on this woman, but I wouldn't say that I didn't, either.

"Hello," I said. "Have you seen Devon?"

"He went home after first hour," she said. "He wasn't feeling good."

His first hour was a free class which he spent helping her with the younger kids from elementary. She spent the first three hours of the day with them and then they were sent back to their school to fend for themselves the best that they could.,

"How did he get home?"

"I took him," she said. That bothered me. Usually, if Devon needed a ride home, or anywhere, for that matter, he called me. She then scooted out a chair.

"Sit with us, Daniel." For a moment I considered refusing, I hadn't even grabbed a tray yet. She seemed to notice this and raised her hand like she was summoning the wait staff. A girl from a couple of grades under me rushed over.

"Do you want a burger or pizza?" said Ms. Lighthorse.

I stood there for a moment dumbfounded.

"Uh..burger?" I said. The girl scampered off.

"Sit down," said Ms. Lighthorse, and so I did.

The table was off in a corner, secluded. Sitting at one end with his neck encased in a metal brace, was Mike Henley. I had known him for almost as long as I had known Devon. At one point he was the captain of the football team and a hell of a quarterback. He was an only child and had been the pride of his family as well as the shining star of our small community. It had been said that his mother, who was running the Oklahoma Medical Center, had already set the wheels in motion for her son to attend Yale. His father was a partner at a law firm in Oklahoma City and had donated quite handsomely to the Blanchard sports fund. The fact that many of us were forced to share books because of budget cuts seemed to matter little to the Henley family; there was no winning in reading.

Four years ago his father had a heart attack while driving back from a football game in Tuttle. Their Escort had left the highway, rolling twice leaving Mike partially paralyzed and unable to complete a sentence with the exception of the occasional On Three, that he would sometimes shout at the most inopportune times. The entire town showed up at his father's memorial dinner, immortalizing the fallen hero as if he had saved them all from some eternal sin. To the side, sitting alone in his new wheelchair was Mike, his back in a cast, his body broken. I remember the look in his eyes: saturated and angry. From that point on his mother slipped into the shadows, quitting her job and retreating to their large home near the outskirts of town. It wasn't long after that Mike became the newest member of Ms. Lighthorse's special class. So much for Yale.

Then there was Linda Wells. She sat gnarled and incapacitated, her body twisted with disease, unable to lift her head, unable to wipe away the steady flow of drool that streamed from her chapped lips. Her fire-red hair was tied to the side and hung down to her warped shoulder. Linda would be lucky to see thirty. But would she consider that lucky? Would I? There had only been one break in the existence of Linda Wells, and that was when Ms. Lighthorse adopted her after both of her parents had fled from the hospital after learning the truth about their baby girl. I hate to admit this, but I kind of understand. Her very presence created anxiety within me and an undeniable urge to look elsewhere while she was being hand-fed and tended to like an oversized infant. The truth is that the silent tragedy that was Linda's life, and the abandonment that came with it, paralleled much too closely with that of my mother's and it terrified me.

Ms. Lighthorse sat there looking at me as I pondered these revelations.

"How has your day been going?" she said, finally.

"It's been kind of hectic," I said.

"I'm sure it has," she said. "I bet you're catching it from all sides."

"What do you mean?"

"With your father being a policeman and Joe Clark's death, I'm sure you're being hounded."

I couldn't argue with her there.

"It was terrible, what happened to Joe," she continued, leaning in closer. "A shame that they don't have any suspects."

Her statement was just that, a statement. I knew then that Devon had shared the information from my computer with her. Ms. Lighthorse placed her hand over mine.

"Don't worry," she said. "I won't say anything."

The girl returned with my lunch and Ms. Lighthorse removed her hand as the girl placed the tray in front of me.

"Thank you, Lydia," said Ms. Lighthorse. Lydia gave her a dreamy smile and then wandered back into the lunch crowd. A sudden gurgle escaped from Linda's mouth. Ms. Lighthorse grabbed a napkin off of the table.

"There you go, sweetheart," she said, wiping the stream from Linda's chin.

I glanced over at the poor girl, with her head locked in place, and saw that her emerald eyes were directed at me.

"She likes you," said Ms. Lighthorse.

Linda let out a grunt.

"I like her, too," I said, forcing a smile. It was then that the warning bell rang, signaling the end of the lunch hour.

"That went by quick," said Ms. Lighthorse. "You barely had time to touch your food."

"It's okay," I said, grabbing the tray and standing up. "I wasn't very hungry."

"Daniel," she said. "Devon's going through a rough spot, right now. It might be better to give him a little space until he works his way through it."

I looked at her for a moment. Devon and I had been friends for as long as I could remember and I was very aware of his struggles. My buddy had often talked about his longing to be normal over the years. And yet, this fork in the road was different and Ms. Lighthorse seemed to know it. Had he confided in her? Or did she sense it?

"I'll do my best," I said. It was all that I could think to say.

CHAPTER FIVE

Dinner And A Nightmare

After school, I considered driving by Devon's house but decided against it. Maybe Ms. Lighthorse was right. Perhaps he needed some time to sort out whatever was bothering him. So instead, I did as I promised, and went straight home. I stumbled through my Algebra homework and caught up on the chapter that I had missed in History. I was just opening the fridge when my cell phone burst out with Father and Son by Cat Stevens.

"Hey, dad," I said.

"Danny boy," he said, and I could hear the effort in his voice. "Have you eaten yet?"

"I was just looking in the box."

"Well hold off," he said. "We're going out. What do you feel like? Italian? Burgers?"

An image of Linda gazing at me filled my mind's eye, causing a shiver.

"Anything but burgers," I said.

"Italian it is," he said. "I'll be there in thirty."

It was more like an hour, but I didn't care. He came in the door still in uniform, a smile chiseled across his face.

"Are you ready?"

"Don't you want to change first?" I said.

"No time. I made reservations at Mario's."

"That's a little pricey, isn't it?"

"What the hell," he said. "It's only money."

The meal was, dare I say, impeccable. The evening was quickly becoming something that I would cherish for the rest of my life, at least this part. We discussed things from the past that had been, up until then, tossed away like an old favorite song. There was even a moment when we were able to talk about my mother without falling off into despair. I think that was important, if not necessary. We needed to be able to talk about her; to relive our memories and share the joy that this woman had given us. And it was only fair.   My mother deserved to be more than just a subject to ignore. I think my father realized it, as well. There is no point in denying that, for both of us, seeing her wasting away in that bed brought a sorrow that we found easier and easier to avoid as time went by. Indeed, it had been almost six weeks since we had last stepped through the doors of the care center. We sealed the end of the meal with a promise to visit her soon and then my father grabbed the bill, took a look, and let out a distressed whistle.

"Should we run for it?" I said.

"I think my badge and name tag might give me away."

*****

We began our forty-minute drive home just as the sun was losing its battle with the western horizon. For a couple of hours, we had managed to put the problems of Blanchard on a shelf, and had temporarily been able to pretend that there hadn't been a murder in the park. I had even managed to forget that my best friend might hate me. We drove on in silence, both of us realizing that our reprieve was coming to an end and that each mile that went by was like a door slowly being shut. It would be a long time before it opened.

*****

That night I lay in my bed, my brain racing, switching from one topic to the next. None staying long enough for any kind of resolution. My father had gone back to the station, his mind was no doubt refocused on the death of Joe. I eventually gave up on sleep and grabbed my phone off of the nightstand, plugging in the earbuds.

19

Within moments I was humming along with The Sound Of Silence. I closed my eyes and let the eerie lyrics take me away, reigning in my thoughts until there was only Simon and Garfunkel's harmonious cry for an awakening.

It must have sent me into a slumber because when I opened my eyes, the music had stopped. I looked towards my bedroom door. The kitchen light was on, casting a faint halo down the hall, creating a silhouette within the frame. I thought at first that it was my father checking on me. But it was all wrong, the shadow was slumped over, barely clearing the halfway point of the frame.

My lamp stood just three feet away but I couldn't move. Chilled air washed over me, and yet I could feel the tickling trickle of sweat on my brow. The shadow began to come forward, thrusting itself towards me with the grinding sound of neglected metal.

"Devon?" I managed to say.

The answer came in the form of a guttural moan. A small sliver of moonlight bridged from my window to the carpeted floor. The intruder broke into this barrier and stopped. Silver rays fell upon a tilted head, stuck as if molded in place. The mouth was open and from the chasm came a thin line of glistening fluid, but it was the eyes that drew my attention. They glared at me with a light of their own.

"Linda," I said. "How did you get in here?"

She continued to cast her fire-like gaze at me, grunting.

"Linda," I said, trying to sit up.

I looked past her and saw that the door was beginning to close.

"What's going on...," I began, but the words were lost in my throat. Linda's eyes continued to burn into me, but her head had shifted. I watched in horror as her face began to remold itself, gone were the paralytic lines that streaked down each cheek. Her jaw lifted, her lips then curled into a smile. Linda placed her hand on the armrest of her chair and pushed herself up. The low light showed a winter fleece blanket wrapping her body. The blanket slowly slid down as she rose, revealing first her bare shoulders and then her bare breasts.

"Don't be afraid," she said, in a voice as clear as the whispering of a winter thaw. "I didn't do it."

But I was afraid. Terrified, in fact. Linda took a step closer, her face capturing the moonlight and within that face was something more. Her mouth had become wider. Crueler. And her hands were like those of a creature built to kill. She came forward, hovering over me as I lay there whimpering.

"I want you," she said, reaching out for me and it was then that I was finally able to scream.

*****

My eyes shot open and I flew from the bed, knocking my little toe against the nightstand. My father rushed in wearing nothing more than a t-shirt and boxers.

"Danny," he said. "Are you alright?"

I stood there with my toe throbbing and my heart pounding.

"Did you have a bad dream?"

To say the least. I reached up and wiped the river of sweat off of my face.

"Do you want to talk about it?"

"I'm fine dad," I said, sitting back down on the mattress. "It was just a nightmare. I don't even remember what it was about."

He reached down and ruffed up my hair and said, "Those are the best kind. I'm down the hall if you need me."

He then turned and left the room, pausing briefly to give me one last look. Of course, I had lied about not being able to remember. The image of Linda Wells standing, her naked body like that of a beast, would be hard to shake.

She likes you, Ms. Lighthorse had said, as if they talked about me all the time. I lay back and curled myself into the fetal position. There was too much shit going on. Joe's murder, the pressure that my father was under, and Devon. Not to mention the oncoming visit with my mother. It was no wonder that my dream took a southern turn. But it seemed so real. I forced myself to close my eyes and placed my thoughts in a stranglehold.   Finally, I was able to fall into a dreamless slumber.

CHAPTER SIX

Goats

By lunch hour the next day, we had our answer about the new regime change. Kyle Bentley lumbered into the room with Steve Kemp and Larry Jones flanking him like a Praetorian Guard. They muscled their way to the front of the line, grabbed their trays, and then lumbered over to a table filled with terrified freshmen who began to excuse themselves as they approached. I sat back in a corner with R.J., pretending to ignore them.

"Look," said Kyle, nodding his head towards Ms. Lighthorse's empty table, his greasy bangs pushed to the side of his prehistoric face. "The retards ain't here."

"Maybe they're out test-driving chairs," said Larry.

This produced a disgusting laugh from all three of them.

"Those guys really are assholes," said RJ. "How have they not been expelled yet?"

"What are you looking at?" Kyle was now glaring at us.

"I was just trying to figure that out," said RJ.

RJ could be quite the ass himself sometimes, but he did have courage and he mostly meant well. There had been a time when he, I, and Devon were very close, but RJ had drifted off into the world of having a girlfriend, which remained cold and eclipsed for me. Still, we were friends, and as it seemed now, closer friends than me and Devon.

"You better watch your mouth, RJ," said Kyle.

RJ blew him a kiss just as Principal Rancord walked into the room. That was the end of it.

I glanced over at Ms. Lighthorses' empty table. Most likely they were on a field trip. Ms. Lighthorse did enjoy taking them away from here as much as possible and with guys like Kyle around, who could blame her? Most of their trips consisted of visiting Native American sites, including the Chickasaw museum and the petting zoo. There were weekend camping trips to the Wichita Mountains, and she always made sure that they made the annual Chickasaw Festival. Devon had told me a lot about these excursions and had said that by far his favorite place was the mountains. This was where Ms. Lighthorse was from originally, and she still had plenty of family that lived around the foothills just outside of Lawton. The place was shrouded in Native American tradition, he had told me, and it was there that they were free to do as they wanted. I had asked him what he meant by that but he wouldn't say. He only smiled and gave me a wink. I figured that Devon was probably sneaking a bottle. Well, who am I to judge?

The rest of the day was like swimming in syrup, the minutes dragging like an overweight slug. Finally, the last bell rang and it was as if the entire school was given an adrenaline shot. The metal exterior doors were flung open and the race for freedom was on.

*****

I arrived home to find that my father was already there. I walked in and he was pacing the living room, his cellphone clutched to his ear. I slunk over to the couch and sat down, placing my bag on the coffee table.

"How many?" he said. I strained to hear the answer but could only get panicked garble.

"I'll be right there," he said, ending the call. He looked over at me, trying to contain the astonishment in his eyes.

"How was school?" he said, reaching for his keys.

"It was fine. What's going on dad?"

"Something's killed a couple of Barry Kemp's goats," he said. "I'm heading out there now."

Barry Kemp was the father of the much-hated Steve Kemp. The

man was a well-known turd, an attribute that he proudly passed on to his son. My father grabbed his keys and made his way to the door, pausing with his hand on the knob.

"How much homework do you have?"

"Just a half chapter of history I need to read," I said.

"Why don't you come with me," he said. "Bring your book and you can read it in the car while I'm dealing with this."

We made our way south on highway sixty-two. My father had both hands on the wheel, his knuckles bone-white, his face contorted with concern. In my entire life he had only asked me to go on a call with him twice: Once to get a cat out of Mrs. Lyle's tree and the other to a car accident, and that was only because I was already with him. For a moment I considered breaking the silence but decided against it. I sat there gazing at the oaks and pines blurring by.

"Something's going on," he said, suddenly. "And I have no idea what it is."

"Does this have anything to do with what happened to Joe?" I said.

"I don't know yet," he said.

Barry Kemp owned a forty-acre ranch just ten miles south of Blanchard. His land sat off County Road 1247 and was bordered by strands of rusted barbed wire. The entrance to his quarter-mile-long drive was guarded by a metal pipe gate which was flanked by a pair of Confederate flags. The gate was open. We pulled into the gravel driveway and saw to our right the family clustered together. Scattered throughout the field were bloody mounds. My father stopped the car and shut off the motor.

"That looks like more than a couple," he said. "You might as well come with me."

Together we made our way to the barbed wire fence. We helped each other through and then walked the short distance over to where Barry stood with his wife and Steve.

A goat lay just a few feet from where they were standing, its skinless body covered with flies. Lifeless eyes gazed up from the swaying grass with terror still locked in place. An image of Joe appeared before me like a magic trick, and I gasped.

"Are you alright?" my father said. "Do you need to go back to the car?"

"I'm fine," I said.

"Took you long enough," said Barry. The man was almost as wide as he was short. His face was the color of an over-ripened tomato, his hair cut in the same military-style as his son's. The Dickey's overalls he was wearing contained the stains of hard work. But it was his hardened eyes that revealed the truth: This man, who looked at fear like it was a foreign language, was scared.

"I got here as soon as I could," said my dad. "Are they all like this?"

Barry pointed to the goat closest to him and said, "If you mean skinned, then yes."

"How many are there?"

"Seven," said Barry. "What the hell could have done this?"

My father broke away and walked over to the goat. He knelt by the edge of the crimson-colored blades of grass. A moment later he stood and walked over to another corpse. I could feel Steve's glare. I gazed over at him and smiled, then turned and followed my dad. My father was pulling out his phone, focusing it on a particularly saturated area. I could see what had drawn his attention. A divot, very faint, pressed in the ground. The outline was blurred, hardly visible at all, and could probably mean anything. My father snapped a quick picture and then moved on to the next goat. We spent over an hour walking the field but all that we could find were skinless remains and broken blades of grass. Whatever it was, had come in the night and had murdered with soundless precision. It had been able to remove the skins from seven goats without alarming Barry or his family. We returned to where Barry was now standing with clenched hands.

"You didn't notice this morning?" said my dad.

"We left here before six, the sun wasn't up yet; June had a doctor's appointment in the city."

"What about you?" said my dad, looking at Steve.

"He went with us," said Barry. "We dropped him off at the doughnut shop across the street from the school."

"What about the dogs?"

"Those worthless bastards never made a sound," said Barry. "I should shoot them for this."

"If you do, I'll be back," my father said.

And he meant it. If there was one thing that he hated, it was people who abused animals.

"I'm just saying," said Barry. "They didn't do anything."

"Maybe they didn't know it was happening," I said, more to myself. "Maybe they didn't hear it."

"Seven goats slaughtered without making a sound?" said Barry. "How is that even possible?"

Yes. That was the question. Much like the enigma of Joe Clark.

"And what about their hides?" said Barry.

"They appear to be gone," said my father.

"No shit, Sherlock," said Barry. "Who around here collects hides? Maybe you should check on that Muslim freak show that moved in over at the Oaks."

Mr. Kemp was referring to the Hernandez family. They had immigrated from Guatemala and were some of the nicest people I had ever met, not to mention Catholic. Not that it mattered. To a guy like Barry Kemp, it wasn't so much the ideology of the person as the shade.

"That's enough of that," my dad snapped. "And I had better not hear about any threats or harassment."

"I don't know what you're talking about," said Barry. "I just want whoever did this caught."

"I'm looking into it," my dad said, nudging me back towards the car. "You call me if you hear or see anything."

"Yeah, whatever," said Barry. "Like it will do any good."

My father ignored the comment and together we braved our way back through the rusted barbed wire.

*****

"That guy's an asshole," I said, as we headed north on sixty-two.

"Language, Danny," said my father. "But you're right. He's an asshole. Always has been."

I gazed out of my window. The sun was beginning to cast the world in a deepening orange. Shadows fell across the highway, threatening the closure of another day. The time change was only a couple of weeks away, which meant long days and less time for skinning. What a strange thought to have. And yet, those goats had found their way into my nerves. The lifeless eyes, stricken with terror and shock, would no doubt be visiting me in the nights to come. Was it any wonder that I yearned for longer days? I wouldn't mention this to my father. I didn't want him to think that he had made a mistake by bringing me.

I snuck a look at him. His face was gaunt in the fading light; riddled with lines like a weather-beaten map. I could see that he was lost in his own horrific revelations. The similarities between what had happened to Joe and the goats were obvious. They had all been removed from their outer shell and the skins had been taken. I'm no detective, but the little amount of blood that surrounded the bodies told me that they were most likely dead before the skinning began. Which was for the best. Plus, it would explain why there hadn't been a sound. But how were they killed? Surely Joe Clark's autopsy had been completed which meant my father must know. Would he tell me? Of that, I wasn't sure, but I decided to try anyway.

"Dad, what do you think happened to them?

He leaned forward, his fingers twisting on the wheel. The headlights of an oncoming car gave his expression an almost ghost-like quality.

"I'm not sure," he said.

"How did they die?"

"I think their hearts stopped."

I looked at him for a moment in disbelief.

"All of them?"

"I know you're wondering what happened to Joe," he said. "And that's what the coroner told me. His heart seemed to have stopped as if it had shorted out."

"What would cause that?"

"She couldn't say for sure," said my father. "Possibly electricity, although there were no signs of a shock."

"Could it have been fear?" I said.

My father glanced at me and I could see that the idea had occurred to him, as well.

"I don't know," he said.

"What about that print?" I said. "What do you think that was?"

"Son, I don't have any answers right now," he said, tapping on the brake pedal, bringing the speed of the cruiser down as we crossed into Blanchard's city limits.

"But I think I'm going to have to make a call."

I decided not to pursue it any further.

CHAPTER SEVEN

Altercation At Lunch

The next morning I turned the corner to find Devon waiting for me by my locker. He was slumped over in his chair, his face hollow and ashen. Even his (Got Milk?) retro t-shirt looked exhausted.

"Hey man," I said. He looked up at me as I approached and I could see dark rings surrounding his eyes. "What's wrong with you?"

"I caught a twenty-four-hour bug," he said. "I didn't get much sleep."

"It looks like you were cast in Dawn of the Dead," I said.

"Thanks for the compliment," he said.

"Are you seriously going to class today?"

"I look worse than I feel," he said. "I just wanted to say I was sorry."

"Don't worry about it. I understand."

He managed a grateful look that warmed my heart. The bell rang out, causing me to jump into action. I flipped open my locker door and threw my bag in.

"Let's get together at lunch," I said.

"Count on it," said Devon, rolling his way down the hall. I grabbed my History book and made a mad dash towards the classroom, again receiving a verbal reprimand for bursting through a door.

The talk in school that day had elevated into pure fantasy. The aliens were here, as anyone with half a brain could see, and were decorating their lavish space ships with the hides of goats. How else could you explain it? But what about Joe? There was an easy answer to that; the aliens had discovered that human skin was simply not conducive to their decor. Perhaps it clashed with the furniture. RJ managed to wait until the third hour before grilling me about what I had learned from my father. I again revealed that I knew nothing. I thought he might hit me.

By the time lunch hour came, I was more than ready. I walked into the brightly lit room and saw Devon parked at Ms. Lighthorse's table. She was reaching over and wiping Linda's chin. I grabbed a tray of spaghetti slop and joined them.

"Hey Dan," said Ms. Lighthorse. "It's good to see you."

"I looked for you guys yesterday," I said plopping down into a cold plastic chair.

"She took us to the Wichita's," said Devon. "Kind of a nature trip."

"That sounds cool," I said. "How come you never invite me?"

Linda let out a grunt. I glanced over at her and saw that her eyes were glued to me. Her body might be devastated but the intelligence that reached out from that green gaze was mesmerizing. Suddenly, the nightmare hit me like a truck and I quickly looked away.

"Hey," said Devon. "Are you okay?"

"I'm fine," I said, grabbing a napkin off of the table and wiping my forehead.

"Maybe we should take you," said Ms. Lighthorse. She then leaned over and patted Linda on the hand. "Would you like that, sweetheart?"

Linda let out a cheerful clack.

"Then it's settled," said Ms. Lighthorse. "A week from this Friday. Will that work for you, Dan?"

I was at a loss. I had wanted to go, especially since Devon had seemed so secretive about what they did there. But now, I wasn't sure. And I wasn't even sure why I wasn't sure. My father and I had finally settled on making a trip to see my mother that weekend but that wasn't why I had reservations.

"I'll have to check with my dad," I said.

"I can talk to him if you would like," said Ms. Lighthorse.

"You don't need to do that," I said.

A metal clang echoed off of the cinder-block wall and I turned to see Kyle Bentley. He had slapped the tray out of a ninth grader's hand, who was now frozen like a cornered rabbit facing a bear. Ms. Lighthorse sprung to her feet and rushed over.

"Mr. Bently, you are going to clean that up," she said.

"Or what? You'll cast an Indian curse on me?"

Ms. Lighthorse stood before him like a tree facing a hurricane. She then smiled and lowered her voice.

"You're already cursed. You're just too stupid to know it."

Kyle's face traversed through the color chart, going from gray to red and then ending on purple. He clenched his fist and for a moment I was sure that he was going to hit her. I started to rise from my chair but was pulled back by Devon.

"If he does it he'll be gone forever," he hissed.

His grip was like an iron clamp on my forearm. I looked over at him, the grin contorting his face was sinister. It was as if he wanted Kyle to strike her. Kyle was an idiot, but he was a very large idiot; six feet two and well over two hundred pounds. He could kill her.

"Let me go," I said.

Devon held on for a moment longer and it was then that Principal Rancord entered the room.

"What's going on here?" he bellowed.

"Kyle knocked over a tray and was just about to clean it up," said Ms. Lighthorse.

Mr. Rancord was an imposing man, having served two deployments during the gulf war, and although he was a couple of inches shorter than Kyle, he could shut him up with a glance.

"Is this true, Mr. Bently?"

Kyle lowered his eyes and said, "I was just going to get the mop."

"Well then step to it," said Mr. Rancord.

Kyle managed to shoot one last venomous look at Ms. Lighthorse before making his way to the janitor's closet. I watched stunned, as Ms. Lighthorse walked back to our table.

"Why didn't you tell Mr. Rancord what happened?" I said.

She slid back into her chair, grabbed a napkin, and proceeded to wipe Linda's chin.

"There's no need," she said. "Guy's like Kyle always come to a bad end. I see no reason to hurry him along the path."

I couldn't help but think about Joe. He had certainly come to a bad end. But not saying anything about Kyle seemed like giving him a pass. What good would that possibly do? Plus, the look he had shot at Ms. Lighthorse radiated pure hate. She had embarrassed him in front of his troll-like friends. In front of the entire high school, for that matter. And that was something that he couldn't allow, not if he wanted to maintain his reputation. It would have to be reconciled. Did she not know that? Ms. Lighthorse was unconcerned. By the time the bell signaled the end of lunch, it seemed as though she had forgotten about the incident.

"Remember," she said. "A week from Friday. We'll leave after school."

I gave her a nod and made sure to stay out of Kyle's reach, who had returned with a mop and bucket.

"You're dead," he hissed, as I passed by. "All of you."

CHAPTER EIGHT

Reservations

We managed to get through the rest of the day without injury or assault. I helped Devon into my retired police car and pulled out of the parking lot without any sign of Kyle. It was good to have my friend back. I'm not going to say that it was like it was before, there was still a chilly wall standing between us, but it was beginning to thaw. Devon sat there on the passenger side, his hand gripping the safety bar. I glanced over and was relieved to see that he was looking a lot better than he had earlier in the day. My arm had developed a bruise from where he had grabbed me at lunch. It hadn't occurred to me then because of the adrenaline, but I don't think I could have broken his grip if I wanted to.

I lifted my arm, presenting him with the evidence of the injury, and said, "Have you been working out?"

Devon looked at the purplish hand-print, let out a low whistle and said, "I'm sorry. It must be from all those years of pushing myself around."

This was true. He had been offered a motorized wheelchair on several occasions but had refused.

"Remind me not to arm wrestle you," I said.

"You can always run for it," he countered.

We both burst out in laughter and I could feel the chill between us warming even more. I turned onto Main and steered us toward the president's streets. Almost every small town has them and they're usually the older neighborhood. This was where my friend had ended up after his father's death. They had lost the big house. Luckily, the loan had been in his father's name, which meant at least his mother's credit had been saved from devastation. They had been devastated enough.

I can say one thing for Blanchard, and I like to think that it goes for most little towns, although I'm not sure; but after the tragedy, this community came together. The house that they now lived in was offered by Mr. Lyle, who owned The Sun Rise Doughnut Shop. Not only did he sell them the house on Jefferson at a very low price, but he had also provided Devon's mother with one of her two jobs. The other job was as an evening cashier at the Tri-City Walmart. She didn't have to work so hard, she made enough for them to get by with the doughnut shop, but Devon had informed me that she was trying to save, trying to make up for the lost time and vanished funds.

"She wants me to go to a good college," he said. "Somewhere far from here."

Maybe that was true. And maybe she was also trying to keep herself occupied. Nightmares, after all, can only catch you when you are asleep.

We pulled into his driveway and I put the car into Park. We both sat there for a moment looking at the peeling white paint on the lap siding.

"We've got to get this place fixed up," he said.

"I don't mind helping," I said.

"We want it to look better, not worse," he said.

"Man, you're an asshole," I said.

"And you're the guy that hangs out with me."

I flipped him the bird and then opened my door.

I brought his chair over and waited as he slid in. Together, we made our way up the ramp. Devon unlocked the front door, and I held it open as he rolled over the threshold.

"Do you want a coke?" he said.

"Does a bear shit in the woods?"

"Think about that a lot, do you?" he said, maneuvering his way into the kitchen.

He returned with two cans on his lap. He threw me one and

then reached for the remote.

"SpongeBob?" he said.

This was a guilty pleasure and one that we swore never to mention to anyone. We sat there watching the yellow guy shrill with each gyration as he moved through his underwater day with a moronic pink starfish. But in our defense, it did offer a harmless way for us to dumb down.

"Do you want to go with us?" he said, suddenly.

"Go where?"

"To the mountains?" said Devon.

I had honestly forgotten all about it. It was an invitation into their world, one that I wasn't sure I wanted to accept. I know that sounds strange and maybe even a bit conceited. But for some reason, it did seem like trespassing. And just what would we be doing in the Wichita's? Sitting around a campfire telling ghost stories? And for two days? Then there was Linda. That piercing look from earlier, that hopeful gleam in her eye. What did she think I would do? Fall madly in love? It was a horrible spin and for a moment I hated myself. She could not help her feelings any more than anyone else.

"I'll have to see," I said.

"If you don't want to go, just say so," said Devon.

"It's not that. I just don't know if my dad will let me. We're supposed to visit my mother Sunday."

"Okay," said Devon and there was a flatness in his voice.

"Do you want me to come with you?"

"Only if you want to," said Devon, taking a long drink out of his can.

"Don't think I can handle it in the woods for a couple of days?" I said.

"I didn't say that. There's just not a lot to do. You'll probably get bored"

"You're by the river, right?"

"It's a half-mile away," said Devon. "I caught a seven-pound large-mouth the last time we were there."

"Yeah you did," I said.

"No, really."

"Where's the proof?" I asked.

"If I knew I was going to have to answer to The Spanish Inquisition I would have taken a picture. But if you don't believe me you can ask Ms. Lighthorse; she was there."

"I believe you," I said.

"Of course, I was more interested in the girls from college who were rafting."

"Really," I said, doubtfully. "Did you manage to get a picture of that?"

"Whatever, Danny. You can go or not. It doesn't mean shit to me."

We said little after that. His statement, either by design or unintentional kind of hurt. We finished our dose of dumbing down in silence. Once the cartoon was over I stood up to leave. Devon was flipping through the channels, his face stoic.

"Do you want me to pick you up in the morning?" I said, taking the keys out of my pocket.

"I have a ride," he said.

Devon's mother reported to the doughnut shop at four in the morning and his list of friends was short.

"With who?"

"Ms. Lighthorse," he said. "I sometimes go in with her to help set up the classroom."

For a moment I considered asking him if there might be more than just a teacher-student relationship going on, but decided against it. It would have been a joke done in bad taste. So instead I opted for, "Cool. I'll see you tomorrow."

CHAPTER NINE

Nightmares And Attacks

I pulled onto Main Street still trying to determine why I felt hesitant about going to the Wichita's. It couldn't just be because of Linda, could it? The indifference that Devon had projected was confusing. His claim that I would be bored conflicted with his tales of large-mouth bass and bikini college girls. It was as if he was using some kind of reverse psychology, trying to spark excitement within me while pretending not to care either way.

Unless he really didn't want me to go.

Why would that be?

These chaotic thoughts were brought to a sudden halt as I turned onto our street and saw the car parked behind my father's city cruiser. I pulled up to the curb and made my way to the front door. I walked in to find my father sitting at our dining table with a manila folder opened in front of him. Across from him sat a very pretty dark-skinned woman wearing a power suit, the shirt opened at the collar. Her chocolate eyes were magnified by a pair of wire-framed glasses.

"Danny," said my father. "This is Field Agent Joyce Green from the Oklahoma Bureau of Investigation."

"Hi Danny," she said, giving me a wave.

"Danny was with me when I saw the goats."

"Really?" she said, pushing the frame of her glasses back up the bridge of her nose. "Not the nicest scene."

"Agent Green is a pathologist and she has had experience with animal attacks."

"Is that what got Joe?" I said.

"Right now we're not sure," he said.

He then looked around the room and said, "Sorry about bringing home my work but the water line ruptured at the station and we're still waiting on Hank."

Hank Miller held the city plumbing contracts and as the lowest bidder felt obliged to take his time.

"No problem," I said. "Did you show her the track we found?"

"I looked at that," said Agent Green. "And I have to say that after twenty years I have finally been stumped."

I talked with them for another couple of minutes and then decided to move on. There was little I could offer so I wandered into my room, closing the door behind me. It was all so crazy, like something out of a Koontz novel. First Joe and then those goats, all of them dead from a seizing heart. How was that possible?

I did my best to forget about it and dug into my homework. I had a chapter review in History and ten problems to solve in mind-altering Algebra. All and all, it took me a little over an hour to complete. By then the agent had left. I went back into the dining room to find my dad still perched over the folder.

"Any luck?" I said.

"She's as baffled as I am," he said.

"She's pretty," I said.

"She's a Field Agent," he said.

"I know, I know. It's just my teenage hormones talking."

"I remember those days," my father said, with a shudder.

I sat down at the table, glancing at the photograph of the goat, and released a shudder of my own. I couldn't help but stare at the poor thing's eyes. Had Joe's eyes been like that? Frozen in terror? I didn't want to know. My father, sensing my anxiety, stacked the pictures and closed the folder, dropping it to the side of the table.

"That's enough of that," he said. "Are you hungry?"

I wasn't, not really. But I figured that his offer was more than just an invitation to a meal. He didn't want to be alone right now any more than I did.

"A little," I said.

We spent the next couple of hours scarfing our microwaved pizza rolls and watching pointless sitcoms and nauseating reality shows. But if you were to ask me what programs we watched, I couldn't tell you. The recent events were flashing in my mind as if on a loop, dominated by the gaze of the goat.

My father struggles to sit through thirty-minutes of television, even if it's a good show, but on this night he sat in his recliner glued to the set, and yet, he seemed distant. I'm sure that he, much like myself, was stuck in his own loop. How could he not be? He was the one responsible for solving these bizarre crimes.

"Do you think that agent will figure out what made that track?" I said, causing him to shake his head as if coming out of a dream.

"She took a copy of the photo with her," he said. "Maybe they'll find something."

"Dad, what do you think is happening?"

"I don't know, Danny. But whatever it is, it scares the shit out of me."

*****

I lay in my bed that night with a quarter moon shining through my window. The only sound was the occasional gust of wind impacting my wall. Another storm was due Saturday. Nothing too severe; just forty-mile per hour gusts and some hail. Nothing to write home about. I forced myself to focus on tomorrow's history quiz. Twenty-five questions about early colonial American life. No worries there. But my mind kept tripping itself up. Tomorrow was Friday: Exactly one week until the trip. I hadn't spoken to my father about it. Perhaps it was because this unexplainable apprehension wouldn't leave. I lay in the silver-shrouded room trying to figure out why.

Would you like that, sweetheart? Ms. Lighthorse had asked Linda.

Her excited answer had left me feeling uneasy and guilty. Why should I care if an incapacitated girl wanted to spend time with me? Was it because I was worried about what other people might say? Was I that shallow? It's not like she could even hug me if she wanted to. I rolled onto my back, placing the crook of my elbow over my eyes, and forced my brain into Park. Eventually, I must have dropped off, because I found myself staring at my reflection in the moonlit water of the Washita River.

Clouds of vapor rose from the murky calm with shimmering beams of moonlight filtering through. From behind me came the sound of bleating goats, distant and fading. I tried to turn away from the stagnation but couldn't move. A sudden ripple from the river acted like a pause button being deactivated, and everything was thrown into motion. I took a step back as murky water near the middle began to bubble, moving its way towards where I stood at the bank. Darkness began to rise from its depth, emerging slowly. Within moments a shadow-laden head cracked the surface, the face hidden by long moss-infested hair. It was a woman, and my blood turned cold as she continued to lift from the surface, her body the color of dirty light, coming closer, and it was then that I saw she was dressed in a tattered bikini. I tried to back away but found that my feet had sunk, the mud now gripping my ankles like manacles. The woman continued to lumber forward to where I was trapped.

"Please don't," I tried to say, but what came out was the bleating sound that I had heard before.

She stopped, her feet still submerged in the current. A pale hand rose from her side, brushing back the hair draped over her face. My mother stood before me, her expression stricken with terror. Electric eyes locked onto mine, seizing me like poison. For a moment I had the sensation of not being able to breathe. My lungs were burning, my heart drumming. Her jaw lowered as if mechanical, and out from her open mouth fell the gutted corpse of a large-mouth bass.

"SAVE ME!" she screamed in a voice that rattled my ears.

The river then exploded from behind her, shooting a wave up into the sky. It crested into a shimmering edge and began to slice its way to where my mother stood helpless. I tried to pull out of the grasping bank but was unable to move. The blade continued its downward motion, whipping the air as it fell. Again I pushed, feeling the stress of stretched tendons and pinched muscles. Finally, the mud gave way. The blade was close, allowing me just enough time to dive for her. I crashed into her body just as the wave crashed into mine. I felt the razor's edge cut into my back, felt myself being severed as I was pushed into the black water. My mother was holding onto me, the horrified look now replaced with a loving smile. Together we began to sink, the distilled silver light fading like a parting friend until there was only darkness.

"Take me to it," she whispered.

*****

I shot up in my bed with the dawn breaking through my window. The clock on my nightstand read 6:28, a full hour before my alarm was set to go off. I reached over and disabled it. There would be no going back to sleep after that dream.

The kitchen floor was like ice. I walked over to the fridge and pulled out the gallon of milk. I made myself a bowl of cereal and sat down at the table. My arm was like a robot; the spoon going up and down with timed precision. There was no taste, no smell.   Perhaps I was in shock. It seemed so real. The water, the scream that my mother had let loose. But it was only a dream. And maybe the reason for the dream was nothing more than my guilt at finally being able to go through a day without thinking about her. Was I wrong for that? I wasn't sure.

I finished my breakfast, put the bowl in the sink, and waited another thirty minutes before preparing for school. I arrived forty minutes early to a mostly vacant parking lot. It seemed as though even the teachers were biding their time. I went through the main doors and stopped at my locker, throwing my bag in. With my history book in hand, I continued to study hall, which was nothing more than the retired gymnasium. Four rows of tables had been laid out, each with a set of chairs. Wire-covered globes hung from steel rafters casting an eerie, archaic glow. The room looked to be empty which, considering the time, was no surprise. I took a seat at the table closest to the door and opened up my history book.

After the convention 177- I began to read, but was then interrupted by the sound of something crashing, which was then followed by an ear shattering scream of "ON THREE. ON THREE."

I flew out of my seat, glancing at the other side of the room, and felt my heart leap into my throat. The back fire door had been flung open. A few feet away from it an empty wheelchair lay on its side and behind it was Mike screaming at the top of his lungs, rocking back and forth in his own chair like a mad man waiting for the lever to be thrown. A pained cry fled across the room, and it was then that I saw Linda lying on the floor, her body twisted and twitching.

"What's going on?" said a voice behind me. I turned to find Ms. Lighthorse and Devon filling the double doorway.

"I don't know," I said. "I think she fell down."

"Like hell, she did," said Devon, pointing at the open back door. Ms. Lighthorse rushed around him, and I followed. We reached Linda and I helped Ms. Lighhorse gently lift the girl from the cold linoleum. Her forehead was scratched and bleeding, but there didn't seem to be any other damage. Mike had settled down, going from a maniacal seizure to silent observation. For a moment I considered asking him about what he had seen, but his answer of 'on three' wouldn't have provided much help.

"That fucking asshole, Kyle!" said Devon, his hands were throttling the wheels of his chair. "Wait until I get a hold of him. I'll kill him!"

"You'll do nothing of the sort," said Ms. Lighthorse.

I have to admit that I agreed with her. For one thing, how Devon thought he could beat a brainless giant like Kyle Bently was beyond me. Secondly, how did he know that it was him? Would he do it? I have no doubt. But it was awfully early in the morning for a kid who was tardy every other day.

"Let me get you to the restroom, sweetheart, and we'll get you cleaned up."

Ms. Lighthorse then pushed the poor girl out of study hall, with Mike following close behind.

"Kyle's going down," said Devon, watching as they cleared the room..

"Man, I get it, but let Ms. Lighthorse handle it."

"Then what?" Devon said, his eyes like fire. "He gets suspended for a few days and then comes back as if nothing happened. He'll probably be a hero to his NAZI friends."

"I know it's not fair," I said.

"No, it's not fair," said Devon, tears welling in his eyes. "None of this shit is fair. And what about Linda? The girl has gone through enough shit. Look at the hell she's in every day, and now, just to add to it, she has to come to school knowing that the son of a bitch who did this to her is telling everyone. Can you imagine? No, this asshole is going to pay."

I listened to my friend's rage, and he was right. But there was one problem; Devon was in a wheelchair and Kyle would kill him. Didn't he know that? I let him go on for another minute or so until he finally became quiet.

"Devon," I said. "You know you can't beat him, right?"

He gave me a look that darkened the room.

"We'll see about that," he said, and rolled out of the retired gym. I watched him wheel through the doorway and then glanced down at the clock on my phone; 7:58. By now the yard would be filling up. I could only hope that Kyle Bently wasn't there.

CHAPTER TEN

Fight

Devon split the crowd like Moses, each kid stopping mid-sentence as he passed by. There was an energy emanating from him, a dangerous charge that demanded attention. I followed behind much like a squire trailing an errant knight.

"What's going on?"

It was RJ, his arm firmly planted around Katrina Caldwell's waist.

"Come on," I said. RJ must have heard the desperation in my voice because he released his true love and fell in behind and I was glad that he did, for it had now become very clear where Devon was leading me. Leaning against the chain-link fence at the end of the schoolyard was Kyle Bently, and with him stood his Praetorian Guard. A cloud of blue smoke hung in the air around them. For them, the school's no smoking policy was just one of the many laws meant to be broken. Kyle looked over at Devon plundering through the terrain and let out a cough-infected laugh.

"What do you want, retard?" he said, dropping his cigarette butt to the ground.

"You think you can do that to her and get away with it?" said Devon, his face the color of the setting sun.

"I don't know what you're talking about, wheels," said Kyle, and I noticed Steve Kemp and Larry Jones beginning to spread out in attack formation.

"Fuck you," said Devon, bringing his chair to a stop a few feet away from Kyle.

"You better just roll on back to that short bus class of yours before you get hurt," said Kyle, taking a step forward.

"Come on Devon," I said. "It's not worth it."

"Stay out of it, Dan. This asshole's going to pay."

"Listen to your boyfriend," said Steve Kemp. "You're already screwed from the waist down. Do you want to be a vegetable?"

By then the entire school was crowding around us, jockeying for position. It would only be a matter of time before one of the teachers saw the crowd and made their way over.

"You think I'm going to fight you?" said Kyle. "Not a chance."

"You're every bit the chickenshit that I knew you were," said Devon.

Kyle looked over at me and I could see disbelief in his eyes. I could also see the confusion. Did he really not know what Devon was talking about?

"Get your boyfriend out of here," he said.

It was then that Devon lunged from his chair, landing belly down on the ground. I watched in shock as he began dragging himself towards Kyle, his fingers digging into the dirt like grappling hooks.

"Get away from me, freak," said Kyle, but Devon refused.

Kyle let loose a panicked kick, aimed for my friend's face. Devon, with the speed of a viper, struck out with his left hand, grabbing the incoming boot and lifted Kyle off of the ground. Kyle's legs flew up, his feet pointing skyward, and hit the dirt. Devon slithered onto his chest, his hands locking around the startled thug's throat, and began to squeeze.

"Get him off me!" Kyle managed to wheeze.

Devon then let go of the terrified kid's neck with his right hand, curled it into a fist, and brought it down. The blow struck Kyle cleanly on the chin, producing a spine-tingling clash of teeth meeting teeth. I watched mesmerized as a couple of molars went flying. Heavy crimson drained from his mouth, pooling in the grass. I then said something to my crippled friend that, up until then, would have been impossible to conceive.

"Devon, stop before you kill him."

He looked up at me, his mouth fixed in a snarl that made me step back. His eyes were glowing like a pair of Silver Dollars struck by moonlight. All around me was quiet; forty-two kids stunned into silence. Even the Praetorian Guard stood motionless, their chins hanging southward, their eyes like ping pong balls.

"Hey!" said a voice from behind. "What's going on here?"

I turned to see Mr. Rancord thrusting through the crowd and just like that, the spell was lifted. Kids began to melt away like snow in spring. Devon rolled off of Kyle's limp body with a cruel smile plastered across his face. I took a couple of steps back but was stopped by Mr. Rancord.

"What happened here?" he asked me.

I told him the truth. There was no reason to lie.

Mr. Rancord waved his hand and said, "Get to class."

I gave Devon one last look and complied. The event quickly took the place of Joe and the aliens. The freakish way that Devon had brought down Kyle was front-page news.

"It was like David and Goliath," said R.J.."You know they took Kyle away in an ambulance?"

I felt my heart sink. This was not good news. Devon could have killed him and maybe he had. A phantom pain surged through my arm from where he had held me back the day Ms. Lighthorse had confronted Kyle. I spent the rest of the morning dodging questions about my friend, counting the minutes until the lunch bell rang.

*****

When at last it did, I walked into the room. Ms. Lighthorse was sitting at the table with Linda and Mike, but Devon wasn't there. I passed on the midday slop and walked over to the table. Ms. Lighthorse pointed to a chair.

"Why didn't you stop him?" she said, as I sat down.

"I tried," I said.

"You should have come to me," she said.

"There wasn't time," I said. "I thought he was going to be killed."

A gurgling hoot brought my attention to Linda. The scratch had scabbed over but there was a slight bump.

"I went to protect him," I said, drawing my eyes back to Ms. Lighthorse.

"Devon doesn't need protection," she said, wiping Linda's chin. "At least not that kind."

After witnessing the fight, I was forced to agree.

"It's his temper that will hold him back," she continued, as if to herself. "It worries me."

"Where is he?" I said.

"He has been sent home," said Ms. Lighthorse. "Mandatory suspension."

Those were the rules at Blanchard High School, home of the Fighting Tigers. If you were involved in an altercation, whether handicapped or not, you were subject to discipline. But who could blame them? Devon had handled the six-foot-tall neanderthal like some kind of old toy. And that look in his eyes. What would the principal have done if he had seen that? Probably a lot more than a three-day suspension. He might have had him committed. Kyle seemed genuinely surprised by Devon's anger, but if he had not assaulted Linda, then who had? Turns out, the answer was much more horrific than any of us could have ever guessed.

Ms. Lighthorse again wiped Linda's chin and then turned to me.

"Have you talked to your father about coming with us?" she said.

"I'm not sure that I can," I said, and Linda let out a low chirp.

Ms. Lighthorse drilled her dark eyes into mine, and I felt my pulse quicken.

"Do you want to come with us, Dan?"

I could have lied, or at least tried to, but I somehow knew that anything but the truth would be recognized for what it was; a feeble attempt to get out of going. Plus, I didn't think it was fair to Ms. Lighthorse.

"I don't know," I said, glancing down at the table.

"It's okay if you don't," she said with a sigh. "I just thought it might help Devon having you there."

"What do you mean?" I said.

"Devon, if you haven't noticed, has become increasingly angry."

Oh, I had noticed, alright.

"And I just thought that maybe if you were to go and spend time with him he might confide in you."

"But I thought you wanted me to give him space."

"I may have been wrong about that," she said. "He's a lot different than the others."

"What does that mean?" I said.

"My other students," she said. "I just think he needs a friend."

"I'm with him almost every day," I said.

She gave me a warm smile and said, "I know you are, Dan. It's just that it's different when you're in the Wichita's and far from here. Don't you ever find this place stressful?"

Joe Clark sitting skinned in the park popped into my head.

"Of course I do."

"There's something to be said for getting away to the mountains," she continued. "I guess what I'm saying is that your friend could use your help."

What could I say? Ms. Lighthorse had painted me into a corner using three coats of guilt. I glanced over at Linda and saw her emerald eyes focused on me.

"I'll talk to my dad," I said.

"That would be great," said Ms. Lighthorse, her smile radiating. "I know Devon will be happy to hear it."

I wasn't too sure about that, but I intended to find out.

CHAPTER ELEVEN

A Trip Confirmed

I left school homework free. It was a rarity that I tried to savor as much as possible. The air was becoming warmer. The flowers were blooming, casting their blanket of invisible pollen throughout the blue sky. Trees metamorphosed from skeletal relics into green works of art. Signs decorated the streets, promoting spring fairs and baseball. And yet a bitter cloud was hanging over Blanchard. The park sat empty. Children had lost their summer rights. The freedom of the changing season had been withdrawn. Murder, I guess, has a way of doing that.

Devon was sitting on his couch completely undressed except for boxer shorts, his misshapen legs curling off of the edge. I had knocked on the door and he had invited me in, but his voice sounded raspy and exhausted. I looked at his face and stifled a gasp. His skin was the color of impending rain, his eyes held the tired look of someone pushing eighty.

"Well," he said, trying to smile. "He won't do that again."

"Yeah," I said. "You got him. He's in the hospital."

"Good," he snapped. "And you didn't think I could do it."

"In all fairness," I said. "I'd like to have seen the Vegas odds."

This caused him to break out into a laugh which quickly turned into a wet cough. His face was bright red and his hands were shaking. After the fit subsided, he lay back his head, drawing in a deep breath.

"Does your mom know?" I said.

"I don't know," he said.

He then pointed at a piece of paper sitting on the coffee table. "But she will. I have to have her sign this before I can go back."

It was a confirmation letter proving that she had been made aware of the fight.

"Will she be pissed?" I said.

"Does it matter? Even if she is, I only see her a couple of hours a day."

"Will she still let you go to the Wichita's next week?"

"She won't give a shit," he said. "What about you, are you going with us?"

"I don't know," I said. "I still have to ask my dad."

"Then ask him," he said.

"Do you really want me to go?"

"Why wouldn't I?"

"I don't know," I said. "I mean, you never talked about it before."

"Yeah, I guess I felt like I wasn't supposed to."

"Why?" I said. "Are you making moonshine or something?"

"I wish," he said. "Did Ms. Lighthorse say something to you?"

"She's worried about you," I said. "She thinks you need to work on your temper."

"I'm sure she does," he said. "She's probably having second thoughts."

"About what?"

"Forget it," he said, with a sigh. "Listen, Dan; I'm exhausted."

I'm not the fastest cowboy on the draw, but I knew an invitation to exit when I heard one.

"No problem, Rocky," I said, standing up. "Call me if you need anything."

I then patted him on the shoulder and made my way to the door.

"Hey, Dan," he said. "You should go with us."

I gave him a salute and said, "I'll talk to my dad."

*****

My homework-free evening was spent alone. My father was still on duty and, of course, Devon wanted to be left secluded in his cave. I watched some Netflix and then perused around on my laptop. All and all, it was very boring. I considered calling Holly Stevens. We shared Algebra class and she would often help me if I found myself facing an equation wall. But beyond that, we rarely talked. Still, she did smile at me when passing in the hall and I had sat with her at lunch on a couple of occasions. Was that a signal? When it came to reading such things my lamp was perpetually broken. I guess what I need is for a girl to walk right up to me and say: I like you, dummy. Maybe then I'd get it.

My father came through the door at around eight. He went over to the fridge and took out a beer then made his way into the living room. By then I was kicked back on the sofa watching The Great Race.

"Tough day?" I said.

"Not so much tough, as uneventful," he said, plopping down in the recliner.

"That's good, isn't it?"

My father took a sip and placed the bottle on his side table.

"Not really," he said. "That agent got back with me about the print."

"What was it?" I said, sitting up.

"They ran every comparative test that they could think of and found nothing."

"How is that possible?" I said.

"It wasn't a very good print," he said.

"Did she have any guesses?" I said.

"Just that it was big," my father said.

We sat in silence for a moment, him sipping at his beer and me gazing at the television, watching but not seeing. There had only been three murders in the last ten years, all of them easily solved. But this was different and even I could feel it. The killing of Joe went beyond the normal passion crimes that we had become accustomed to, like when Mr. Gerard found out that his wife was secretly planning to leave him for some guy out of the city and planned on taking their jointly owned Easy Stop convenience store with her. Mr. Gerard had been served the divorce papers at nine-thirty on a Tuesday morning and by ten was walking into the store with a double barrel twelve gauge shotgun in his hand. The part that always got me was the fact that he blew their dog in half first. I had gone into their store on many occasions and had seen him playing with that Cockerel Spaniel like it was his kid. I guess when the levee breaks it doesn't matter who you are. Mr. Gerard's next shot made his wife unrecognizable.

By ten-forty-five, Mr. Gerard was sitting in the back of my father's cruiser. He had never even considered leaving town. He was found on his front porch with a cigar in hand when they arrived to arrest him. And it made sense: Mr. Gerard was pissed so he killed his wife. But with Joe and the goats, there was nothing but unanswered questions. Where was the motive? Joe, I could kind of understand, but what had a herd of goats ever done to anyone?

I couldn't help but think that it had to be an animal. The way the bodies had been left seemed inhuman. And yet, where were the killing wounds, or the skins, for that matter?

"How was school?" my father said, bringing me out of the fog.

"It was fine. No homework."

"I heard there was some trouble with Devon." You could tell a secret in this town and then go to the store and by the time you got there have someone recite it back.

"Yeah, he got into a fight with Kyle Bently."

My father raised an eyebrow and took a long drink from his beer. I'm sure he was trying to imagine how that was even possible. He placed the beer down and leaned forward.

"Are you saying that Kyle jumped him?"

"Just the opposite, actually," I said.

"Why would Devon do that?"

I told him about what had happened to Linda and how Devin was sure that it had been Kyle.

"And he just jumped out of his chair and crawled at him?"

"That's exactly what he did. Now Kyle's in the hospital."

My father leaned back with a sigh, his brow furrowed.

"I'll check on him tomorrow," he said. 'You know his parents can press charges if they want. Hell, they can go after the school."

That thought hadn't occurred to me. An image of my friend being dragged to the back of my father's car gave me a chill.

"Well, Kyle did try to kick him first," I said.

"That's good to know and it might change everything if they decide to do something. Can anyone else verify that?"

"RJ was standing right next to me," I said.

"Okay, then we'll see what happens."

He then finished the rest of the beer and began to stand.

"Dad, Ms. Lighthorse invited me to go to the Wichita's next weekend."

My father settled back into his chair.

"Do you want to?" he said.

"I'm not sure," I said. "We were supposed to go see mom."

"That can wait until you get back," he said. "Why wouldn't you want to go?"

"I don't know. Maybe it's because of what's going on here. Ms. Lighthorse is adamant that I go. She thinks it will help Devon get through his problems."

"What kind of problems has he been having?"

My father's concern for Devon was genuine. He had been on the scene when Devon's father had killed himself. Since then he had taken a special interest in my friend.

"I'm not sure. He does seem angrier than he used to be."

"Well, honestly Danny, that's understandable."

"What do you mean?"

"Think about it. You both are seniors now. Your prom is in two weeks and soon you'll be off to college."

"Yeah," I said. "But what's any of that have to do with Devon?"

"Who are you taking to the prom?" he said.

It was a disarming question and one that I hadn't thought of, at least not lately. As I mentioned before, I'm a little awkward when it comes to the opposite sex.

"I don't know yet," I said, finally.

"But you will be going, right?"

"I guess so," I said. "I'll probably ask Holly Stevens, if she isn't already going with someone else."

"And do you plan on dancing?"

"Well, it is the prom," I said.

"And what about Devon?" he said. "Is he going?"

"I haven't talked to him about it. What are you getting at?"

"Only that Devon will not be dancing," he said.

It was then that I understood and it made me feel terrible. Here I was prescribing self sorrow for my lack of communication skills, feeling sorry for myself as I walked to my car, drove my car, and then walked into whatever place I had driven my car to. Taking for granted the everyday activities that my friend could never be a part of. I realized that we rarely talked about girls, and if we did it was to only comment on how they looked. But as far as a relationship went, like that of RJs, it was never discussed. Perhaps that was a part of why he was pissed at me. Had I been using his disability as a crutch? As a comfort blanket for my shortcomings? Devon probably realized this and harbored a festering resentment. How could he not? His good friend was tossing away gifts that he would never have.

"What should I do?" I said.

"I think you should go," he said. "I think he needs you now more than ever."

"Then the Wichita Mountains it is," I said.

"Good," my father said, lifting himself off of the chair. "I'm going to jump in the shower and go to bed. I've got an early day tomorrow."

I watched him leave the room silently thankful for his wisdom. He had pointed out something that should have been obvious and it made me feel like shit. The prom, the last month of high school; was all an end to an era, one that should be celebrated with dancing and romance. But for my friend, it only meant another page in his life that must be left out. He would be forced to watch as the other kids swayed to whatever music was blaring in the gym. Forced to sit as the punch flowed and the girls giggled. Yes, I could certainly see why he would be angry.

For a moment, I considered calling to let him know that I was going, but by now, his mother would be home from work and no doubt chewing him a new one for the fight at school. Instead, I sent him a short text. Within minutes it was returned: Great was all it said.

CHAPTER TWELVE

Packing And A Video

The rest of the weekend was as uneventful as Friday night. There was one exciting detail; I did call Holly, and to my surprise, she agreed to go with me to the prom. I was hoping for a little more emotion in her voice, but it sounded like a business transaction:

"Hey, Holly. It's Dan...Dan Lee."

"Yes, Dan."

"If you're not already going with someone, I'd like to know if you'd be my date for the prom."

"That would be fine, Dan. What time will you pick me up?"

"Uh...seven?"

"That will be fine."

And that was that. The prom wasn't for another two weeks but at least I wasn't going alone. That was good for another round of guilt as I thought of Devon. There was no one for him to call, except for Linda, maybe. This ending of high school was creating changes that I wasn't prepared for. For a moment I wished that I could turn back time, back to when our only concerns were completing homework and staying out of Joe Clark's reach. But Joe wasn't coming back, nor were the good old days.

*****

The week snailed by. Most of my time was filled with practice finals and chapter reviews. Very dull. Kyle was released from the hospital Wednesday, his jaw still wired shut. His parents did indeed threaten a lawsuit but thanks to video taken from someone's phone, which showed Kyle clearly trying to kick the handicapped kid in the face, they decided against it. Devon returned to school Thursday morning as somewhat of a hero. His mother had given him an ear full but that was the extent of it.

"King Leonidas returns," said RJ, as Devon rolled into the lunchroom.

The indistinguishable chatter fell off to an eerie silence, like some kind of presence had been sensed. I had been sitting by RJ and his one true love waiting anxiously. Devon shot us a smile, grabbed a tray, and made his way over to where Ms. Lighthorse and her class sat. I followed him over and grabbed a chair.

"How are you, Dan?" she said.

"I'm good. My dad said I could go with you,"

"That's what Devon told me. I'm glad to hear it."

"I'm not sure what I should bring."

She sat back in her chair, her hands intertwined on the table.

"Just the normal things you would bring on a camping trip; a toothbrush, a change of clothes. We have fishing rods and tackle if you would like to try the river."

"Should I bring a tent?" I said.

"You won't need it," she said. "We have quarters there for us."

I looked over at Devon.

"So we're going to be roomies?"

"You won't have to," said Ms. Lighthorse. "There's more huts than kids."

"Plus, I like my space," said Devon. "And you snore."

"Cool," I said, though I was a little disappointed.

I figured Devon and I would be staying up all night like we used to do when we were younger. Just another change that I would have to get used to.

"We'll leave here after school tomorrow," said Ms. Lighthorse. "I'll be driving the van. You're more than welcome to ride with us."

I didn't like the idea of leaving my car at school for two days unattended. Plus, if I'm being honest, I didn't want to be stuck up there with no way out. Stupid, I know, but what if my dad needed me?

"That's okay," I said. "I can follow you."

"Whatever you want," said Ms. Lighthorse. "We're just glad you're coming." Linda let out a hoot in agreement.

****

I spent part of that night packing a bag. It was a strange time of the year for planning. The days were reaching the upper eighties but at night you could still feel the retreating winter's chill in the air. They had changed the forecast to only a slight chance of rain for early Saturday morning, which usually meant that if it did come it would be bad. I made sure that I included my boots and parka along with my water shoes and swim trunks. My father came into my room just as I was struggling to zip the bag.

"Are you running away?" he asked, with sarcastic hope.

"You're not that lucky," I said.

"Aren't you only going for a couple of days?"

"That's the plan, but I like to be prepared."

"How you weren't a boy scout I'll never understand. Just be careful. Don't break anything."

"I will," I said. "We're not staying in tents. Ms. Lighthorse says they have huts."

"That's interesting," my father replied. "I know the old Wichita tribe used to have a lot of those when they had the land, some of them are still there, but I didn't know that the Chickasaw did. It's not a part of the Chickasaw Nation."

"How well do you know Ms. Lighthorse?"

"Not very," he said. "I know that she's pretty high up with the tribe and that she went to an Ivy League school; Harvard or Yale. It was one of those. She certainly takes her job seriously. She put Blanchard on the map, as far as that goes."

"Why does she only have three high school students?"

"She used to have more," said my father. "This was when you were little. Devon probably remembers. They grew up and moved on, I guess. As to why her class is so small now, I really couldn't say. Blanchard's not exactly anyone's idea of a thriving metropolis. Maybe most parents with special needs kids prefer to stay where they're at."

That would make sense. Not to mention Oklahoma's deterring weather.

"When are you leaving?" he said.

"Tomorrow, right after school. But I'm going to drive and I'll have my phone on me. I just hope I get a signal."

My father pulled out his wallet and took out two twenties and a ten.

"Here," he said. "This is all I have on me."

"I've got some money," I said.

"Take it anyway, just in case."

I snatched the bills out of his hand.

"You don't have to tell me twice," I said.

"You make me proud," he said, and then left the room.

I finally finished zipping the overstuffed bag and placed it on the side of my bed. I thought about what my father had said. Up until then, I hadn't considered that the Wichita mountains weren't a part of the Chickasaw Nation. Strange that Ms. Lighthorse, who was full Chickasaw, had family there. But maybe they had been intertwined somewhere in the past. I made my way over to my laptop which was sitting on the small corner desk. I grabbed it, flipping it open as I flopped onto my mattress. Thanks to my early Oklahoma History class I knew a little about the five civilized tribes: The Chickasaw, Cherokee, Choctaw, Seminole, and Creek. It was a label that I always found rather misleading, considering they had all been driven off their land under the threat of death. What was so civilized about that? But I didn't know much about the tribes that were already here.

I turned on the computer and typed in Wichita Tribe. A row of information filled the screen. I clicked on one that read Wichita: The Dying Tribe. It read like an obituary dedicated to both the people and their way of life.

Once, they had been a peaceful thriving group, unaware of the Spanish storm rising from the south. Then they met Coronado, offered their hospitality, and were repaid by murder and sickness. It was the redundant tale that had inflicted so many other Native Americans. But for the Wichita's it was utter devastation, leaving them, in the end, with no more than three hundred citizens scattered throughout

Kansas, Arkansas, and Oklahoma.. The last person who spoke the original dialect was a woman who had died twenty years before, taking their language with her. To me, that was the saddest part. It solidified the end. Strange that she never passed on the language to someone else. Perhaps she couldn't find anyone else. Or worse; nobody cared.

There was an old video of the woman. I clicked on it expecting to see a Native American wearing the leather hides and beads of her people but was shocked to see that she was silver-haired, wearing a cotton dress, and staring at the camera through a pair of horned rimmed glasses. She looked like anyone's grandmother circa 1970.

"My name is Abigail James and I am the last speaker of the Kitikiti'sh, or what you would call the Wichita tribe."

She then went on in her native tongue, the meaning dubbed in. The words flowed with rhythmic consonants, each ending with long and short sounding E's. It was musical, and I found myself transfixed as she told of the different legends dear to her people. She talked of the Great Spirit and of the animals that had meant so much. She then spoke of darker myths; one being of a man whose dead wife had returned, another of how a snake fooled a cunning coyote. But it was the story about the vengeful beast that got my attention: A skinchanger who walked amongst them as if one of them, but was a creature with an insatiable appetite for killing. It was always watching. Looking for those who wrongfully persecuted others. Those were the favored victims of the beast. Its touch like electric death, its reward; the covering of its victim; a shroud of victory with which it decorated its walls like a hunter's trophy.

I'm not one to fall into supernatural traps just because I can't explain what's going on, there's enough of that in the world already, but I must admit that as I listened to the woman tell this tale I couldn't stop the chill from climbing my spine. But what happened next had me swearing off any and all horror movies for years to come. I looked over at the empty chair at my corner desk and felt my heart skip in my chest. Joe was sitting there, his head tilted back, muscles and sinew shining in the room's artificial light. The woman's voice seemed to become louder, overpowering the sounds of the wind from outside, crushing back the television that my father was watching. It was then that Joe's head moved, his chin dropping, his mouth still locked in an eternal scream. I raised my hands and covered my eyes, stifling back a surging scream of my own. The room went quiet. I slowly lowered my hands. The chair was empty. The video had been completed and was offering a re-play.

"Hell no," I blurted out, slamming the laptop shut.

*****

That night I lay with the blankets up to my chin. The room was sitting at a comfortable seventy-degrees but I couldn't stop shivering. The old lady had gotten to me, how else could you explain the visitor? What I saw was nothing more than an illusion created out of suppressed fear. Yes, the idea of a sadistic murderer running loose in our small town was always there. But it was there for everyone. Were they seeing corpses in their bedroom too? Maybe they were, but I wasn't about to ask. Maybe Ms. Lighthorse was right: what I needed was to get away from here. I closed my eyes and forced them to remain shut. I began counting sheep but soon found myself imagining goats. I then flipped on the lamp sitting on the nightstand and grabbed the book that I had been stumbling through for over a month. It was called Hearts In Atlantis, by Stephen King. After reading a couple of pages I realized that I had made a bad decision and put it down. There was no way I was turning that lamp off. Not tonight. My eyes kept wandering over to the chair. It was empty. Of course, it was empty. It had been empty. But the cold sweat resting on my forehead begged to differ. Finally, I rolled over on my side, away from the cold wooden support, eventually falling into a dreamless slumber.

CHAPTER THIRTEEN

Pencil Of Chaos

It was hard not to laugh. Kyle lumbered into the lunchroom that Friday with his pair of guards flanked on each side, their eyes shifting from one student to the next, looking for any sign of disrespect. It was as if a fallen Dictator had returned to reclaim a country that had moved on. I watched him enter from a corner table with Devon, unable to ignore the flitting eyes of my fellow students. They darted from Kyle to Devon in anticipation, hoping for an immediate rematch. But they would be disappointed. Devon looked up at Kyle only once and then continued to concentrate on his slice of pizza. Kyle pretended not to notice us and led his troops to an empty table on the other side of the room. His chin still held a purplish-yellow blotch, his eye contained a dark crescent, and his jaw was wired. The hospital had kept him for four days and I was surprised to see that he was back at school so soon. Steve and Larry waited until their leader was sitting and then pushed their way to the front of the line. They grabbed their trays and also an extra can of Pepsi, making sure that they took a straw.

I gazed back over at the big beaten kid and caught him looking over our way. He quickly averted his eyes.

"Man," I said. "You really messed him up."

"To hell with him," said Devon. "Did you bring your stuff?"

"It's in my car," I said. "Are you riding with me?"

"No. I'll go with Ms. Lighthorse and Linda."

A week ago I would have thought that strange, but much had changed since then. Kyle could confirm that. I again looked over at the big kid. The other two were now sitting with him, their three heads close together, whispering back and forth. Perhaps they were laying out their plans for the future. Would they dare jump Devon? I remembered how Devon effortlessly threw Kyle and wondered if the three of them would be enough. I looked over at my friend, his hair was much longer than it had been at the beginning of the year, it fell in dark streams to his shoulders. His face was sharper, almost cruel. It seemed to match his newfound attitude.

Devon doesn't need protection, Ms. Lighthorse had said. At least not that kind.

A transformation had come over my friend. A transition that left me feeling baffled and scared. Our conversations had declined into three or four-word sentences usually followed by long pockets of silence. I didn't like it. And I didn't like the fact that Devon seemed to care less.

The terror group quickly finished their lunch and, without looking once our way, left the room. It was a spectacle of false acquiescence and it scared the shit out of me.

"They're planning something," I said, more to myself.

"Let them try," Devon said with a mouth full of pizza.

For a moment it was like sitting next to Kyle. The barbaric nature was the same. Devon's eyes caught mine, and in those eyes, I no longer saw the docile, reserved friend from my past. Within his gaze stirred a boiling hatred. An animal who had finally felt the freedom of being unleashed, who had tasted blood and wanted more. I stood up and excused myself. I could feel Devon's eyes burning into my back as I left the lunchroom and wondered if they glowed silver.

*****

I found Ms. Lighthorse in her classroom. She was with Linda who grunted as I walked in. Ms. Lighthorse and Linda had taken their lunch back to the room. It was so she could continue packing for the trip. She had Linda's bag sitting next to her desk along with a row of pill bottles. Mike Henley had stayed home from school for the day. He wasn't going on the trip so there was no reason for him to be there.

Mike had only gone once to the mountains and, according to Devon, had somehow managed to disappear for five hours. It was only after Ms. Lighthorse had given up the search and was about to call the authorities when he appeared out of the woods, his face scratched and the wheels of his chair covered in mud. That was it, as far as his mother was concerned. Never again. Considering he was all that she had left, who could blame her?

"Hi Dan," said Ms. Lighthorse. "Are you packed and ready?"

"Yes," I said.

My voice was shaking.

"What's wrong?"

I didn't know where to begin. Kyle was back and this shit wasn't over. Devon was becoming deranged, hoping that the future felons would try something. Not to mention there was still a killer loose and my father had no idea who or what it was.

"I'm just tired," I said, finally.

"If you don't want to go, you don't have to."

"It's not that," I said.

Ms. Lighthorse pointed at a chair. I made my way over to it and sat. She took the one next to it. Her dark eyes looked into mine and all I wanted was to hide within the comfort of her gaze. She placed her hand on my wrist, and I could feel the warmth of her skin crawling up my arm.

"It's been a tough couple of weeks," she said. "But it will get better."

"I know," I said. "I just feel like everything is changing so fast."

"That's because it is," she said. "Both good and bad."

I thought back over the year, trying to weigh those good things against the bad, and was coming up short.

"We all change, Dan," she said, and I wondered if she might be reading my mind. "Some go on to do great things, some just survive. Then some only look for a way out. And through it all, the world continues to spin."

I couldn't help but glance at Linda.

"I guess you're right," I said, doubtfully.

"Think about it," she said, leaning closer. "Every season ends and then begins again, right?"

I nodded my head.

"But none of them are really the same. Winter dies, and with it, many things and yet winter will return but those things are gone forever."

"Are you saying to just value the time we have?"

"Yes," she said, removing her hand. "And value those who are still around when the next winter comes."

"It's just that there are so many bad things happening."

"Like what?" she said.

"Well, first of all, my friend is acting like he wants to kill someone."

"Devon is changing," she said.

"And do you think that's good?"

"I think it's necessary and unavoidable."

She then grabbed a pencil off the desk and tossed it. It flew for a few feet and then hit the vinyl floor, bouncing first right and then left and skidded to a stop near the back wall.

"Why did you do that?" I said.

"That pencil is much like Devon," she said. "I had control and then I let it go and for a moment it followed my direction right up until it hit the floor. After that, it did what it wanted and all I could do was watch."

I thought about that. It went along with the uneasy feeling that had been sitting like a stone in my gut. Ms. Lighthorse was right. We were all being tossed out like rescued birds, each of us released by those who loved us. Their control was coming to an end and soon they would be forced to watch as we made our own way. But did this explain Devon's behavior, or did it simply trivialize it? I wasn't sure. Then, as if on cue, he was at the doorway.

"Did I miss something?" he said.

"We were just talking about the trip," said Ms. Lighthorse.

"Are we taking the elementary kids?"

"Not this time," said Ms. Lighthorse.

"Are you expecting something?" said Devon.

Ms. Lighthorse glanced at me, then at Linda, and said, "I can only hope."

* * *

*****

Normally, I would count down the excruciating minutes of my last hour, watching the long hand of the ancient Traditional clock as it dragged its way slowly closer to the small hand resting on the number three. But on this day I found myself wanting the minute hand to slow down, hoping that the clocks throughout the school would break. I can't explain this apprehension. I should have been excited about the trip. I should have been looking forward to finally being able to spend time with my friend at the place that he loved best. But I couldn't, and I think Devon knew this. Perhaps he even felt happy about it. When the pencil hit the floor it went where it wanted. Devon was hitting the floor and I could only hope that it wasn't rock bottom.

The bell startled me. Voices echoed off of the walls with exuberance. Another Friday had come to an end. Another week had closed, meaning that summer was that much closer. The hallways were filled with a mass exodus. Grinding hinges of flung opened doors flooded over-excited conversations. I barely noticed any of this as I stopped at my locker. My only homework for the weekend was a chapter in English. I pulled the book out but left my bag. I shut the panel and placed the lock. Yellow heated light flooded my vision as I lumbered my way out into the parking lot. I could see the van parked at the side door of the school, the handicap lift was lowered. I climbed into the Corsica and inserted the key. The motor turned and then fired. Not once had this relic from my father failed to start. Today it wouldn't have been such a bad thing. I idled over to the rear of the van, coming to a stop just as Ms. Lighhorse opened the side door to the school. She gave me a quick wave and then made sure that Linda cleared the threshold.

I lowered the passenger window and said, "Do you need help?"

"We're good," said Ms. Lighthorse.

She then helped Linda mount her wheelchair onto the lift. Linda's face was twitching with joy. Within moments she was inside the van. Next came Devon. He thrust himself onto the lift and glanced over at me as it began to rise. There was no smile, or thumbs up. After he was in, Ms. Lighthorse slid the door shut and folded up the lift. She gave me another smile and then walked around to the driver's side.

Five minutes later we were on our way to the Wichita Mountains. A place where wildlife roamed and the river never ran dry. A place where my life would soon change forever.

CHAPTER FOURTEEN

Settling In

I followed the van off of the interstate and into the park. To my right stood a herd of buffalo, their massive heads lowered as they grazed on spring grass. The road had narrowed into a shoulder-less two-way, its yellow line faded. Moments later, Ms. Light- horse brought the van to a near stop and turned onto a dirt trail bar ely wide enough for the van's wheels. I followed her, carefully avoiding the back spray of small rocks. Ahead I could see the road ascending, winding its way towards higher elevations. The plains had become jagged cutaways, creating an eerie tunnel effect, casting deep shadows across the road as we continued to climb. Bent pines burst through the rocky sidewalls, leaning precariously over the road creating an illusion of being lifted. After another twenty minutes, the narrow route opened up into a valley surrounded by cliffs. The pine trees straightened and were joined by oaks and cottonwoods. At the center of this field sat a dozen round structures. They were spaced out four to five feet apart and were covered in weathered hide held together by thick stitching. They were not TP's, but they were close.

Ms. Lighthorse came to a stop in front of the nearest one and I parked behind her. I opened my door and immediately felt a chill riding the breeze. Winter had not fully surrendered up here where the air was thinner. Ms. Lighthorse climbed out of the van and I helped her with Linda. Devon, of course, needed no help.

"Okay," said Ms. Lighthorse once they were out, "everyone pick a house."

I watched Devon roll his way over to the third hut closest to us. Ms. Lighthorse then pushed Linda over to the second one. I stood there watching them, feeling like a stranger in a strange land, which I guess I was, but I also felt a little unwelcome.

"Dan," said Ms. Lighthorse, coming out of Lisa's hut. "Would you help me get some firewood?"

I followed her through the row of shanties. A shoulder-high stack of cut pine stood just behind the furthest hut and I held out my arms while Ms. Lighthorse loaded. I carried the wood back to where a small pit had been dug just on the other side of the van. After three trips Ms. Lighthorse informed me that it was enough.

"So, campfires and ghost stories?" I said.

"Do you like ghost stories?" said Ms. Lighthorse.

"Who doesn't?" I said.

"I might know a tale or two if you're interested."

"I can't wait," I said.

"Why don't you see what Devon's up to while I get Linda's things."

"You don't need help?"

"I'll be fine," she said. "Go talk to Devon."

I made my way over to his abode, stopping just outside of the fur-covered flap.

"Hey man. Are you decent?"

"Is that a joke?" he said.

I pushed my head through the slit and asked if I could come in.

"Entree," he said.

The inside was way more spacious than it looked from the outside. Arched petrified limbs interlocking up to where a small sliver of sunlight lasered from the rounded peak. Throw rugs had been placed on the dirt providing a comfortable place to relax.

"These are cool," I said.

"And old," he said.

"Chickasaw?" I asked.

"No," he said. "Much more ancient."

"Who built them?"

He gazed at me, his eyes narrowing. He began to speak but stopped abruptly. He then threw up his arms and said, "I'm not sure."

I didn't believe him. He knew, although why he didn't want to say was beyond me. Perhaps it was a part of the secret that he had withheld for so long. I guess I thought I wasn't supposed to, he had said, when I had asked why he never talked about this place. And now he was still holding out.

"Maybe Ms. Lighthorse knows," I said. "I'll ask her later."

"Yeah, maybe," he said, with a yawn.

The flap was suddenly flung open. Ms. Lighthorse entered the hut with Devon's duffle bag and dropped it at his chair.

"Are you comfy?" she said.

"Golden," said Devon.

"Good. Let's get you settled in, Dan," she said, holding the flap open.

I went through and made my way to my car. I grabbed my bag off of the passenger seat and followed her into the fourth hut.

"Here we are," she said, as I entered. "There's an outhouse straight back from here, but just make sure you knock first."

"I will," I said.

"I have plenty of water in the van so help yourself."

I nodded my appreciation.

By then the sun was falling behind the western ridge. A coyote rang out with a lonesome cry and was soon answered by another.

"I love to hear them sing," she said. "Did you know that's what they're doing?"

I listened to the anguished wails echoing off of the cliffs and was forced to stifle a chill. I know that they are mostly harmless but it had been a long time since I found myself so far out and in the open. It was humbling.

"I didn't know that," I said.

"Yes, and soon it will be like a choir. We're lucky; they don't usually get so close."

I wasn't sure if lucky was the word that I would have chosen.

"Get settled in," she said. "I'm going to start working on the fire. We should be roasting hot dogs within the hour."

She turned to leave.

"Ms. Lighthorse," I said, causing her to pause. "How old are these structures?"

"Hundreds of years," she said.

"Who built them?" I said. "Was it The Wichita?"

Ms. Lighthorse smiled and said, "This will be a good story for the campfire, and it might even have a ghost or two in it."

She then left the hut before I could say anything more.

*****

I checked my phone; no signal. This was not surprising considering we were half a mile up and forty miles away from the nearest town. I sat down on the fur-covered ground. The inside was much like Devon's with archaic limbs overlaid with hides. I briefly wondered if it was buffalo, or maybe elk. The smell of growth filled the air, carrying with it the sound of beckoning red-tail hawks and threatening crows. Infant leaves chattered in the wind and I felt my eyelids becoming heavy. I lay back, using my duffle bag for a pillow. I was finally here; the place that Devon had talked so little about. It was because of this place that I would sometimes spend weekends alone enveloped in jealousy. And here I was, just as alone and without the sanctuary of social media.

From outside came the crackling of a flame. Ms. Lighthorse had succeeded in getting the fire going. Dancing rays of orange snuck through the door-flap of my hut and with it came an aroma of burning bark.

"Let's cook these dogs," Ms. Lighthorse called out.

I lay there for a moment longer with my eyes shut. Maybe it was because of the crazy week, or maybe it was just being away from the madness, but right then I felt as though I could sleep for days. I heard the faint squeak of wheels turning, growing louder, and stopping just outside of my hut.

"Are you coming?" said Devon.

"I'm on my way," I said, forcing myself to sit up.

The flames were leaping into the air. Smoke billowed, rotating up into a deepening sky. A coyote bellowed as I sat down and was answered by another.

"Sounds like the Bee Gees," I said. Ms. Lighthorse burst out with laughter and I could see Devon smiling from across the pit. Linda sat with her head cocked to the side, her red hair covered with a stocking cap. She was wrapped in a fleece blanket that sent visions of the nightmare racing through my mind. I found myself scooting closer to the fire. Broken cliffs jutted around us, their shadows creeping eastward as the sun fell behind the time-battered peaks. Darkening pines surrounded by shrubs and ivy edged along our open valley, blocking most of the wind. Ms. Lighthorse handed out skewer forks and then opened a package of hot dogs. I heard my stomach rumble. I hadn't eaten since lunch and had barely touched my food then. Ms. Lighthorse placed a sack of buns and a bottle of mustard down near the fire. There were also chips and sodas. No one spoke during the first round. Ms. Lighthorse helped Linda with her hot dog, swiping her chin after every other bite. I tried to ignore this.

After Linda finished, Ms. Lighthorse wiped the remaining grease from her chin and said, "Dan would like to hear a story. You asked me about the huts. Do you still want to learn about them?"

"Absolutely," I said.

Why not? There was still going to be a whole other day to kill.

I could see Devon's eyes glowing in the flame, they were narrowed as if studying me. Linda let out a jovial hoot and Ms. Lighthorse patted her knee.

"What do you know about the Wichita tribe?" she said.

"Only that they were here before the five civilized tribes," I said. "I watched a video about them. It was kind of sad."

"Everything's sad when it comes to Native Americans," said Devon.

"This is true," said Ms. Lighthorse. "But the Wichita's weren't the first ones here. Have you ever heard of the Loshinka tribe?"

I had never even heard that word before and told her.

"They have been mostly forgotten," she said. "But long before the five came from the east and before the Wichita were driven south the Loshinka were here."

"What happened to them?" I said.

Ms. Lighthorse offered a smile, and said, "Now we come to the story."

* * *

CHAPTER FIFTEEN

A Tale By the Fire

"It is said that there is magic within these mountains," she began. "Even now, you can feel it if you try. This was what Loshi saw in his waking dreams. He was a medicine man within his tribe. He had been born with a clubbed foot, which, as far as his people were concerned, meant that he had been touched by The Great Spirit. He was revered for his visions and it was because of these visions that he led two hundred of his people out of an arid land we now call Arizona. For he had been shown a prosperous country, filled with wild game, rivers, and canyons. But it wasn't just this that caused the exodus. The vision also tasked him with creating a balance with this new land, a place where Father Sky and Mother Earth could meet. Do you know what I'm talking about Daniel?"

"It sounds like a Medicine Wheel," I said.

"Very good," said Ms. Lighthorse. "Also known as a Sacred Hoop."

"How long ago was this?" I said.

"Around the time the Incas fell."

"Wait. You're saying this happened in the sixteenth century? How do you know this?"

"The legend has been handed down by my people."

"How would the Chickasaw know this?"

"Do you want to hear the story or not?" said Devon.

I nodded, thinking this might not just be another ghost story concluding with a BOO, after all.

"They arrived just as fall was turning into winter and were soon struggling to survive.   There were animals, but they were scattered, many of them migratory. Still, they had faith in Loshi and continued to trust him. Loshi seemed not to be worried about their hardships, his only concern was finding the right place to construct his wheel. Eventually, he did find a spot centered around a lone cottonwood, with branches canopied out like a ceiling. Under his direction, the Loshinka gathered what stones they could find and within a month they had the wheel completed. Things did seem to improve, but just barely. One year went by, and then two and still they struggled."

I found myself staring into the swirling flames as she spoke, captivated. In the distance, a terror-stricken scream was cut short in the darkness. Something had come to a gruesome end.

"Then one day a wounded man staggered out of the woods wearing a dented metal chest plate and a crested helmet, his skin as pale as the moon. At first, the Loshinka were sure that he was a spirit coming to save them. Loshi was not stupid and could see that many of the stranger's injuries looked as if they had come from the same weapons that they themselves carried. But he wasn't completely sure, so he would sit with the man, listening, studying the stranger's language, until he was able to comprehend much of what the stranger said, and it wasn't good. The man kept pointing at the golden rings that he wore on his fingers, demanding to be taken to where such things could be found. Loshi only shook his head, pretending not to understand. Eventually, the stranger was back on his feet, wandering through the village, as if it was his kingdom. The man offered nothing and did little else but consume what small amounts of food they had, often demanding the company of a young woman. But what could Loshi do? The stranger was thought to be a God."

"Who was he?" I said.

"No one knows," said Ms. Lighthorse. "But if I had to guess, he was probably a deserter or a survivor of some battle."

"A Spaniard," said Devon. "It would fit the time."

"Regardless," continued Ms. Lighthorse. "Loshi had seen enough, and one night as the man was perched beside a fire fondling a terrified girl, he decided that something must be done. He came over and sat across from the stranger. This seemed to anger the man, so he pushed the girl away and began to threaten Loshi, promising to return with more just like him and destroy their home.

"Loshi only nodded and grinned, feigning ignorance. He then tapped the man's golden ring and pointed off into the woods. The man's face lit up and he demanded to be taken to this place of riches. The next morning Loshi led him into the woods as the rest of the tribe watched, unsure of what they should do. Loshi was disabled, after all. The next day came and went, and then another until the people decided that they would send out a search party the following morning. But that evening Loshi returned, and he was alone."

"Pay attention," said Devon. "This is where it gets good."

"But he had brought something with him," Ms. Lighthorse continued. "Strapped to his back were two sacks of seed. One contained corn, the other wheat. He handed his people the sacks and instructed them on what was to be done. He then limped his way home and wasn't seen again for two days."

I felt a moral coming.

"By the end of spring, they had an abundance of both wheat and corn. But that was just the beginning. The crops brought in deer and soon they had all of the meat that they could want. They began to thrive and it wasn't long after that that the small community began to grow. The women were caring for two and sometimes three children at a time."

Ms. Lighthorse leaned back on an elbow, her dark eyes focusing on the dancing flames.

"Then came Anchita," she said. "The girl with twisted legs. Her mother was horrified and blamed herself. But Loshi, being the medicine man, had cared for the mother during the pregnancy and reassured her that she was not to blame and that he would take the child to the Sacred Hoop to see what could be done. So he left the village, the infant curled in one arm. This time he was gone for a week, and when he returned, he seemed different. His face was lighter and his hair had lost much of its gray, he still walked with a limp, but it was only slight. Of course, they wondered what had happened to the child but no one dared to ask."

"He killed her?" I said.

"Hold on," said Devon. "She's getting to it."

"Anchita was just the first," Ms. Lighthorse said. "Another child was born a month later with both of his arms missing. Again Loshi took the child and returned alone. Now his hair was darker and his foot seemed to have straightened."

A sudden slice of wind cut through the treeline, producing sparks from the twisting fire. I felt my skin goose within my jacket and wrapped my arms around my chest.

"Are you cold?" Ms. Lighthorse said.

"I'm fine,' I said, through chattering teeth.

"Where was I? Oh yes, soon more children were born with deformities and each one was taken away by Loshi, never to be seen again."

"How many?" I said.

"There was never any count," said Ms. Lighthorse. "But enough for the Loshinka to believe that something was seriously wrong. It wasn't just the deformed babies that had them spooked; Loshi was changing; His skin had become pale and his limp was completely gone. He was now disappearing for weeks at a time, and rumors began to spread. How is it that he seems to look younger? And what of his foot? These questions only gained in urgency as more and more children were taken. One night they decided to find out. They rushed into Loshi's home only to find that he was gone. But something was there: A crested helmet lay in the center of his hut. The people knew this helmet, had at first revered and then feared it. It was then that they noticed it wasn't empty."

"Let me guess," I said, with more bravery than I felt. "A severed head."

"Close," said Ms. Lighthorse. "It was tiny bones taken from the bodies of the children."

"Wait," I said, leaning towards her. "Are you saying he was collecting them?"

"Only parts," said Ms. Lighthorse.

"What was he doing with them?"

"That was the question the Loshinka wanted to be answered so they sent two of their bravest into the woods to find out. The next day Loshi returned but the two men didn't. Another day passed and the people became nervous. They sent another group out to search while

Loshi watched from the opening of his hut. It is said he was smiling. By that afternoon the group returned, their faces stricken with horror."

"They were dead," I said. "Loshi had killed them."

"Yes and no," said Ms. Lighthorse. "They found the two men less than a mile away from the village, their skins had been removed, but that was just the beginning of the tale. They found tracks, prints unlike anything they had ever seen before, and decided to follow them."

At this point, I began to think that Ms. Lighthorse was summing up a joke. One of very bad taste considering what had just happened in town. I glanced over at Devon and saw that his eyes were locked onto me, studying my reaction. Ms. Lighthorse didn't seem to notice and continued.

"They followed the odd tracks and it wasn't long until they found themselves at the wheel."

"Their wheel?" I said.

"Yes," said Ms. Lighthorse. "As the scouts drew closer they began to feel uneasy. The air had soured and there was no sound. It was like stepping into another world; one of utter loss. They say that one of the men began to cry and that another simply fainted."

"This doesn't sound like a medicine wheel," I said.

"But it was," said Ms. Lighthorse. "Only it had changed."

"What do you mean?"

"The scouts came to a stop at the edge, none of them daring to cross over. And it was then that they learned what Loshi was doing with the children. Scattered between the granite and sandstone edging sat tiny skulls. But it was the center of the wheel that had them paralyzed. What once was a plush and healthy tree was now a large and twisted trunk, its branches stripped and empty, like skeleton fingers. Leaning against the ruined trunk was the stranger, his face carved into a grotesque grin, and above him, hung like a pair of drying blankets, were the fresh skins of the murdered scouts."

I found myself clutching the sleeves of my coat. I felt like a little kid. I can only imagine what Devon was thinking.

"How the hell is that a medicine wheel?" I said. "And why would this evil Loshi guy make it?"

"It didn't start out this way," said Ms. Lighthorse. "But let's move on: The men were horrified by what they had discovered and were unsure of what they should do. It was then that the skins began to move, lifting like a pair of sails and the men ran. They returned home and told the people what they had found. Of course, they were angry and rushed into Loshi's home, but he was gone."

"What happened to him?" I said.

"No one knows," said Ms. Lighthorse.

"So that's it?" I said. "He just disappeared? What happened to the Loshinka?"

"That remains a mystery, as well."

"Maybe they went back to Arizona," I said.

"Maybe, although there is no record of them returning."

"And you think these are their huts?" I said, with disbelief. "How is that possible?"

"The Wichita's arrived here and found these burned skeletal structures and decided to rebuild. But they didn't stay long. They said this glade was cursed by a bad spirit and so they continued south. Of course, these huts have been repaired since, I've helped with that myself. But the frames are original."

I gazed over at the shadowed structures. The rounded tops, much like the surrounding mountains, were weathered and beaten down. Could they really be five hundred years old? I glanced at Devon and saw that he was now focused on the flame. A low grunt came from Linda and I watched as Ms. Lighthorse adjusted the blanket that was covering the girl. A chill raced down my spine and it wasn't just from the falling temperature.

"Do you believe it?" I said, finally.

"I do," said Devon, looking up from the fire.

"It's just a story," said Ms. Lighthorse. "And you wanted one."

I guess I had, although if I could do it over I would have requested a campfire song. A distant flash drew my attention to the west. Within moments a low rumble broke through the darkness.

"It's going to rain tonight," she said.

I felt my heart sink as I pictured myself drenched inside the archaic structure.

"Don't worry," Ms. Lighthorse said. "These homes stay dry."

She then reached into her bag and pulled out a thermos, and said, "Who wants hot chocolate?"

I nodded my head and gratefully took the steaming styrofoam cup from Ms. Lighthorse. The sweet liquid warmed my throat, producing a shiver. Another round of yipping wild dogs met the approaching thunder. For a moment, all I wanted was to be away from here. There was no rational explanation, except for the fact that Ms. Lighthorse's story seemed to have scared the shit out of me. I gazed around the wall of black circling the perimeter of our site as the strengthening wind rattled the branches of the unseen trees.

Devon and Ms. Lighthorse spoke about next week's class plan as Ms. Lighthorse continued to take the occasional swipe at Linda's chin. I looked over at the girl in the chair and realized that her eyes were locked onto me. I gave her a quick smile and drew my gaze back to the flame. The flickering dance was hypnotic and I soon found myself struggling to stay awake. I glanced down at my phone and saw that it was only ten after nine. Much too early for me to feel this tired. I again looked over at Linda. She was smiling, her teeth reflecting blood-red from the fire. I felt my lids beginning to close. A brief warning shot through my mind - Linda was smiling. I tried to look at her once more but found that my lids were now shut tight, padlocked.

"I don't feel good about this," I heard someone say from far away.

"Let's get him inside," said another, it sounded like Devon.

"I'll help," said yet another.

I felt arms sliding under my shoulders, locking around my chest. A set of hands gripped my ankles and together they lifted.

"Get the door," one of them said, and I was sure that it was Ms. Lighthorse.

"I've got it," said the other voice. Darkness was sweeping towards me like the oncoming storm front and there was no way to fight it.

"I do like him," the voice continued.

"He's not one of us," said the voice that sounded very much like Devon.

"But he could be," said the other, and then I was out.

CHAPTER SIXTEEN

A Visit to the Wheel

An explosion propelled me to my knees. A blinding flash of blue sliced through the gaps of my hide-covered home and was quickly followed by another rib-rattling bomb. The cold wind whistled through the seams of the hut, encircling the inside. I wrapped the blanket around me, noticing that I had been stripped down to my underwear. How had that happened? I hadn't been drunk, hadn't smoked anything, and yet, my head was pounding. I had been fine until Ms. Lighthorse's hot chocolate. Had she put something in it?

I don't feel good about this.

Someone had said that.

But had they? It was like a shroud had been placed over me, distorting facts and fiction, melting them together. I reached around blindly until I found my pants and pulled my cell phone out of the pocket, hitting the flashlight app. I stepped into my jeans, walked over towards the opening, and froze.

The flap waved like a flag in a hurricane. Another strike of blue revealed a slumped-over shape just outside of the doorway. I raised the light of my phone and was rewarded with a pair of emerald reflections. Linda sat just outside, her body slumped, her head tilted. I knew then that I was lost in another nightmare. And yet, this was different from before. For one thing, the fear that had had me clutching my blankets was absent and I was able to move. Gone were the signs of her disease but gone also was the transformed brow of the beast. She was just Linda. Or Linda as she should have been.

She stood up, wrapped in a fleece blanket, just as a gust burst through, tossing her copper hair.

"Dan," she said with an oddly deep and musical tone. "Walk with me."

As if it had heard her, the blustering wind began to fall away. The violent lightning that had been blasting like artillery just moments ago fizzled into calming lights.

"Please, Dan," she said, holding out her hand.

I was fully aware of the unconscious trap that I was in and for a moment considered trying to pinch, or maybe slap myself. But what would be the point? This was not a nightmare and Linda was no monster. If anything she was beautiful. The most beautiful girl I had ever seen. This thought brought with it a sense of shock as well as shame. As a guy knowingly trapped in a dream, I found it hard to come to terms with what my mind had devised. Linda, a crippled girl, now stood before me as my definition of desire. What did this say about me? Perhaps I should pinch myself, after all. Instead, I took her hand and she led me out of the hut.

We walked together between the van and my clunker towards a bank of trees. I hadn't put on my shoes and the wet grass felt cold. Its damp blades slid between my toes, tickling with its gentle touch. Above us the clouds had begun to break, allowing light from a three-quarter moon to reveal the landscape around us.

"Where are we going?" I said.

"It's a surprise," she said, without looking at me.

Her hand was warm. It clutched mine with a purpose, her grip tight but not uncomfortable. We broke through the tree line and she veered us slightly left and together we started making our way up the side of a pine needle-covered slope. My breath was soon coming in burning gasps and my legs were stiffening. It was a strange sensation for a dream but perhaps I was trying to make it as real as possible. Linda continued to lead, her face turning towards mine only once. She led me until the tall pines ended at a clearing. I could see jagged shapes rising within the low light of the moon, circular patterns running along the surface of the ground with spokes shooting towards the darkened base of some massive tree that sat at its center.

"Is this the medicine wheel?" I whispered.

Linda released my hand and stepped over the line of large rocks that made up the circumference.

"It is," she said.

The story of The Loshinka broke through like a train and I stumbled back. But these were not bones rising from the ground. The lines looked to be made of granite and appeared to have markings etched across them, but in the dim light, it was hard to tell.

"How did you find it?" I said.

"Ms. Lighthorse brought us," said Linda.

"So Devon's been here?"

"Many times," she said. "It has made us better. It wants us to stay."

I gazed up at the shadowed hulk that sat at its center.

"Why?" I said.

"You ask too many questions," she said. "Just know that it's here and that there is magic within these mountains."

She then reached out, took my hand, pulling me into the wheel. I was sure that I would feel some kind of electrical surge or nauseating wave but there was nothing, only the warmth of her skin touching mine. Linda then lowered me down with her, and together we sat gazing up at the moon, her hand locked in mine and her head resting on my shoulder.

"This is much better than the last time," I said.

Linda looked up at me.

"What do you mean?"

"The last time you became a monster."

"Is that what you think of me?" she said, pulling her hand away. "That I'm a monster?"

"Not at all," I said. "Dreams are just dreams. I can't control them."

"And you think that you are having one now?"

"Of course," I said. "But I like this one."

Linda retook my hand and placed her head back on my shoulder.

"And in this dream you had, the one where I became a monster, what happened?"

For a moment I held my answer. Strange, considering I most likely wouldn't remember any of this once I woke up. But for some reason, I didn't want to say. I didn't want to risk hurting her feelings any more than I already had. I decided to tell her some but not all. I tilted my face to where I could see her bare legs sticking out past the blanket and felt my pulse quicken.

"You said that you wanted me," I said, finally.

Her hand released mine and found its way to my thigh.

"That doesn't sound so bad," she said, giving my leg a squeeze. "What else?"

I thought back, trying to block out the image of her horrific transformation and how she had risen from her chair naked with an intention that had been very clear. Should I tell her? Another part of the dream burst through, shattering the moment and she felt me shiver.

"What is it?" she said.

"You said you didn't do it."

Linda pivoted her body until we sat facing each other.

"I didn't do what?"

"You didn't kill Joe Clark," I said.

A sudden flash of silver shot from her eyes, reminding me of Devon's as his rage toward Kyle was released. I pushed myself away from Linda. Her hand shot out bullet fast and grasped my wrist.

"Do you think that I did?" she said, her mercurial eyes cooling.

"It was a dream, Linda," I said. "Just like now."

Linda scooted herself closer, pushing me until my back lay on the pebble covered ground. She crawled up my body, her blanket falling to the side. She then threw one bare leg over me. Her face now floating just inches from my own, her long red hair providing a curtain of secrecy.

"You don't feel like a dream," she said.

I couldn't respond. As if on their own, my hands found their way around her waist. She lowered her face and I felt the warmth of her lips press against mine. Her tongue broke through, exploring until finally enticing my own into a lust-filled duel. We made love within the medicine ring, alternating our positions as synchronized partners might do, her cries matching mine. At one point, I thought I heard the sound of something whipping in the wind, like wet sheets, but as I slowed my rhythm she gave me a sudden painful scratch across my back.

"Ouch," I cried out.

"Not yet," she said, looking up at me. "Don't stop yet."

*****

We made our way back to the huts in a fog of exhaustion. The fact that I was lost in this dream of Linda, made love with her like a guy who was accustomed to the act, left me numb. Of all of the girls that I could possibly dream about, why had I picked her?

Because it's not a dream, said a voice.

That, of course, was ridiculous. We neared my hut and I could see her chair still sitting there in front of the opening. We paused long enough for her to reach up and kiss me.

"I love you, Daniel," she said.

She then grabbed the handles of the wheelchair and pushed it toward the black mouth of her abode. I watched until she vanished into the darkness then made my way into my hut, tripping over one of my shoes. The blankets still lay as I left them, rumpled and tossed. After smoothing them out I lay back fully expecting to awake. Instead, I found myself walking through the park.

CHAPTER SEVENTEEN

Spectral Warning

It was empty. The early morning birds were chirping from tree to tree. I was near the creek and felt mild regret at not breaking yet another rule by bringing my pellet gun. Eight was the immediate number that came to mind. That was how many squirrels I had managed to plug since receiving the Daisy pump last Christmas. A relatively low number when compared to the Blue Jays and Cardinals but good enough to continue what I liked to call The Numbing. For others it might seem like an insane notion but I knew better. A conscience can be detrimental for a man such as myself and by the time summer rolled around I would be ready. Just a couple of more months and I would be able to leave this piss-ant town and my piss-ant family. The Marines had called and I was more than happy to answer. They would be my new family and I would be their new killing machine.

There had been moments, especially after a good ass whooping provided by my father, that the thought of suicide seemed like a viable option. But if I was going to take myself out I sure the hell wouldn't be going alone. My miserable father would, of course, be first on the list, and then my mother for being stupid enough to choose him. Yet, these were all just adolescent fantasies that lost their appeal over time. It wasn't that I couldn't do it, I think that the rotting carcasses that littered the park were proof enough of that. No. It was the fact that I knew I was meant for something more. The world was an evil place filled with men just like my father, and our country needed protecting. This was the creed that sustained me. All I needed to do was not get into any more trouble. To keep my nose clean for the rest of the year. Kyle might not agree but he was a prison term waiting to happen, much like my father had been. Hell, maybe I would even apologize to that teacher and her retard class. Perhaps I was growing up, after all.

Then I heard something behind me. Probably just those punks from middle school. For a moment I considered hiding and waiting for them to come by. How I used to love terrorizing them, sometimes chasing them all the way to the school's entrance door. But I decided against it. Just two more months and I would be rid of this cemetery town. Better not to risk it. So I continued on, the sound of footsteps from behind gaining. I stopped and looked but could only see the swing set and paint-depleted restroom. A sudden chill, very unmarine-like, seized my spine. I turned and began to walk, moving quicker.

"Joe Clark," a voice said and it was then I knew that I was in danger. I turned and it was there, standing as tall as any nightmare could. Fur covered its body, its eyes burned silver like a pair of raging harvest moons. I wanted to run but was frozen except for the urine that had been released within my jeans. Its gorilla-like arm reached out slowly as if the thing had no concern. I watched the claw-riddled hand open and could do little else but shut my eyes, trying to pretend away the heated talons tightening around my throat.

An explosion of light burst through my skull and then all was dark.

*****

Swirling blue mingled with green and yellow, like diluted water colors thrown on a canvass. Bitter wind swept over my body and I felt myself being lifted, rising in some soundless tempest. Within moments I found myself hovering above a twisted slide, its red iron gleaming from the rising sun. A scream ripped from below. Joe sat on the bench, his blood decorating his skinless body in abstract crimson patches. His face tilted towards the sky...towards me.

"Pan has found his Rodelero, and there will be more," he said. "Dan...Dan..."

CHAPTER EIGHTEEN

Dan Begins To Die

"...DAN."

My eyes snapped open to find Ms. Lighthorse leaning over me with her hand on my forehead. I lay wrapped within my blanket, my teeth chattering like one of those wind up toys. Sweat was pouring into my eyes but I was freezing.

"Dan, you're ill," she said. "Stay here."

She then made her way out of the hut. The sun was beaming through the opening and I could feel warm air rolling through, caressing my chilled face, but it only made it worse.

Ms. Lighthorse was back within seconds, a small medical bag in her hand. She unzipped the side, pulled out a thermometer and placed it under my tongue. She looked around and found one of my t-shirts lying next to the wall and made her way over to it.

"Take off that wet shirt and put this on," she said, coming back and lowering herself beside me just as the thermometer began to beep.

I took the shirt from her and began to sit up, slowly removing the saturated T as she grabbed the thermometer from my mouth.

"A hundred and three," she said, with concern. "We need to take you ..." she began, but then gasped.

"What happened to your back?"

"What is it?" I said.

Ms. Lighthorse took her cell phone out of the back pocket of her jeans and snapped a picture and then showed me. A jagged scabbed line was running from my left shoulder to my spine.

"How did this happen?" she said.

Linda did it while we were having sex, was what I almost said, but was able to catch myself.

"I don't know," I said, finally. "Maybe I slept on something."

"Can you stand up?" she said.

I threw off the blanket and it was as if I had suddenly stepped into the Arctic. I rose to my feet, wrapping my arms around my shivering body.

"Look at your feet, Dan," she said.

I gazed down at my green-stained toes. The cuffs of my jeans were laced with dried blades of grass and small chips of dirt.

"Did you go out last night?" she said.

"No," I said, putting on the dry shirt and collapsing back onto the floor. "It was storming."

But was it?

She looked down at me. For a moment I was sure I had done something wrong. But what it was I couldn't say.

"We need to get you out of here," she said, making her way out of the hut.

I lay there roasting and afraid. It had been a dream. How could it not have been? The scratch on my back had probably caused it. But where did it come from? I sat up, running my hand over the layered blankets that made up my mattress and could feel nothing. There was no stick or stone hidden within the folds. Of course, even if there was, it wouldn't explain the fact that my toes were grass-stained.

*****

I packed my things the best I could, not bothering to fold anything. The internal furnace continued to rise, causing me to feel detached. Ms. Lighthorse came in after everyone else was loaded in the van and found me staring into nothing with a pair of dirty shorts clutched in my hand.

"You can't drive," she said.

I considered arguing but found that my throat was far too dry. Instead I watched in a semi-coma state as she picked up my bag. She then grabbed my hand and led me out of the hut, much like Linda had done in my dream.

I struggled into the vehicle aware of Linda's emerald eyes following me. She sat in her chair, strapped behind the passenger seat of the van like an astronaut awaiting countdown. Beside her was Devon, his chin resting on his hand as if observing some kind of science experiment.

He turned his face towards Linda and said, "What did you do to him?"

"Enough," said Ms. Lighthorse, climbing into the driver's seat. "She didn't do anything."

Devon leaned forward, placing his hand on my forehead, and then withdrew it quickly.

"He's burning up," he said. "He needs a doctor."

"That's exactly where I'm taking him," said Ms. Lighthorse.

There was the low rumble of the motor coming to life and I found myself falling sideways onto the seat. I lay there as the van began to move, my skin constricted, my head throbbing.

Ms. Lighthorse navigated through the bumpy terrain, my body flaring with each washed-out gully. The silence within the van hung like an ominous cloud. Something had happened and it seemed as though I was the only one who didn't have a clue as to what it was. Not that it mattered at the moment. At this point, my mind had become a runaway train, zipping along, each thought being tossed aside with blurring speed. I closed my eyes and hoped that the smooth feel of pavement would come but instead I heard the crunching sound of something solid being flung against the bottom of the van. It took a few moments longer than it normally would have for me to realize that what I was hearing was rocks. There had not been a gravel road on our way to the campsite, it had gone from pavement to dirt trail with nothing in between. With a pain-infected struggle, I was finally able to sit up. In the distance, I could see Mount Scott cresting over a row of smaller mountains. The narrow gravel road that we were on snaked its way ahead for miles until disappearing between two jagged bluffs. On either side of the road waved endless blades of switch-grass, rolling like tides of an ocean.

Even though an inferno was raging in my mind it was clear to me that we were not heading back to Blanchard. Perhaps she was taking me to Lawton, the town did have a fairly good-sized hospital. That thought sent a chain reaction of dread throughout my already shivering body, which then careened into a terrifying question: Was I going to die? I had been sick a few times as a kid, had suffered through a couple of battles with the flu, but I had never felt anything like this. The burning wasn't just in my head, in fact, it seemed to be centered at my left shoulder. What could have done that? How could it have become infected so fast?

"You should lay back down," said Devon, from behind.

I turned my head as much as I could to look at my friend. His eyes were wide and his fingers were drumming on the arm rests of his locked-down chair.

"Where are we going?" I managed to cough out.

"To get you help," he said.

"But where?"

"To a doctor," he said.

"What happened to me?"

I could see the conflict in Devon's face. He started to open his mouth, let out a sigh and shut it.

"You know something, don't you?" I said.

"You need to lie down," said Ms. Lighthorse. I turned and saw her dark eyes in the rear-view mirror aimed at me.

"We should tell him," said Devon.

"It's not for us to decide," said Ms. Lighthorse.

"But if he begins to fade."

"He won't," she said.

Suddenly, Devon turned to the drooling Linda and said, "Couldn't keep your hands off of him, could you?"

I was just able to fling my arm out and brace myself against the driver's seat as the van came to a sliding stop. Ms. Lighthorse undid her seat-belt and turned, her eyes radiating black rage. Devon was glaring back at her with an anger of his own.

"You knew she was going to do this," he said. "You even helped her. And now look at what's happened."

"Nothing has happened," she said.

"Really?" said Devon. "Look at him. Why did she have to take him inside of the wheel?"

"Devon, this is not the time or place," said Ms. Lighthorse.

An anguished moan pierced through the angry barrage. I looked over and saw a tear trailing down Linda's cheek. Ms. Lighthorse left her seat and came to rest on her knees next to me. She leaned over my seat and wiped Linda's eyes.

"There, there," she said softly. "It's not your fault."

"The hell it isn't," said Devon.

A bizarre sort of sorrow released within me.

"It's okay," I said. "Just tell me what's going on."

"I will," said Ms. Lighthorse, making her way back to the driver's seat. "But first we have to get you some help."

As if to agree, an explosion erupted in my skull, causing me to cry out. I fell forward, again bracing myself against the driver's seat. The pain was like an electrical current, racing down my back, splitting at the waist. My legs kicked out as the fire rushed towards my bare feet.

"I'm sorry."

I was able to tilt my head and saw that Linda was now out of her chair, leaning towards me, her hand gripping my injured shoulder.

"You should be," said Devon, unlatching himself and then hopping over the passenger seat, his legs working just fine. "Were you trying to make him like us?"

"I didn't know this would happen," said Linda, her green eyes drowning in tears. Even though the pain scratched at my skull like a captured lion, I could see that she had returned to the beautiful girl from the night before. I wanted to console her, to tell her that I didn't blame her for what was happening. I tried to pivot around, tried to reach out for her but was unable to turn. It was then that a numbness embraced me like I had jumped into freezing water. I would have collapsed to the floor of the van had Devon not been there to hold me back.

Panic took hold and I tried to cry out but could only manage a dry whisper.

"I can't move," I said.

Devon carefully lay me on the seat, his face shining with worried sweat. Linda sat back in her chair, lowering her face into trembling hands.

"He's going," said Devon.

"Hang on Dan," said Ms. Lighthorse, slamming down the gas pedal. "We're almost there." The crunching gravel sounded distant, as if it were coming from the other side of an insulated wall. The golden sunlight darkened and then began to gray.

"Try to stay awake," said Devon.

The pain was gone. I attempted to snap my fingers, I could feel my hand wanting to comply, but there was no sound. Another round of panic gripped me and I let out a hissing groan.

"You'll be alright," said Devon. "Mother Gina will know what to do."

CHAPTER NINETEEN

Spiritual Journey

Devon's words sounded as if they were coming from underwater. I found myself struggling to breathe. The van came to a stop but I hardly noticed. Everything was overcast and my body was filled with the tingling of billions of nerves shutting down. I heard a grinding hinge and felt the early morning breeze trying to slap me back to whatever reality this was.

"What's happened?"

I tried to focus on where this new voice was coming from but was unable to turn my head. A hand, like rough leather, rested on my head for a moment, lightly massaging my brow, and then it was gone.

"Get him to the lodge," the voice said.

Both of my arms and legs were gripped and I felt myself being lifted. In the distance, I could just make out the hazy peak of Mount Scott, its rocky sides a swath of dull earth colors. It soon vanished as the natural light was replaced by the low-lit walls of domed rock. A musty smell, like old rotten clothes, mixed with burnt sage, infested my senses as I was gently placed on a hard surface. The temperature seemed to have jumped forty degrees.

"Leave us for now," said the stranger's voice.

By then whatever was happening to me was near complete and every sound was like a tinny echo growing further and further away. A bluish light suddenly flared to my left, casting dancing phantoms on the curved ceiling.

"Don't be afraid," the voice said.

From the corner of my eye, I could just make out a shapeless form hovering near the flames. The shadow then seemed to melt, rushing over the floor like an oncoming wave. I wanted to back away, wanted to flee from this madness but could only watch in terror as the raging void seized me.

****

I opened my eyes to a cloudless blue sky; the kind that chases away all nightmares.

"Sit up. We don't have a lot of time."

It wasn't the words that sent my heart plummeting; it was the voice. The stranger was still with me. I sat up to find a blue fire burning just a few feet away and beyond that sat a young copper-skinned woman. Her face was a portrait of sharp, artistic features. Long black hair was tightly bound behind her head. Covering her thin body was a one-piece tunic made of faded hide. Mixed colored beads of red and yellow crisscrossed from the shoulders down to a rusted dolomite-edged hem. Resting across her lap was a wooden bow and to her left sat a quiver filled with white fletched arrows.

She was looking at me with eyes that resembled Ms. Lighthorse, only they seemed older, wiser. Around us was a ring of melded pine and cottonwoods, their limbs interwoven and shifting like some giant swirling blanket. From behind the foliage curtain came a muffled sniffing. The woman looked over at where a sudden snap broke through the breeze.

"Do you hear that?" she said, turning her gaze back to me. "It is trying to find a way through."

"Who are you?" I said.

"That doesn't matter, right now. What does matter is that it smells blood."

"What do you mean?"

"You are dying, and it knows it."

A thunderous sound, like a falling tree, came from behind me. The woman jumped to her feet, releasing an arrow. It went through the treeline as if it had been shot through smoke and a yelp, like a pain-stricken dog, was soon followed by fading, hobbled steps.

"It will be back," she said.

"What was it?" I said, trying to control the trembling that had now seized me.

"No time for that either," she said, dropping the bow and reaching into a pocket on the side of her tunic.

She pulled out a broken hand-sized chip of stone. It was flattened to an edge on one side like the remains of an ancient hatchet head. The woman held it out and began to come towards me.

"Hold on," I said, "What are you going to do with that?"

The girl stopped within reaching distance and said, "Let me see your shoulder."

"You're not touching me with that," I snapped.

"It's your choice," she said.

A faint howl sifted through the tangled wall of trees.

"You're not doing anything until I get some answers," I said.

The woman scowled at me for a moment, her hand clutching the jagged stone.

"I hope you're worth all of this," she said, plopping down in front of me.

Another roar came, sounding much closer.

"It's coming back," she said. "I won't be able to keep it out much longer. Ask your questions but know that if it breaks through and you haven't let me complete what needs to be done, I will leave you."

"What is it?" I said.

"A hunter. A tracker. A deal maker."

"I don't understand," I said.

"It has traded its misery for the misery of others."

These cryptic answers had my mind spinning.

"Did it kill Joe Clark?"

"I do not know that name," she said.

"He was skinned and left in a park," I said.

"It would fit the profile," she said. "The skin is an offering."

"An offering to what?"

"That answer will take more time than we have. For now just know that this thing, this it, has fallen into a snare, like so many others before it."

"Like Loshi?" I said.

"Heard of him, have you? Yes. Perhaps even us."

A violent impact came from just beyond the shifting green to our right.

"We are out of time," she said, leaning towards me, the stone held out in her hand. "Will you allow me to do what needs to be done?"

"What exactly are you going to do?"

"You have been wounded by one that has been touched by the wheel."

"Linda," I said. "Is she like that thing?"

"I hope not," said the woman.

"You don't know?"

"I don't know everything," said the woman. "Now, take off your shirt and let me see that shoulder."

"Who are you?" I said, pulling my T over my head.

Instead of answering she placed the stone on the scratch. The pain was like stepping into a fire and I clenched back a scream with my teeth. Another crash came from the treeline and the green wall began to break away. The woman ignored the disaster unfolding before us and continued to press the stone against my cooking flesh. I was roasting from the inside out and was amazed that the woman was able to withstand it, amazed that I hadn't burst into flame.

It had managed to push a teeth-laden muzzle through the thicket and was snapping at the woven branches.

"Don't look at it," the woman said, her eyes focused on the stone.

I tried not to, but the roars, combined with the sharp snap of breaking limbs, disrupted any hopes at concentrating on anything else. It would be free of the entanglement at any moment and then what? I looked at the bow and quiver lying ten feet away. Could she reach them before it got to us? I didn't think so. An image of Joe sitting on the park bench, skinless and alone popped into my mind's eye. But it wasn't Joe gazing up at the cloud filled sky; it was me.

"Done," she said, placing the stone back into her pocket.

Only then did I realize that the feeling of being deep fried had vanished. So, too, had the creature that had come so close to breaking through the wall of trees.

"It's gone," I said, pulling my shirt over my head.

"It missed its chance," said the woman.

I turned towards her and stifled a gasp. Her flawless copper skin had shrunk into deep, ash-tinted crevices. The black, tightly bound hair now hung loosely at her shoulders, gray and brittle. Only her eyes seemed unchanged.

"Still think I'm pretty?" she said, slowly rising to her feet.

"Uh...well...," I stammered.

"Don't you already have a girlfriend?" she cackled. "Isn't that why we're here?"

She then turned and limped her way back to the bow. With a muffled grunt she bent over and picked it up off of the ground, then grabbed an arrow out of the quiver.

"It all comes with a price, you know," she said, notching the arrow. "I've paid many times over."

I watched as she lifted the bow and pulled the arrow back. She then gave me a wink and pointed the glistening tip directly at my chest.

"What are you doing?" I said.

"Saving your life," she said, releasing the arrow.

I could do little else but close my eyes as the shaft whistled through the air. But there was no pain, no impact. The only thing I felt was the temperature suddenly rising. I risked a look and saw that I was sitting up in the dome surrounded by layered sandstone. The blue flame had turned to orange and just beyond it was a shadowy figure slumped over in a chair. A burst of sunlight sent bolts of agony throughout my skull as a door to the side was flung open. Ms. Lighthorse rushed in with Devon and Linda following close behind.

"Mother Gina," said Ms. Lighthorse, coming to a stop next to the motionless person.

Within moments my eyes had adjusted and I saw that it was an old woman. She looked to be in her eighties, if not older. She was wearing an oversized Sooner t-shirt that hung past faded Wranglers. She had beaded moccasins covering her feet which were resting on a pair of metal stands. It was then that I noticed she was in a wheelchair.

"Mother Gina, are you okay?"

Ms. Lighthorse had dropped to her knees in front of the woman, placing the lady's wrinkled face in her hands. The woman shook her head and let out a weak groan. She then reached up with a thin arm and brushed Ms. Lighthorse's hands away.

"I will be," she said. "Get me out of here."

Ms. Lighthouse grabbed the handles of the wheelchair and pushed the old woman out of the heat. I watched for a moment, trying to come to terms with what had just happened. The illness was gone, which was strange considering a few minutes before I was sure I was going to die. In fact, I felt as if I could happily run from here to Blanchard without so much as breaking a sweat. I began to follow Ms. Lighthorse but was stopped by Devon's hand on my shoulder.

"I'm sorry I didn't tell you," he said.

I looked at my friend who was standing eye to eye with me for the first time. Clarity had returned, allowing me to evaluate my recent discoveries and I realized that my feelings were mixed. On one hand I should be happy that Devon was able to walk, had been walking for a while, it seemed. But that led to the other hand, which was curled in anger: Why had he not told me? We had shared far too many tragedies for him to keep this from me. How could he not trust me? He knew I had broken into my dad's official web-page, damn it. Suddenly he jumped, turned a circle, and landed on one knee with his arms spread wide.

"TA DA!" he cried out.

I felt my face start to crack, my lips curling upward. My best friend was kneeling before me, his eyes twinkling with a joy that was both foreign and incredible to see. Whatever anger I had been feeling was gone, much like the illness that had brought me here. An explosion of laughter erupted from my dry throat and soon tears were flowing down my cheeks. It felt as though my stomach was about to rupture. After a few moments, I was able to regain some control and said, "You're an asshole."

"And you're the guy that hangs out with me," he answered back.

And just like that, the bridge had been repaired.

"I'm just glad you're better," he said, rising to his feet.

"What happened to me?"

"Come on," he said, motioning me towards the door. "That's a question for Mother Gina."

CHAPTER TWENTY

Mother Gina

I followed Devon out of the dome and realized just how far up in the Wichita's we had come. Mount Scott loomed less than three miles away. Of course, I was being hauled around like a corpse when I last saw it. But what was even more bizarre was how it seemed as though we had fallen back a hundred years in time. Surrounding us were run-down houses topped with weather-beaten roofs like the shanty's from the dust bowl era. Boarded windows sat within paint-depleted walls. There were no fences separating the properties, only stacked stones with an occasional rusted post.

"Who are these people?" I said.

"They are Ms. Lighthorse's family," said Devon.

"How can they live like this?"

"This is their land," said Devon.

"Why haven't they fixed it up?"

Devon stopped and looked at me, his expression bordering on aggravation.

"You really have to ask that?" he said.

I knew what he meant. Even now there were promises being broken and land being stolen. Still, Ms. Lighthorse was Chickasaw, one of the most well off tribes in Oklahoma, their people had some of the biggest casinos in the state and were pretty good at taking care of their own. It didn't seem as though they would let any member of the tribe wallow in the dark age domiciles that now stood before us.

"Come on," said Devon. "Let's find everyone else."

I followed him past a tarpaulin-covered house with its front door hanging by one leather hinge. A sound of breaking glass and a stifled yelp came from inside. I began to slow down.

"Ignore it," said Devon, continuing on without giving the house a glance. "It's just Crazy Carl having one of his fits."

It was strange watching my friend maneuver through the jutting sandstone and dried scrub grass. Obviously, he had been here many times before, as had Linda... And there it was. Thanks to the near-death experience and the shock of seeing Devon up and walking, I had managed to forget about the night before. But the truth always finds a way, it is said. And so it had. I followed my friend, my helpless compadre who wasn't so helpless after all, with a sick, guilty knot resting in my stomach.

Couldn't keep your hands off of him, Devon had said.

He knew what we had done. Apparently, he had expected it. Again, the question of why he kept all of this a secret flashed in my mind. If he had just told me, all of this could have been avoided. No way would I have made this trip. Plus, I would have avoided Linda at all costs.

Would you have?

The memory of her warmth said otherwise. I followed Devon towards a small hut near the edge of the rundown village and had just cleared a small sandstone barrier when the front door was flung open. Ms. Lighthorse stepped out and following close behind her was Linda. I looked up at the girl then quickly looked away.

"What's going on?" said Devon.

"She's trying to recover," said Ms. Lighthorse, shutting the door. "We should let her be."

Ms. Lighthorse began to walk past us, motioning for us to follow when a raspy voice stopped her mid-stride.

"Send him in."

Ms. Lighthorse stared at the closed door, her face tight with concern.

"Are you sure that's a good idea?" she called back.

"I'm not sure of anything anymore," the voice answered. "Send him in...just him."

Ms. Lighthorse waved me towards the door, but I hesitated. There was an inarticulate fear that seemed to have frozen me in place. I gazed over at Linda and saw that she was staring at me, her emerald eyes wide and anxious.

"Go Danny," said Devon. "I don't think you have a choice."

I took a step towards the door and reached out for the tarnished knob with my heart racing. It felt as though I was preparing to jump out of an airplane. I turned the handle, pushed the panel, and stepped over the threshold.

*****

The room was dimly lit by dust-infested beams of sunlight shooting from ripped towels doubling as curtains. Wafts of molded wood blended with sage and cinnamon. Cracked walls contained archaic paintings depicting herds of buffalo and Bob-Tailed deer, while others leaned more towards the spiritual: Eagles exploding out of lakes of fire and wolves caught midway in some sort of lycanthrope transformation. Dream Catchers had been placed throughout the room, staggered in an almost battle formation. Near the center of the room was a tarnished oak coffee table and next to it a weathered leather couch, torn, with its foam interior bubbling out in places. Resting on it was Mother Gina, her arms folded across her sunken chest like a corpse prepared for viewing. She tilted her head towards me as I entered.

"Close the door and sit down," she said, nodding towards the wheelchair off to the side.

I did as she commanded, the pulse in my temple going up a notch. We looked at each other for a moment in silence, long enough for her to remind me of the wasted features of my mother. But that wasn't quite fair; my mother's condition was the result of an unfortunate accident and deserved pity. This woman lying before me exuded a power that regarded such pity as a dishonor. There could be no doubt that she had saved me from whatever had inflicted my body, and no doubt that she had stopped the creature trying to kill me.

It always comes with a price, she had said.

Was she paying that price right now? Paying for saving me? A sudden wave of guilt shook me and I had to look away.

"You did nothing wrong," she said, as if reading my mind.

"What happened?" I said.

"You were taken into the ring," she said. "Injured while being watched."

"Watched by who?"

It was then that I remembered the sound of the wet sheets fluttering in the darkness and it brought with it images of the skinless scouts who had died while searching for their mad leader.

"Was it Loshi?" I said. "Was that what was trying to break through?"

She looked at me with narrowed eyes, then struggled to sit up. I leaned forward, lightly taking her elbow until she was able to center herself.

"The story of Loshi has been altered many times over the years. Each version widening further and further from the truth."

"But the Loshinka did come here?"

"Oh yes, in fact, they're still here," she said.

That caught me by surprise. How was that possible? According to Ms. Lighthorse, the tribe had vanished into obscurity. The woman watched patiently as I mentally traversed the maze that she had placed before me. And then it struck me. The connection was quite obvious, actually. And it explained why these people remained reclusive and in poverty.

"You're Loshinka," I said.

The woman cracked a sideways smile and said, "Clever boy."

"So the story that Ms. Lighthorse told wasn't true?"

"I wouldn't go that far," she said. "Loshi did exist and he did bring us from Arizona."

"But what about the sacred wheel and the white man? Was any of that real?"

The woman let out a sigh and rested her head against the back of the couch.

"Now we come to it," she said, in an almost whisper. "This is a choice that I must now make. But you have been touched."

Mother Gina then fell silent, closing her eyes. I sat there on the edge of her outdated wheelchair, trying to control my breathing. After a moment I had to consider the possibility that she had fallen asleep. I was about to call out to her when she suddenly lifted her head, her dark gaze catching and holding mine.

"We never built the wheel," she said. "We only repaired it."

"I don't understand," I said.

"The wheel was already here, although it had been damaged."

"But who made it?"

"That is a good question. And even after all of these years, we still don't know."

"But what about the murdered children?" I said. "And the white man?"

"Most of that is true," she said. "Although the number of children has seemed to have grown exponentially."

"Did Loshi kill the white man?" I said.

"I believe that he did," said Mother Gina. "And I think that's where the trouble began."

"But why would Loshi kill the children?" I said.

"I don't think he did, at least it wasn't just him."

"The white man helped him?" I said.

The confusion by then was making me dizzy.

"Yes and no," she said. "Loshi knew that his people were in danger and that if he let the man leave he would come back with more just like him. So he had to be stopped and for Loshi that meant committing an act that, up until then, was unthinkable. Loshi was a healer, not a killer. This was why he led the man to the sacred wheel. He figured that whatever spirit dwelt within the ring would protect him, perhaps forgive him, for what he was about to do. But I think he was wrong."

"You think that whatever was in the wheel made Loshi go crazy?"

"I think that whatever was in the white man made the wheel go crazy," she said. "Ninety percent, Daniel. That's how many Native Americans died because of the diseases the Europeans brought."

"I read about that in class," I said.

"But there is more than just physical ailments that can be passed on. The man held within him cruelty and greed that had, up until then, never been experienced in this land. Neither Loshi nor the sacred wheel was prepared for the evil that his murder would release."

"Wait. Are you saying this man, whoever he was, infected the wheel?"

"I'm saying it's possible," said Mother Gina.

"The creature that attacked us," I said. "Is it real?"

"There is something out there," she said. "Something that has given itself over to the blackened part of the wheel."

"You said that this creature was a deal maker. What did you mean by that?"

"This creature, as you call it, didn't start out that way. Much like Loshi before, it was driven by a purpose that left it helpless."

It was then that the memory of Devon flinging Kyle into the air shuttered in my mind like an old black and white film. And his eyes, the way they flashed cold silver. This was a possibility that I didn't want to consider, and yet it confronted me like a mile-high wall.

"Do you know something?" Mother Gina said.

Maybe I did, but I didn't want to admit it, not even to myself.

My father had told me once about the method for solving a murder. I was working on a paper for my English class. It had been an open assignment, the subject left to our choosing. I had picked Ted Bundy, not because of any sick fetish, but because I wanted to understand what made a man like that tick. Plus, I knew that Mrs. Shelly was an avid suspense reader and I figured that alone would boost my grade. It seemed to have worked, it was the only A I received that semester. My father was the first step in my tedious research and he was happy to help. He began by telling me about motive. That was the most important one. Did the suspect have a reason to commit murder? Devon had certainly hated Joe Clark and with good reason, but enough to kill him?

Then came the means. Would the suspect be capable? After watching the one-sided fight between Devon and Kyle there was no doubt. And finally; opportunity. Was the suspect in the area when the murder took place. I thought back to the morning Devon had called me with the news. He had seemed genuinely surprised and he was already at school, but that didn't mean that he couldn't have done it before. Perhaps he was calling me for an alibi. But that was ridiculous, why would anyone suspect him in the first place? And then there was the atrocity of what happened to Joe after he was dead. Would Devon skin him? It's an offering, the old lady had said, but she didn't say to whom.

A sick feeling clutched my stomach as I tried to come up with more reasons why it couldn't have been my friend as opposed to why it could. I was falling short.

"What about these offerings," I said, at last. "Who's receiving them?"

"That is something that I can only guess at," said Mother Gina.

"I'm willing to listen," I said.

Mother Gina gave me another slanted smile and said, "I believe that the violent greed of Loshi's enemy is demanding to be honored with tribute, except gold now means nothing to what it has become."

Her words acted like a trigger and I was again floating in the park, gazing down at the skinless corpse of Joe Clark. In that bizarre dream, he had issued a warning. I struggled to remember what he had said, it had seemed so foreign, so nonsensical. Then it came to me.

"Who is Pan," I said. "And what's a Rodelero?"

Mother Gina leaned towards me, her gnarled hands resting on her bony knees.

"Why do you ask?"

I told her about the dream, and how it at first seemed that it was me walking through the park.

"And you're sure that these were the words this boy spoke?"

"As sure as I can be," I said. "But what do they mean?"

"A good question and one that we must find out."

"But surely that was only a dream," I said.

The old woman gave me an impatient look that made me feel about as small as a microbe. Her silent point was well taken. There were things at work here that considered the realm of unconsciousness inconsequential, just a minor barrier to be casually crossed. The sooner I accepted this fact the easier it would be to continue with the real struggle. But did I really want to be a part of this struggle? And what exactly was this struggle? The best-case scenario was that I was involved in a mass delusion, where these people tricked themselves into some kind of psychosis and committed murder. But both Devon and Linda were walking, and that went beyond any parlor trick. Which led me to the worst possibility: My friend was a killer.

"What should I do?" I said.

"You must find out what you can about the warning you were given," she said. "Use your internet, or Google, or whatever it is you use. And you must keep your eyes open. It has seen you, it knows who you are."

"Are you saying that it will be coming for me?"

"I'm saying that you got away. You're probably the only thing that has."

That was something I hadn't considered; being marked by some skinning monster. It seemed as though the choice to help her was really not a choice at all, not if I wanted to survive.

Two weeks ago all I had been concerned about was maintaining my just above average GPA and having the nerve to ask Holly Stevens to the Prom. That now seemed like another life; a life that was quickly fading into some soon-to-be-forgotten dream. But what she was asking of me went beyond simple observation. What if this help that I did provide led me to conclude that my best friend was indeed a murderer? What would I do then? What would she do? Kill him? Could I live with myself then? And if I didn't help her and he did kill again, what then? Would that be any better?

Sudden anger erupted within me. Anger towards this woman, towards Ms. Lighthorse, towards Linda and Devon. Towards the entire Loshinka tribe. But it wasn't just anger that had me clenching my fists...It had seen me.

"I'll do what I can," I said, at last.

"Good," said Mother Gina. "It's best if we keep what was said here known only to us."

Yes, considering everyone waiting outside the front door could be the wolf in sheep's clothing. I rose from the ancient chair and began to make my way towards the door.

"Daniel," she said.

I turned around to see that she was again laying back on the ripped couch, her eyes closed.

"I don't think that what happened to you was an accident."

"What do you mean?"

"I think that you were touched for a reason," she said.

Her words did little to comfort me. If anything, they only made this nauseous clutching at my gut squeeze a little harder. I considered pursuing the conversation but decided against it. Mother Gina had begun to snore.

I opened the front door and was forced to cover my eyes against the blazing April sun. Ms. Lighthorse stood at the edge of the porch with Devon and Linda flanked on each side.

"What did she say?" said Devon, and I couldn't help but notice the worry in his wide eyes. Was that the expression of guilt or genuine concern? I hated that my mind had automatically shifted into the suspicion gear.

"What she said was meant for Daniel," said Ms. Lighthorse. "It's time for us to head back. We still need to get our stuff and pick up his car."

CHAPTER TWENTY-ONE

A Flat In The Mountains

We loaded into the van and made our way down the trail-like road blanketed in silence. At one point Devon tried to lighten the mood by mentioning the school dance.

"You think I should jump up from my chair and start break dancing or should I give it the evangelistic approach?"

Here he raised up his arms and said, "I'm healed."

"You can't do either," said Ms. Lighthorse, her dark eyes flaring at him from the rear-view mirror.

"I'm just kidding," he said, his arms falling to his lap. "We all need to lighten up. Danny's better and Mother Gina will be alright."

"Who are you taking to the dance, Dan?" said Linda.

"You might want to be careful how you answer that," said Devon, giving me a sly smile.

"I'm not stupid, Devon," said Linda. "I know he can't take me."

But she was wrong, technically, at least. I could take her. I could roll her into the decorated gymnasium and ignore the sideways glances and muttered insults. Pretend that whatever was being said had little effect on me, but it would be a lie. The Linda that I had been with, the Linda that now sat behind me, was forbidden to make an appearance. Just as Devon was.

"Daniel," said Linda. "I won't be mad."

"I was going to take Holly Stevens, but now I don't know."

Linda's hypnotic greens searched my face. My expression

remained poker steady until, finally, she smiled and looked away. Guilt can alter tides, and I was now wondering how I could possibly enjoy myself on the dance floor with Holly while knowing Linda was sitting on the sidelines. I found myself trying to come up with an excuse to back out of the date with Holly. Perhaps she would take the news as nonchalantly as she had taken the invitation, but somehow I doubted it.

"Don't change your plans," said Ms. Lighthorse. "Don't change anything."

"Is it not his choice?" said Linda.

"Was any of this?" said Ms. Lighthorse.

Linda let out an angered grunt but said nothing.

The frigid silence returned and we spent the remainder of the journey cocooned in our own thoughts. I again thought of my father trying to come up with an answer to the death of Joe Clark. My horrific nightmare of strolling through the park was gaining relevance. I looked over at Devon and saw that he had a slight smile zipped across his face. It made me shudder. There would be more killings, I was sure of that. More unsolvable murders that my father must face. Could I allow that knowing what I knew? The short answer was no. My father had been through enough. My mother was a living corpse, and yet he refused to give up on her. Refused to move on with his life. But could there be another way?

An image of her coming out of the river blasted like a spotlight before me.

Take me there, she had said as the water took us down.

Strange that it had taken this long for me to at least consider the idea. My mother lay silent forty miles away, helpless and waiting for the welcoming release of death. But did it have to be that way? Could this be the reason I had been touched? I wanted to believe this, I wanted it with all my heart, but somewhere deep inside a warning light was flashing in fire orange neon: STAY AWAY!

*****

Ms. Lighthorse drove us around the final bend, bringing us to a stop behind my Corsica.

"What the hell happened?" she said, shutting off the motor and climbing out. I leaned forward in silent shock, gazing through the front windshield. I could see shredded rubber littering the ground around my rear wheel. I jumped out of the van and made my way over to the retired patrol car, my heart thrumming.

"Do you have a spare?" said Ms. Lighthorse.

"That was my spare," I said, silently cursing myself for not replacing it.

By then both Linda and Devon were standing next to me.

"What could have done this?" said Devon. "A cougar?"

"Why would a cougar attack a tire?" said Linda.

"Maybe it had rabies," said Devon. "Or maybe it doesn't like Firestone."

"This wasn't done by a cougar," said Ms. Lighthorse.

"Then what?" said Linda.

"I don't know," said Ms. Lighthorse.

She then gazed up at the sun tilting towards the west, and said, "I think we should head back."

"What about his car?" said Devon.

"There's nothing we can do about it now," said Ms. Lighthorse.

I heard all of this, but it barely registered. This attack wasn't random. How I knew this I couldn't say, but I was sure of it. The creature had tried to get to me but was stopped, and now it was angry. But it wasn't stupid. I would have to come back, it had made sure of that, and I was sure that it would be waiting for me when I did. And yet there was a silver lining surrounding my disaster; Devon had been with me, so that pretty much crossed him off of the killer list. Or at least I hoped it did.

CHAPTER TWENTY-TWO

Back Home

I got into the van in a state of surrealism, vaguely aware of the others taking their appropriate places. Ms. Lighthorse backed away from my injured car and steered us out of the ancient glade.

"I can bring you back tomorrow if you'd like," she said.

"That's okay," I said. "I'll have my dad bring me."

At least with him, there would be a gun handy.

The grinding dirt was replaced by the smooth whine of asphalt. We crossed under the welcoming sign for Mount Scott, and the air became heavier, like a moist weight. The information center for the park, with its empty lot, appeared and then disappeared on my left as Ms. Lighthorse continued to steer us out of the Wichita's.

The mountains were fading in the side mirror when I suddenly heard choking erupt from behind me. I turned to see that Linda was shaking in her chair, her arms whipping out, hands curling and uncurling.

"What's going on?" I said, leaning over and catching one of her flailing hands.

"She'll stop in a second," said Devon.

Within moments she seized, her breath catching in her throat. Her head then tilted like a broken limb, her jaw becoming slack with a stream of drool trickling down her chin.

"Once we leave the foothills we return to our miserable selves," said Devon.

"I'm sorry," I said.

Less than twelve hours ago she had taken me into the wheel and I had gone willingly. Now she slumped in a helpless state; unable to speak, unable to laugh...unable to do anything but watch as the uncaring world went by. I reached up and wiped a tear from my cheek. If Devon noticed he didn't say anything, and for that I am grateful.

Little else was said for the remainder of the trip. I think for them it was a moment for re-acclamation. For me, it was like watching a family age before my eyes, which forced me to again think of my mother. She lay where she had been the day before and the year before and so on, and here I was holding the key to the fountain of youth. The thought of bringing her to the wheel produced an indescribable terror. And yet the thought of not trying held guilt that I knew would stay with me for the rest of my life. Was I prepared to live with that? Could I live with that? This was a choice that I couldn't make alone. I would have to tell my father. But would he believe me, or would he think that I had cracked? The only thing I could do was show him, and for that, I would need help. I gave my friend a glance and saw that his eyes were closed, his breathing deep and calm. Linda, too, was sleeping, her hands twitching on her lap.

"They're recovering," said Ms. Lighthorse. "These trips take a lot out of them."

I only nodded, then turned my face towards the window just as Ms. Lighthorse crossed into Blanchard.

*****

I watched the van turn off of my road. Ms. Lighthorse had made me promise that I would call her if my father wasn't able to take me back to my car. Through it all, I kept sneaking glances at the back of the van. Neither Devon nor Linda moved, it was as if they had died.

It was a little after two in the afternoon and my father wasn't home. He was no doubt still searching for clues on dead-end roads . I made my way into the house, passing the spotless living room and immaculate kitchen until finding myself alone in the welcoming clutter of my sanctuary. I was suddenly terrified, as if something was coming, like a midnight storm, or a faceless monster. This fear wasn't baseless. How could it be after all that I had seen? And my dad was in the middle of it; lost in an evil forest, chasing for a truth that didn't exist. I had to talk to him.

"Hey, buddy," he said after the second ring, but his voice sounded rehearsed. "Sounds like you've got a pretty good signal."

"I'm back," I said. "Dad, what's wrong?"

There was a pause.

"It's your mom," he said.

"What happened?"

"I can't talk about it right now," he said, his voice trembling. "I'll be home in an hour."

I could hear my pulse pounding in my head as he ended the call. I stood there for a moment with the cellphone welded to my ear. The choice I had to make about my mother had become immediate. Was this the plan all along? And if so, whose plan?

I slumped on my bed feeling as if I were a piece in some game and had just been moved. The chair that had held the phantom of Joe Clark, like something out of a Dickens novel, sat motionless in the corner. I had hoped that it had been a nightmare, but after the trip to the mountains, and all of the madness that followed, I was sure that he had been there.

Mother Gina seemed sure that he had.

Use your Google, she had said.

I glanced over at my computer, the dark screen was like a cold mouth of a cave daring me to enter. I didn't want to.

Pan has found his Rodelero!

Those words meant nothing to me, and yet just thinking them sent a shiver down my spine. I rose and made my way over to the computer, walking as if my time of execution was at hand and lowered myself into the swivel chair. The monitor came to life with the slightest touch of the mouse. I stared at the screen with my fingers hovering an inch above the keyboard..

I typed the word Pan. The screen came alive with information concerning cooking, some long-ago forgotten movie and a breakdown about an ancient Greek God that appeared to be half man and half goat. I skimmed over the Wikipedia definition and learned that He ruled over fields, woods and fertility. But this God was worshiped long before the Loshinka arrived, and was part of a culture half a world away. I backed out of the page and typed in Rodelero and felt my heart skip. A drawing of an armored horseman appeared with a sword held high. Surrounding him were depictions of scantily dressed natives fleeing for their lives.

I scrolled down and began to read: Blood-thirsty killers, who followed and served the leaders of Spain. They slaughtered millions of people as they butchered and tricked their way through Central America in search of gold. A sudden gust of wind slapped my window, causing me to jump in my seat. I looked through the pane of glass and saw that a cloud had covered the midday sun, casting a shadow over the neighborhood. I forced my gaze back to the screen and tried to focus on the words and not the fear that the image had produced. The more I read the more it correlated with the story of Loshi. He had taken a stranger, a dangerous man, into the wheel and murdered him.

Probably a Spaniard, Devon had said.

Was that man a Rodelero? And if he was, who was Pan? Surely not the Greek God.

Again I typed in Pan, but could find nothing that connected with Rodelero, or Spain, for that matter. I was missing something.

*****

My investigation was brought to a stop by the sound of the front door being opened. I clicked off the page and shut the computer down.

"Dan?"

"I'm here," I said, making my way out of my room and into the kitchen where I found my father popping the top off of a bottle of Coke.

"Where's your car?" he said.

I explained how the car had a flat, leaving out the events from the night before and my near death experience. He sat at the table, his eyes focused on the bottle and as I spoke I couldn't help but notice the death-like grip he was holding the Coke with. The anxiety he was struggling to keep capped was obvious, and I quickly wrapped up my tale.

"We'll get a tire tomorrow," he said. "I got a call from the center earlier today."

"What's happened?"

"Your mother stopped breathing," he said. "They thought she was gone, but three minutes later she opened her eyes."

"Well that's good, isn't it?"

"The doctor said it meant that her body was finally beginning to shut down. She said we should expect this to start happening more and more until...", but he couldn't finish.

I pulled out the chair across from him and sat. I tried to think of something to say, but came up empty. My father reached up and wiped a tear from his eye, leaned back and said, "It's going to be a long haul. I don't know if I'm ready."

My next thought might seem twisted, if not a little selfish, but we were already involved in a long haul, it's just that we had become used to it. Perhaps the truth was that we were both hoping for a quick retreat for my mother. Not just for her, but for us, as well. Yes, selfish, indeed. The magical, sinister wheel, again entered my thoughts, connecting itself to our misery like a virus penetrating a cell. Of course, she would be forced into a time consuming death, one riddled with guilt-laden opportunities and many chances for a decision. Plenty of time to reconsider whether or not I should take her. Another moving piece.

My father stood up, swigged down the last of the soda and tossed the bottle into the trash.

"I have to head back to the station," he said. "We'll go get your car tomorrow, but I want to stop by and see your mother on the way."

Without another word, he left. I sat there for a moment, not even trying to fight back the cold fear growing within me. We would see her tomorrow, see her ailing face, watch for signs of her breathing suddenly coming to a stop, knowing that there would be nothing we could do.

If that were only true.

It was a struggle to finish out the rest of the night without going back on line. The Rodelero was key, I was sure of it, but I had seen enough for now. I lay in my bed with my bag still resting to the side, packed and forgotten. My thoughts turned to Devon. My plan had been to see if he would go with me and my father back to my car. To see if he would show my father what the wheel could do, and then leave it up to my father. Now, with my dad nearing breakdown, I wasn't even sure if I should tell him at all. But I was sure of one thing; bringing Devon into the picture at that moment was a bad idea. The last thing my father needed right now was some fantasy story. Another thought struck, causing me to sit up. What if it didn't work? My mother was not a Native American, that lineage came from my father. What if the wheel was biased?

I lay back and gazed up at the fading light through my window. The sky still held the filtering gray clouds, causing the day to look further along than it really was. I didn't like the illusion; it made tomorrow seem that much closer.

At some point exhaustion must have flipped a switch, because the next thing I knew my father was shaking my shoulder.

"Come on, kid," he said. "We've got a lot to do today."

CHAPTER TWENTY-THREE

The Center

We found a used tire at Scott's Wheels. Scott Larkin had gone to school with my father and was kind enough to meet us, even though it was Sunday. He mounted it on an old rim, and made me promise to come back for a new one. We thanked him and made our way towards the center.

The building was like a pair of super sized box-cars meeting at a squared entrance that doubled as both office and entertainment room. The outside was done in stucco, which was aged to the point of falling off. We stepped into the lobby and were immediately assaulted by wafting waives of chemicals and detergent. Rose Peterson shot us a smile as we approached the welcoming desk. She was an older woman and had been there the day my mother arrived.

"Hey guys," she said in a voice trained to deny the truth. "It's been a while."

"Too long," said my father. "How are you, Rose?"

"I'm doing good," she said.

"Has there been any change?"

"Nope," she said. "It's as if it never happened."

After a minute more of small talk we made our way down the left wing. The narrow hall was painted dull gray with metal doors lined on each side. A feeling of being constrained trickled over me, a sensation of claustrophobia that I had never before experienced. I forced myself to take a deep breath. My mothers room sat at the end on the right side. I let my father take the lead and hoped that he wouldn't notice something was wrong. He stopped at the door with his hand resting on the knob.

"Dan," he said. "This could be the last time we see her, so you need to talk to her and tell her that you love her."

I could only nod. My father opened the door. Mote infested light beamed through the window at the far wall, creating an almost angelic glow. I followed my father into the room, each of us pulling a chair closer to where my mother lay facing the sunlight. At the head of her bed stood a wide monitor, its screen displaying the painfully slow beating of her heart. Her breath came with an even slower rhythm bordering on gasps. My father took her hand in both of his.

"I'm so sorry, Helen," he said. "I knew better."

This had been the albatross, the cross that my father had struggled with over the years since the accident. The guilt of having participated in a digital conversation that had changed our lives forever was corrosive. And now the tragic conclusion was at hand. He wasn't ready for this, he had said, and it was then that I realized that I wasn't ready, either. My mothers motionless eyes remained focused on the golden light from the window. Did she see it? Could she feel its warmth? These were questions that no one could answer. I gazed at her face, so different from the image from my childhood that I held on to. This woman looked like a stranger compared to the memory.

"You should say something," my father said.

I scooted the chair closer and took her other hand. It was cold and dry, like aged paper.

"Mom," I said. "I love you."

The words were a trigger, releasing free-falling tears. She would die soon.

But did she have to?

If I said nothing about the wheel it would become my own albatross to bear. Together, my father and I would be sentenced to walk through the darkness, each weighed down by our unshareable grief. I looked up and saw that his shoulders were slumped, his head lowered with my mothers hand now resting on his cheek. It was more than I could take.

"Dad — ," I began but was interrupted by a sudden wet choking cough coming from my mother. Her face had become the color of a storm-covered sunset. Her grip on my hand was like an iron clamp.

"No," said my father, shooting up from his chair. He rushed for the door, slamming it open and disappeared out of the room. My mothers hand continued to tighten, turning my fingers purple.

"Mom," I said. "You'll be alright."

Her head swiveled, her blood-shot eyes locking onto mine.

"Loshi is losing," she said in a cracked voice. I felt my heart shift to light speed. Her eyes continued to laser, her breath coming in heaves. From outside of the room I could hear nearing footsteps.

"He needs our help!" she said, and then, as if I had dreamt it all, her head dropped, her eyes drifting back to the sunlight.

My father rushed into the room followed by a woman wearing a long white coat and a young nurse. I was pushed out of the way as they surrounded the bed. The doctor took my mothers wrist and gazed up at the monitor. My father fell to his knees at the head of the bed.

"She was choking," he said.

"That's not surprising," said the doctor. "But she seems fine now."

My heart was still in live-wire mode. I stood there with my nails digging into my palms, trying to come to terms with what I had just witnessed. The thought of sharing the information with the doctor never entered my mind. Somehow, I knew this went beyond any medical science.

"Are you okay?" said my father. I looked over and saw the concern on his face.

"It just scared me a little," I said.

"Why don't you wait outside," he said, tossing me the car keys.

*****

I walked out into the humidity with my phone in hand. I scrolled to Devon's number and placed the call.

"Hey man," he said. "How's Linda?"

I ignored the comment. I had intended to honor my promise to Mother Gina and had said nothing about the evil that seemed to be wandering around in the mountains and in our town. Of course,

Devon had been the prime suspect then, but after watching the transformation upon our return, I decided that it wasn't possible. At least, I hoped it wasn't. Besides, I had to talk to someone, this was beyond out of hand.

Devon listened without once interrupting, not even when I mentioned taking my mother to the wheel. There was a long silence after I finished the tale and I wondered if he had hung up.

"Devon?"

"I'm here," he said, finally.

"I don't know what to do."

"Don't say anything to your dad. Let me talk to Ms. Lighthorse."

"Do you think we should?"

"I don't think we have a choice," he said. "You said Pan and Rodelero, right?"

"Yes," I said.

"I may have an idea who Pan is," he said. "I'll call you back."

The line went dead.

I unlocked the patrol car's door and climbed into the passenger seat. The temperature was hovering in the low eighties and the sky was near cloudless. But, the chill that had seized me refused to let go. Outside seemed dark, shaded by fear and the unknown. Everything revolved around the Sacred Wheel: The place where my injured car awaited my return, the place where I had almost died. The place that my father and I were soon going to be. A shudder raced through my body just as my father walked out of the building.

CHAPTER TWENTY-FOUR

Back To The Mountains

The first twenty miles were spent in silence. My father looked to have aged ten years since we had arrived at the center. For him, it had been too close. She had almost died with us sitting right beside her. These thoughts were no doubt playing over and over in his mind. My thoughts tended to be a little more on the terrified side.

Loshi is losing. He needs our help.

How I wanted to tell him. To share with him the madness that I had stumbled upon. But to tell him would only add to the chaos, providing another thing for him to worry about; his son's sanity. Devon had said to wait until he could talk to Ms. Lighthorse. Would she know what to do? Perhaps she would talk to Mother Gina, if anyone could help, it would be her.

"Are you okay?"

My father had broken free from his mental maze and noticed the anxiety etched across my face.

"I've been better," I said.

"I'm sorry," he said. "I shouldn't have panicked."

"I didn't notice," I said.

"We have to be prepared," he said.

He was right about that. Something was coming, something we were not ready for. Could we ever be ready? I didn't think so. I gazed at my father. His hands were locked onto the steering wheel as if it were a ledge. I looked at the clock on my phone: 12:42. We were less than an hour away from my car. I suddenly realized that I wasn't a hundred percent sure of how to get to it.

That was good, it gave me an excuse to text Devon.

It took less than five minutes for his response. It was a step by step route ending with the narrow turn off.

Have you found anything out? I typed.

Not yet, was his reply. I'm waiting for Ms. Lighthorse to call me back.

After missing one exit and having to turn around, we finally found the narrow path-like road. The hanging rocks seemed to be reaching out, hardened traps waiting for a mistake. The trees stood like ancient sentinels, their budding leaves waiving us in. My father navigated the final turn, leading us to the row of huts. He parked the cruiser behind my Corsica. The shredded rear tire still lay scattered in the grass.

"What happened?" he said, shutting off the motor and opening the door.

I pissed off a monster, I wanted to say but settled for, "I'm not sure."

My father looked at me in disbelief. I couldn't remember the last time I had lied to him. There was never any reason to, and, although this fib was for his own good, it still hurt. He popped open the trunk and then walked around to the back of the cruiser, pulling out the tire and floor-jack.

"Let's get this done," he said.

He wanted to get back to town. Time, after all, was running out.

"I can do it," I said, grabbing the handle of the jack.

"They grow up so quick," he said, managing to smile.

The humor was automated, shallow, but at least he tried.

"Make sure to loosen the lugs before you lift it," he said, turning towards the huts.

"These look old."

"They are,' I said, grunting under the strain of physical labor.

"You stayed here?"

"Only one night."

"Not exactly a Hilton," he said, making his way to the one Ms. Lighthorse had stayed in.

The last lug-nut felt as if it had been welded on. I was forced to use my foot as well as both arms, in order to get it to budge. Finally, after the sharp pain in my lower back retreated, I was able to place the jack under the frame. The car was up and the tire was off. I glanced over at where my father had been and froze: He was gone. A bolt of fear burst through me. I placed the replacement tire on while cursing myself for being so stupid. There was a monster out here. Had I forgotten? I dropped the car, pulled out the jack and then ran over to the hut. It was empty. They were all empty.

My eyes drifted over to the treeline, the place where terror awaited. I gave the empty hut one last wishful look and then made my way over to where the woods began. Checkered patches of dirt glimpsed through saw-grass, revealing a path leading up into the thickening oaks and pines.

"Dad!" I cried out.

No response. I took a deep breath, counted to five and stepped onto the trail. The air grew heavier, the trees blocking most of the wind, creating a natural wall. An eerie silence fell over the woods; there were no chirping birds or limbs rattling. It was as if everything had been placed on pause. The only sound was the occasional crack of my foot landing on a stray stick, amplified and startling. The trail continued to climb, weaving through the trees like an endless road to nowhere. Linda had led me up here, and yet, I could remember nothing of the journey. The time it took for the climb was unattainable, as if it were a part of a dream that I couldn't recall.

I considered calling for my father again and was about to when I suddenly crested a ridge. Chunks of granite and sand-rock lay before me, slithering in an arc, webbing out here and there. At its center stood a haggard cottonwood, its limbs barren, untouched by life. At its base was a shadow, its identity hidden from me by both fear and darkness. Suddenly it moved, causing a gasp to leap from my throat. The shape rose and then turned towards me. It was my father. He stood there with his hands locked together, like a man in prayer. He stared at me for a moment as if I was a stranger. He then shook his head like he was coming out of a dream and began to walk to where I stood frozen.

"Hey buddy," he said. "This place is pretty cool."

He stepped over the perimeter and placed a hand on my

shoulder.

"Are you okay?" he said. "You look a little sick."

"I'm fine," I said. "Are you okay?"

"Getting better," he said. "Did you get the tire on?"

"I'm good to go."

"Then let's go," he said, giving the cottonwood another glance. "I'm getting hungry."

My dad then patted my shoulder and began the long walk back to the cars. I stood there watching him descend, unsure of what, if anything, had happened. The place scared me and that fear made me assume the worst. Still, there was magic in these mountains, I had seen it, and not all of it was good. A chill crept over me at that thought, motivating me to move.

CHAPTER TWENTY-FIVE

Nightmares Of The Father

I received a text message from Devon as I was pulling into my driveway demanding that I call him ASAP. The line only rang once before he picked up.

"I know who it is," he said, his voice jumping an octave.

"What are you talking about?" I said, opening the front door and making my way down the hall.

"Pan," he said. "I know who he is."

The dirty clothes in my room appeared to be breeding. I tossed a pair of shorts and a rumpled button-up shirt off of the chair at my computer and sat down.

"Well, don't leave me in the dark," I said.

"His name is Panfilo de Soto, and he was the worst of the worst."

"Not the de Soto?"

"No," said Devon. "You're thinking of Hernando de Soto, he died somewhere in Louisiana. Panfilo managed to make it further into the country, although nobody knows how far."

"Why do you think it's him?"

"It fits," said Devon. "Here, check this out."

He then sent me a link on my phone. I turned on my computer and typed it in. A portrait revealing a pair of narrow eyes flanking a sharp saber-like nose filled the screen. It was quite possibly the cruelest face I had ever seen.

"Whoa!"

"Yeah," said Devon. "How'd you like to be the artist who had to paint that?"

"Do you think he tried to make him look friendlier?"

"I don't think that's possible."

"But how do you know it's him?" I said.

"Read the article," said Devon.

The information came from two survivors who had managed to find their way back to Mexico. They told of a luckless journey, filled with brutal natives unwilling to bend the knee and how they were forced to fight for their lives through harsh climates and savage attacks. Through it all, Panfilo refused to give up. Gold had been found, Cortez was drowning in it, and Panfilo was sure that this land held just as much, if not more, than the southern discovery. He was also sure that the barbaric natives held the key. They knew where to find it and once a few were tortured the others would have no choice but to tell them what they wanted to know.

The Spaniards continued on, their numbers falling from four hundred to forty- eight, as they plundered from the Mississippi River west. At some point the gunpowder was gone and all but one of their horses had died. Finally the men had enough and demanded that Panfilo turn back. He refused. The men waited until their leader had drunk himself into a stupor and then quietly packed their things and left, taking with them the remaining horse. It was the last time that anyone saw Panfilo de Soto alive. The men were questioned and, although many believed that they had killed de Soto, were never charged.

I pushed myself away from the desk and leaned back in the chair. All of this sounded so crazy. Here we were discussing the possibility of some evil spirit from the seventeenth-century infesting a sacred ground cherished by a people long gone. But they weren't gone, not really, just forgotten.

"What should we do?" I said, finally.

"I talked to Ms. Lighthorse and she said she was going to talk to Mother Gina. Until then we keep our eyes open and do nothing."

That sounded fine to me. What, if anything, could we do? We ended the call after agreeing to meet in Ms. Lighthorse's classroom before the first hour. I glanced at my phone and saw that it was after six. It was time to take a break. To shift gears I typed in Tea for the Tillerman by Cat Stevens and tried to ignore the claw -like tension that seemed to be scraping at my back. I turned up the speakers and made my way over to the bed, free falling onto the mattress as Where Do The Children Play soothed my poster-filled walls.

Will you tell us when to live or will you tell us when to die, the song said. Beautiful, really, but for some reason it chilled my blood.

Loshi is losing. He needs our help.

*****

My mother hadn't spoken in years and yet somehow she had managed to blurt out a warning, using a name that she had never heard. How could that be? Had the Sacred Wheel reached out to her? Had it channeled itself through a dying woman and sent up a flare just for me? What did it expect me to do? A sudden ring erupted from my phone, causing an embarrassing squeal to spew forth from my throat. I answered without checking the number.

"Hello," I said, my voice shaking.

"Dan?"

It was Holly. Her voice held the professionalism of a military commander. I quickly covered the phone and cleared my throat.

"Hey," I said, hoping my voice had recovered. "What's going on?"

"I'm sure you know that the prom is next Friday."

Is it not his choice?

Linda's voice echoed within my mind, sending waves of guilt, causing me to grip the phone until my knuckles turned white.

"I didn't forget," I lied.

"Good," she said. "I just wanted to let you know that if you wanted to grab something to eat first I would be good with that."

"Okay. How about Carlitos?"

"That would be fine," she said. "So I should expect you at five-thirty?"

"That will be fine," I said.

"Good. By the way, you could sit by me tomorrow at lunch."

"That sounds fine," I said.

"Until then," she said, and then the line went dead.

I lowered my phone, gazing at it as if it were some kind of alien artifact. Talking to Holly had that effect. It was then that I heard the front door open. I left the ramshackle comfort of my room to find my father tossing his keys onto the kitchen table.

"Hey kiddo," he said, making his way to the fridge.

"What's going on?" I said.

"Just fishing," he said.

And yes, he was. The murder of Joe Clark was eating away at him and there was nothing I could do, at least for now.

"No luck?" I said.

"Nothing," he said, grabbing a beer and sitting at the table. "It's as if I'm chasing a ghost,"

Not a ghost, dear papa, but a demon.

"I'm taking tomorrow off," he said, after a long drink. "I'm going to spend some time with your mother."

"Do you want me to go with you?"

"No, you don't need to miss school. I'll call if something's up."

With that, he finished his beer and left the room. I sat there for a moment, my thoughts running like wildfire. He had found his way to the wheel. Had stood at its center with the rotten cottonwood enveloping him within its shadow. For a moment it hadn't looked like him. Someone else was standing there; dark, unafraid and hungry. This was what my heart was telling me and yet he had been there, looking like a tourist. We had, after all, left the ring together. There had been no attacks, no voices whispering from the shadows.

So why was I now sitting at the table terrified?

I left the kitchen, noticing that his bedroom door was closed. I made my way to my sanctuary and lay down. I trained my ears for any sound, but all that I could hear was the light beating of the wind against my bedroom window.

*****

A scream caused me to bolt from my bed. My room was enshrouded in darkness. I reached over and turned on my lamp, sure that it would reveal at least one ghost, but the room was clear. It had to have been a nightmare, and no surprise there. I walked over to my window and gazed out at the murky shadows that seemed to have swallowed the world. There was no moon, no stars, the sky had been covered by silent, invisible clouds. From the reflection in the window I could see the chair that Joe had sat in. It was empty. I closed my eyes before that had a chance to change and turned away from the glass, pulling the curtains closed.

My phone said 2:32 AM. Somehow I had managed to pass out before eight and had remained in a coma for over six hours. I sat back down on the bed not sure if I would be able to go back to sleep. A moan sent the hairs on the back of my neck to attention. The sound was muffled and low. Another cry soon followed and I made my way out of the room, pausing in the narrow hallway, my heart jackhammering in my ears. The moans had now become barely audible sobs and they were coming from my fathers room. I stood with my ear pressed against his door.

"Dad?" I said, giving the panel a gentle knock. "Are you okay?"

There was no answer. There was no sound at all, it was as if the heavy blackness of the outside world had found its way in. The memory of Devon's father was suddenly there. His self-inflicted end brought on by unspoken anguish acted as fuel for my already erratic mind. I burst through the door and stopped mid-stride. My father stood facing his window, his arms hanging, his shoulders slumped.

"Dad, are you okay?"

The shadow that was him slowly turned, and I swear that, for a moment, it was as if there was more than just one person there. It was like a blurred image that began to split, one part falling away until it seemed to evaporate, like flickering waves of heat.

"She doesn't have to," my father whispered.

I had heard enough. I reached over and flipped the light switch. The beams shattered the darkness, revealing a man bent with his eyes closed. It was as if my father had come back from the future thirty years older.

"Dad," I said, rushing over to him.

The lids of my father's eyes fluttered for a moment and then opened. He rose to his full height, widening his shoulders until the illusion of age was gone.

"Dan," he said. "What are you doing in here? Did you have a bad dream?"

"Not me. You were."

"I was?" he said, running his hand through sweat- drenched hair. "I don't remember it."

"That's the best kind," I said, putting my arm around his shoulders. "Do you want some water?"

"I'm fine," he said, allowing me to lead him back to his bed. "Wow, I'm exhausted."

He lay back, resting his head on his pillow and shut his eyes. I stood there for a moment listening to his low, steady snores. The image of that splitting shadow still gripped my nerves.

She doesn't have to, he had said.

She doesn't have to, what? Die? No, she doesn't. I suddenly felt duped. This offer had been made to me, and I had hesitated. Was the wheel now bypassing me for a more sure bet? Was it being offered to my father? To hell with what Devon and Ms. Lighthorse said, my father needed to know the truth, and if he refused to believe me I would make Devon back me up no matter what it took. For a moment I considered waking him and spilling the proverbial beans. But he looked so peaceful and nightmare free. I turned to leave the room unknowingly making one of the worst mistakes of my life.

CHAPTER TWENTY-SIX

Threats And Empty Calls

I came into the kitchen just as the sun was clearing the eastern horizon and felt my heart sink. A note with two twenty- dollar bills had been left under the salt shaker.

> *Danny,*
>
> *I've got to go to the city after I see your mother. I won't be home until late.*
>
> *Here's some money for food.*
> *Love Dad.*

We did not lie in this family, at least not much, and yet I knew that what I was reading wasn't true. My cell still sat on my nightstand, its battery fully charged and ready.

"Hey kid," he said, after the third ring. "You're up early."

"And you're gone early," I said.

"Yeah, I've a few things to do at the station before I head over to see your mom."

"Dad, are you okay?"

"I'm fine," he said. "Why do you ask?"

"Last night," I said. "Your nightmare."

"I'm sorry about that," he said. "It was one of those falling dreams. You know, they seem so real."

Another lie. Unless he truly didn't remember. Or wasn't

allowed to. The truth of Joe's murder was still unknown to him and telling him was why had gotten out of bed an hour before my alarm was set to go off.

"Dad, I need to talk to you," I began.

"Danny, it'll have to wait. I've got to get a hold of Pearson so he can cover for me."

With that the line went dead.

I completed my breakfast for no other reason than ritual. After placing the dirty bowl into the dishwasher, I made my way to the bathroom and turned on the shower.

The mirror above the sink began to steam over, slowly covering the frightened image of a young man. I removed my clothes and stepped into the water, pausing briefly as hot-water slapped against my skin. For a moment I considered not going to school and tracking my father down. And what if I did find him loading my mother into the car? What would I do then? How could I stop him? The truth was, I couldn't.

I lowered myself into the tub, interlocking my hands around my knees, allowing the warm stream to caress my neck. The plan was to go to Ms. Lighthorse's class early in order to discuss Devon's theory of Pan, but that had taken a back seat as far as I was concerned.

Would Ms. Lighthorse believe me? And even more urgently; would she help me?

I turned off the water and stood, reaching past the curtain and grabbed a towel off of the nearby rack. I took one step out of the tub and froze. Staring back at me was the mist covered mirror and written across it in finger-like print were the words;

HE IS GOING

I stood there for a moment desperately trying to get my heart rate under control.

The ghosts had returned, had quietly intruded without a sound. Had it been Joe?

I left the room without looking back.

*****

I found Devon and Ms. Lighthorse sitting at her desk.

133

"Dan," Ms. Lighthorse said, as I entered the room. "Come in and shut the door."

I pulled the panel until I heard the lock catch and then made my way over to an empty chair.

"Devon was filling me in on this Pan guy," she said, as I sat. "What do you think?"

"I think I have a bigger problem," I said.

They listened to my story without interrupting. I told them of my nightmare about Linda and how I had lived vicariously through Joe at the park and then concluded with the writing on the mirror from this morning.

"And you think this was Joe warning you?" said Devon, doubtfully.

"He was there before," I said.

"But why would that asshole want to help you?" said Devon.

"Maybe he wasn't as bad as he pretended to be," said Ms. Lighthorse.

"I don't know," said Devon, shaking his head.

The thought of his arch-enemy switching to the good guys was understandably hard to swallow.

"Would it even work?" I said. "I mean, she isn't even Native American."

"Neither is Mike,' said Ms. Lighthorse.

"But that was only once," said Devon.

"That's because we only took him once," said Ms. Lighthorse. "And look what happened."

"You mean Mike was able to walk?" I said.

"Yes, and he was gone for hours," said Ms. Lighthorse.

"Well, it could be a good thing, right?" said Devon. "What if it did heal her?"

"Could it?" I said.

"I don't know," said Ms. Lighthorse, leaning back in her chair.

"What about the dreams?" I said. "Is that normal?"

"It never happened to me," said Devon.

"There's something else at play here," said Ms. Lighthorse. "Mother Gina made that clear."

"No shit," I said, unable to contain myself. "It killed Joe and now it's coming after me."

"We don't know that for sure," said Ms. Lighthorse.

"What should we do?" said Devon.

"I want you to try and call your father at lunch, Dan," she said. "Until then there's not a lot we can do."

She then turned towards Devon and said, "Now, tell me about Pan."

Devon filled her in on what he had learned.

"What do you think?" I said, hoping that Ms. Lighthorse would say that it was ridiculous.

"At this point, anything is possible." she said. "And it does make sense, as far as it goes."

"But how can we prove it?" I said.

"I'm not sure that we can," said Ms. Lighthorse. "But maybe Mother Gina can."

The thought of that old woman limping her way into that ring on her own filled my heart with dread.

"She can't go up there," I blurted out.

Ms. Lighthorse looked at me with a sly smile and said, "You, of all people, know that she has many ways to travel."

"So we do nothing?" said Devon.

"For now I'm afraid that's all we can do."

"What about my dad?"

"Call him at lunch and then we'll go from there."

*****

The morning dragged on like rush- hour traffic. R.J.'s attempts at disarming me of information had receded to one quick question. I again assured him that I knew nothing. He gave a quick humph and then proceeded to tell me about his date with his one true love. I couldn't help but wonder what he might say if I told him about my trip into the ring with Linda.

By the time lunch-hour arrived my shoulders were sore from my rigid posture. Slamming lockers and sudden howls of laughter were causing me to jump. Forced deep breaths and counting to ten didn't seem to help. The call I was to make to my father was like a countdown to an execution; each minute that ticked by felt like a moment closer to certain doom.

I walked into the cafeteria, bypassing the food line and barely noticing Holly's startled look as I passed her table. Ms. Lighthorse sat at the center of their table flanked by Devon and Linda, with Mike Henley perched at the end. He was wearing a ridiculous Oklahoma University football helmet.

"Aren't you going to grab a tray?" said Ms. Lighthorse, as I sat across from her.

"Not hungry," I said, pulling my cell from my front pocket and scrolling to my fathers number.

I pushed send and waited. I didn't have to wait long, the call went straight to voicemail.   I ended the connection and tried again with the same result.

"He's turned his phone off," I said.

"It could be because he's at the clinic," said Ms. Lighthorse.

"Or because he's up in the mountains," I said.

"We don't know that, Dan," she said.

No, we didn't. But it felt right.

"I should go to the clinic," I said.

Linda let out a low grunt, causing me to look into her blazing green eyes and I suddenly longed to lose myself within her emerald shine.

"I don't think that's a good idea," said Ms. Lighthorse.

"Why?" I said, forcing myself to break away from Lisa's gaze.

"One; you're studying for finals. Two; you're not even sure if your father is taking her. And three; if you are right, it might be better if your father didn't know."

"Why?" I said.

"I don't want to say anymore, at least for now," said Ms. Lighthorse, nodding her head towards the main part of the room. "Besides, you need to go say hello."

I turned to see Holly still sitting, now alone, at her table. I gave her a weak smile, which she answered by giving her wrist a few light taps. I held up my index finger and then turned back to Ms. Lighthorse.

"I don't know what to do," I moaned, rising from my chair.

"Wait until after school and try again," said Ms. Lighthorse. "If he doesn't answer, come see me. I'll be in my class."

I turned and made my way over to Holly. She pushed out the chair closest to her, I lowered myself, hoping that the smile plastered across my face didn't look as fabricated as it felt.

"Is everything alright, Dan?" she said.

I glanced over at the table and saw Linda watching us like some kind of British spy.

"I hope so," I muttered.

That seemed to be the extent of Holly's empathy as she turned the conversation to the upcoming dance. According to her, she felt it was important that, considering we were going together, we wore matching colors.

"For the photo's," she said. "It is our senior year, after all. We need to match."

I sat there nodding my head, pretending to be interested as the heat from Linda's anger continued to burn. It was no wonder that I never saw Kyle and the Goons approach from behind.

"Look at this," said Kyle, nudging my shoulder with his hip. "The retard lover is trying to get lucky."

"Why don't you stay with your own kind," said Larry Jones. "I thought you liked them in chairs."

"Why don't you guys go back to the boys room and then you can get lucky," said Holly, surprising me.

"Good one, blondie," said Kyle. "Just remember, I know where you'll be on Saturday. If you're not careful, you might get lucky."

"Okay," I said, rising from my chair, hoping that Ms. Lighthorse would notice.

"Okay, what?" said Kyle.

An earth trembling "ON THREE" suddenly echoed off the walls.

I looked over to see Mike Henley's football helmet crashing to the floor, but that's not what caused Kyle and his cronies to step back. Devon had cleared half the distance to my table and was coming on strong, like a chariot mounted centurion. The memory of being thrown to the ground and knocked out cold must have still been fresh in Kyle's mind, triggering panic, because he quickly turned, plowing both Steve and Larry out of the way, and rushed for the exit. The two of them exchanged a confused look and then followed.

Devon came to stop next to where I was still standing with my hands clenched.

"I'm glad you're my friend," I said, lowering myself back onto the chair.

"As well you should be," he said. "You know they're planning something, right?"

Of course they were, in their twisted minds they were behind on points.

"We need to be ready," said Devon.

He then threw up a hand and said, "Looking good Holly, can't wait to see you at the dance."

With that my best friend gave me a knowing grin and turned back to where Ms. Lighthorse was now picking up Mike's helmet.

"He's so weird, sometimes," said Holly.

Sometimes, I thought.

CHAPTER TWENTY-SEVEN

A Retreat To Mother

A strange thing happened at the end of that school day; RJ asked if I wanted to hang out. He hadn't done that in so long that I had just figured it was a page turned and forgotten. For a moment I considered asking if his bond of eternal love was developing cracks but decided against it. Instead, I told him that I had to get home to meet my dad. He shrugged and said, "You might ask about Joe Clark."

I assured him that question was near the top of my list. We split up in the parking lot and I watched as he climbed aboard his F-150. He drove by me, placing his hand to the side of his head, emulating a phone while mouthing 'call me'. I gave him a thumbs up and then pulled the cell out of my front pocket, finding dad's number.

Straight to voicemail.

I made my way back through the front door, following the sky-gray floor of the hallway to Ms Lighthorse's room.

"Still no answer?" said Devon, as I walked through the doorway.

"Straight to voicemail," I said.

Linda sat near Ms Lighthorse's desk, her head lowered as if she were asleep.

"Is she okay?" I said.

"She will be," said Ms. Lighthorse.

"I'm going to the clinic," I said.

"You should," said Ms. Lighthorse. "I'm going to see Mother

Gina."

"Do you want me to go with you?" said Devon.

"No," said Ms. Lighthorse, giving Linda's shoulder a reassuring squeeze. "Linda and I can manage. I think you should go with Dan."

I'm sure she wanted Devon with me to make sure I didn't do anything stupid.

"Call me once you know," she said.

"And you call us if you learn anything," said Devon.

I gave Linda one last look and then Devon and I left the room.

*****

The parking lot at the center was empty except for a couple of cars, my fathers cruiser was nowhere to be seen. I pulled into the spot nearest to the handicap- ramp and quickly helped Devon with his chair. We made our way to the front sliding doors. The rush of the air - conditioned breeze flooded over my face as the glass panel opened, creating goose pimples over my skin. Rose was perched at the center desk like an ancient watcher. She looked up as we approached, allowing a thin smile to creep across her face,

"Dan," she said. "Here to see your mother?"

"Is she here?" I said.

Rose's smile faded for a moment.

"Why wouldn't she be?" she said.

"Has my father been here?"

"Not since yesterday. Is something wrong?"

That was a good question. Could my father have snuck my mother out? There was a fire escape near the end of her hall, but the odds of someone not noticing seemed slim.

"Nothings wrong," I said. "We'll just go see her."

The squeak of Devon's wheels were amplified in the narrow hall, causing my already pounding heart to kick up a notch.

"Do you think she's gone?" said Devon.

"I don't know," I said.

We stopped at her door. The light blue metal panel stood before us like a gateway into another realm. One drop of sweat rolled off of my brow and trickled into my right eye. I reached up and brushed it away.

"Should I open it?" said Devon.

"I'll do it," I said, grabbing the knob. I turned the handle and pushed the door. The room held the fragrance of honeysuckle and bleach, a synthetic attempt at pleasantry. I passed through the doorway with Devon squeaking close behind. The light from the window was much like it had been before; with rays of dust- infested gold filling the small cube. I stopped mid- stride with a gasp. The bed lay with rumpled sheets piled in disarray, the pillow at the head of the bed had been folded as if to allow someone to sit up.

"Well, that's good," said Devon.

I looked over at my friend, wondering what kind of sick joke he was trying to pull and then gazed back at the empty mattress, prepared to let him have it. But she was there. It wasn't a folded pillow I had seen, but her head. The rumpled sheets were nothing more than her covered feet. I let out a shuddering breath and made my way over to one of the guest chairs, collapsing into it.

"Are you alright?" said Devon, moving his chair towards me.

"For a moment, I thought she was gone."

"Maybe your dad did go to the city," said Devon.

"Maybe," I said, but it felt wrong.

Everything felt wrong.

"What do you want to do?"

My friend sat in his mobile chair, his eyes focused on me, waiting for an answer. I had no answer. My father hadn't been there, and yet his phone was off. Why?

"Do you think he went to see that cop from the city?" said Devon.

That was a possibility I hadn't considered. Maybe the agent had found something. Perhaps that was why my father's phone was turned off. But he said he was going to visit my mom first and had never arrived.

"I don't know," I said, finally, answering both Devon and myself.

"He could be in a meeting," said Devon. "I'm sure he'll call you when he can."

We sat in the room with only the sounds of beeping machines and muffled voices from other rooms breaking the silence.

My mother lay there with her eyes closed, her breath

mechanical. Her face had the shrunken pose of death, her skin reminding me of worn out paper. She was the same age as my father and yet she could have passed for his mother.

"Do you think it could help her?" said Devon.

"I don't know," I said.

"But what if it could?"

"What are you saying?" I said, turning towards him.

Devon looked over at me, his hands now rubbing together like some kind of mad scientist.

"What if the wheel could save her?" he said. "Look at what it's done for us."

"Mother Gina said that the wheel was sick," I said. "And what about the warning from Joe. And don't forget about my tire."

"But it still works," said Devon. "You and Linda can vouch for that."

"That's not funny."

"All I'm saying is that there is a chance," said Devon. "If she stays here..."

He didn't finish the sentence. He didn't have to. My mother's time was running out. It had come down to days. Possibly hours. Devon knew this, and I could see the familiar grief in his eyes. He knew the terrible weight of this kind of loss. He knew what the long term effects could be. In truth, his mother had never been the same since his father's death. She had retreated into a dark place after her husbands suicide, weighted down by guilt, anger, and the constant question of why? Though not exactly the same, it was eerily similar to what my father and I would soon have to face.

"Would you?" I said, finally.

"Would I, what?" said Devon.

"Knowing what we know, would you take her?"

"Yes," said Devon.

"But what about what I saw last night in my father's room?"

Devon leaned back in his chair.

"It could have been nothing," he said. "You said it was dark."

"Okay," I said, giving him that. "But what about when my mother suddenly spoke? And don't tell me I was imagining that."

"Maybe that was her telling you that she wants to go."

"That's not what she said."

"Loshi is losing and needs our help. Isn't that what she said?"

"That doesn't mean she wants to go," I said.

"Dan, if she doesn't, she dies."

Back to that hideous fact. I sat with my thoughts swirling like a storm blown feather. The what if's spinning like a casino wheel. Did she want to go?

Loshi needs our help, she had said, not Loshi needs your help.

"Let's go," I said, rising from the chair.

""Where to?"

"We're going to make a stop at the police station," I said, just as my phone began to ring.

"Is it your dad?" said Devon, rolling out the door behind me.

"No," I said, looking at the number. "It's Ms. Lighthorse."

CHAPTER TWENTY-EIGHT

No Answer

I answered the phone and asked her to wait until I could get outside. Devon followed close behind as we made our way back down the hall, offering Rose a quick wave, and then passing through the sliding door.

"I'm here," I said.

"Was your mother there?" said Ms Lighthorse.

"Yes."

"Good," she replied with a sigh.

"Maybe he wasn't lying about going to the city," I said, hopefully.

"I'm sorry Dan, but he was."

"How do you know?"

"We passed by him as he was coming out of the narrow turn off to the huts. It was obvious where he had been."

"But why would he go to the wheel alone?"

"I don't know Dan. Mother Gina will try to find some answers for us."

"When is she going?"

"She has already left," said Ms. Lighthorse.

"But how will she contact us?"

Of course, they had no phones.

"She has her ways, Dan, you know that. Until then, just go on as if nothing is happening."

Easier said than done. It wasn't Ms. Lighthorse, or any of them, for that matter, being visited by ghosts. Had they considered that? The fact that I was now sleeping with my nightlight on mattered little.

"Dan, are you there?"

"Yes," I said. "I'm not going to say anything, at least until we talk to Mother Gina."

"Good," said Ms. Lighthorse. "Is Devon still with you?"

I told her that he was and handed him my phone. He took the cell and pivoted away from me, lowering his voice. I unlocked the car and popped the trunk, preparing it for his chair, all the while trying to catch pieces of what he was saying. All that I could hear was Devon's occasional okay and a couple of uh-huh's.

The call ended just as I was moving my bumper jack to the side.

"Here you go," he said, rolling up beside me and handing me the cell.

"What did she say?"

"She's worried about you."

"I'm worried about my dad," I said, in an exasperated voice.

"She thinks it would be better if I stayed with you, at least until your father gets back."

If he gets back, I thought to myself.

"Devon, what the hell is going on here?"

"I don't know," he said, wheeling himself over to the passenger side. "How about a pizza? My treat."

I could do little else but shake my head and help my friend into the junker. I put his chair in and closed the trunk, pausing to give the clinic one more look before climbing in and starting the motor.

Devon ordered a pie from Telly's as we made our way back to my house. We didn't speak. What was there to say? All we had were questions without any answers and time was running out. But maybe there was someone who had an answer. Someone who had met the very demon that we were trying to find. But would he come if summoned? Did I really want him to?

*****

We were in my room. I was sitting on my bed working on a slice of pepperoni, barely registering the taste. I was watching Devon scroll through the history of Conquistador's and their various horrific

145

excursions on my computer.

I gazed over at the chair where Joe had sat. I couldn't help but wonder if he was there now, watching us, laughing at us. But would he be laughing? The shadow of Joe was much different than the physical Joe. The message on the mirror and the vision of his death had not been threats but warnings. Would he know what this thing wanted with my father? A chill filled my blood as I sat there contemplating. Was I really going to do this?

After a few moments Devon switched off the screen and turned his chair to face me. The sun was sinking, casting a deep orange glow throughout my room. My friend sat studying my face. I'm sure he could see the lines of concern, attributing it to my father, and he was mostly right. But mixed in with that worry was the knowledge of what I was about to do. I considered telling Devon, and yes, having him there as I requested the company of his dead foe did carry with it a sense of comfort, but would Joe show up? Somehow, I knew that he wouldn't. A bridge had been built, but it was only big enough for two. It was then that the front door opened. The familiar sound of the key chain hitting the table was soon followed by my father's voice.

"Danny, you home?"

I felt my breath catch in my throat. An expression of fear washed over Devon's face, mirroring the flood of emotion that suddenly consumed me. It lasted for a second, and was quickly replaced by concern.

"Yeah, dad. I'm back here with Devon."

"You guys better not be on those kinky sites," he said.

"We're not...anymore," I said, rising from the bed and making my way out of the room.

Devon followed close behind, we turned the corner of the hall to find my father sitting at the kitchen table with a beer in his hand.

"How are you Devon?" he said, with a quick nod of his bottle.

"Better, if I could have one of those," said Devon.

"It's important to have a dream," said my father, taking a swig.

"How was the city?" I said, pulling out a chair.

"It was fine," said my father, his eyes lowering. "The agent thinks she might know what's been wreaking havoc around here."

"Really?" I said. "What is it?"

"I'll know more tomorrow," was all he said.

"Look, dad," I began.

"Hey, Dan," said Devon, cutting me short. "I'd better get home."

"That's probably a good idea," my father said, finishing off the rest of the beer.

He then lifted himself from the chair and tossed the empty into the trash.

"Run him home, Dan. I'm turning in early." My father then left the kitchen without saying another word.

*****

I dropped Devon off. We had discussed little on our short trip to his house, besides both agreeing that my father was lying. We also promised to be the first one called if either of us heard from Ms. Lighthorse.

The house was dark when I returned. My father was obviously not lying about turning in early. I sat in my car, parked beside his cruiser, with my mind racing. I knew what I needed to do but was terrified to try. How was I supposed to do it, anyway? I didn't have a Ouija board or any kind of incantation book. Should I go into the bathroom and say his name a few times into the mirror? I didn't know. Finally, I made my way into the house, pausing briefly at my father's closed door. All was quiet on the bedroom front. I then went into my room, sat on the edge of my bed and stared at the wooden chair.

"Joe," I whispered. "Are you here?"

Nothing. The room was as silent as silent could be.

"Joe," I said again, thinking of all of those ghost hunting shows and beginning to feel like an idiot. "Give me a sign."

The chair sat empty. I glanced at the clock on my phone: 9:13 PM. Not exactly the witching hour. After another ten minutes I gave up and lay back on the bed. My mind bounced around like a super ball, going from Mother Gina, to my father and then to the beast running loose within our town. Occasionally I would glance at the chair but it remained empty. My phone was nearing the end of its life so I reached over and plugged it in. The shadows on the ceiling cast

Rorschach shapes; animals and long reaching daggers of dark. From outside a gust a wind caressed my window, momentarily breaking the silence, and then vanished.

Joe was a no show. But did I really expert it to work? Maybe he was busy. Could ghosts be busy? Perhaps he was haunting what murdered him. Most likely not. Even the dead might think twice before harassing whatever that was. By the time ten-thirty rolled around I was ready to surrender. I plugged in the earbuds and let the soothing sounds of James Taylor chip away at the wall of tension throbbing in my head.

CHAPTER TWENTY-NINE

Conversations

HELLS BELLS by AC/DC burst through the unconsciousness, causing me to bolt up in my bed. The alarm on my radio clock had suddenly blasted to life. I slammed my hand down on the top of the plastic box, missing, and then slammed it down again.

2:00 A.M. flashed digitally like a neon sign.

I grabbed my phone and saw that it wasn't a mistake; it was exactly two o'clock. When did I set my alarm for two?

"Hey Dan," said a whispering voice to my right.

I turned and choked back a scream. Joe sat on the chair, his skinless face tilted to the ceiling, his vein- infested hands resting on chipped kneecaps. His chin slowly lowered until ping-pong sized eyes, blemished red and ashen, pointed directly at me.

My breath was frozen in my lungs. I forced myself to exhale, clutching my blanket like a three year old waking from a nightmare. The smell of saturated soil, like dirt that had cradled a sewage line for decades, filled my nose, causing my vision to blur.

"Give me a second," I managed to say, wiping my shaking hand across my face.

"If this isn't a good time..." he began.

"No, I'm fine," I lied. "I just need to wake up."

"Don't take too long," said the ghost of Devon's horror. "I don't have all night."

"Joe, you have to help me," I said.

"I've been trying to," he said. "Or haven't you noticed?"

For a moment he sounded like the old Joe that we all hated.

"I know you have," I said. "What can you tell me about the wheel?"

Joe lifted his wasted hands off of his wasted knees and leaned forward. I could see the burst vessels purpling deep within his unblinking orbs. It took everything I had not to cringe.

"Only that it is evil, and that it is getting stronger."

"But what does it want with my dad?"

"I don't think it gives a shit about your dad," he said leaning back. "Just like it didn't give a shit about me. It only wants the desperate and the pissed off. Everyone else is just decoration."

"But they say the wheel wasn't always like that," I said.

"Maybe not, and yet here I am."

"Have you seen what it is?" I said.

"It is death," he said. "I can't tell you anymore than that."

He then leaned towards me, extending out his hand and said, "But I can show you."

I looked at his hand. The whitish red membrane that was once covered by skin seemed to glow and I felt my stomach become a knot. I remembered the jaunt he had revealed to me before in the park and wasn't sure if I was prepared for something like that again. But if it held answers what choice did I have? I reached out slowly, as if reaching out toward a flame, trying not to let the fear raging through me win. I grabbed his hand and all went dark.

******

I opened my eyes to find the cottonwood tree standing before me. A dull violet glow pulsed from behind, imbuing it with a living look, like a heartbeat. But the light was cold; dead. A nauseating breeze struck me from behind and I heard the sound of something flapping. I looked up and saw what looked like a sheet, hanging from one of the higher branches. Then the cold light began to focus, becoming brighter until one violent beam fell upon the branch. And that was when I saw my face, only it had been stretched, draped over the limb.

I knew then that my life was over. All I wanted was to escape, to leave that place, but I couldn't move.

Then it spoke.

No more, it said. My soldier has seen to that.

But there was something else there. Something struggling to come forward and for a moment the pinpoint light separated, becoming weak and broken. Another voice erupted with only one word.

RUN!

And I did. I ran out of the ring; a dark runner lost in a dark world. There is no light at the end of a tunnel. No stairway or pearly gate. There is only a rotten, hollowed out tree, and it leads to the devil.

*****

At some point Joe must have released my hand, because I found myself laying in a fetal position at the side of my bed. I glanced up at the wooden chair and saw that it was empty. I struggled to my knees and rolled onto the mattress, my hair soaked in sweat. I looked over at the clock: 4:47 AM. I had been on the floor for over two hours. Maybe that's why Joe had left; he was tired of waiting. I switched on my reading lamp and stared at the ceiling. What he had shown me still had my heart pounding and I forced myself to take deep breaths until it fell below triple digits.

I played back in my mind what I had been shown, trying to avoid the more gruesome parts, but it was impossible. I had been there in real time, had seen the blood dripping off of the branch, and heard the sticky flap of the skin. And ghosts do feel fear, I had learned that, as well.

No more, it had said. My soldier has seen to that.

Was that what this thing called the killing beast, its soldier?

My stomach felt like lead so I decided to grab a small glass of soda. I walked out into the hall and stopped. A light was sneaking from under my fathers door. I walked over and listened. There was no sound. I gave the panel a low knock but it wasn't answered. I turned the handle, gently pushing the door open. His bed was made, looking as if it had been untouched. His bathroom door was wide open. I then rushed into the kitchen. It was empty and his keys were gone.

Maybe he went in early, I thought to myself, allowing the part of my brain that specialized in denial to have its say.

But I knew better. By the time I returned to my room it was nearly five-thirty. I sat on the edge of my bed staring at my phone, debating, but there really was nothing to consider. I placed the call only to have it go straight to his voicemail. This man, who made his living by answering calls, was blocking mine. Never had that happened before.

CHAPTER THIRTY

Changes

I arrived at school forty minutes early and was glad to see Ms. Lighthorse's van. The thought of sounding insane had become a thing of the past. All secrets were now being laid out, like abstract paintings. The revelation that was shown to me by Joe did little to tamp down my fears, but it certainly justified them. There was no way I could allow my dad to take my mother into the wheel. Devon was sure that it could help, but he hadn't witnessed the horror that I had while being possessed by Joe's spirit. If he tried to argue I would shut him down. I would have to.

My resolution quickly evaporated once I walked into the classroom. Ms. Lighthorse was sitting behind her desk, her beautiful face now a mere shell of its former glory. On one side of her was Linda, her piercing eyes drilling into mine. On the other was Devon, his arm draped around Ms. Lighthorse's shoulders.

"What's going on?" I said, grabbing a chair.

"Something has happened to Mother Gina," said Ms. Lighthorse. "She hasn't come back."

"Do you think it got her?" I said.

There was no reason to be specific; we all knew what it was.

"I don't know," said Ms. Lighthorse. "But I do know I need to go."

"What about the little kids?" said Devon. The elementary students would be arriving at any moment.

"Your right," Ms. Lighthorse. "I'll have to wait until lunch."

We sat there for a moment in silence, each of us lost in our own thoughts. The Mother Gina that I had met, the one on the other side, seemed more than capable of taking care of herself, at least when it came to whatever that beast was. But that wasn't the real enemy, the beast was nothing more than a servant. Would Mother Gina be able to handle its master alone? I didn't think so. I glanced up at the clock hanging on the wall. There was only ten minutes left until the first hour bell rang.

"I had a visitor last night," I said.

"Was it Joe?" said Devon.

"It was," I said. "And he showed me something."

They listened to my story, their expressions switching from disbelief to concern. Linda shuddered in her chair as I recounted the skin draped over the branch. The fear that Joe had been feeling was overwhelming and it was still resonating within me. I was forced to clench my hands in order to stop them from trembling.

"Are you okay?" said Ms. Lighthorse.

"I will be," I said, and concluded by telling them about the other being that had saved Joe.

Ms. Lighthorse sat back, her dark eyes narrowing. Devon adjusted his chair, pivoting towards me. There was no question of it being believable, we were beyond that, the only thing now was to figure out what should be done.

"Mother Gina went to the wheel," said Devon, almost to himself.

Linda let out a worried coo.

"She suspected something was wrong," said Ms. Lighthorse.

"But she didn't know this," I said.

"What should we do?" said Devon.

"What can we do?" said Ms. Lighthorse. "I'll go up there after the elementary kids go back."

"You're not going into the wheel, are you?" said Devon.

"I don't know."

"You can't," I said. "Not alone."

"I'll go with you," said Devon.

"Absolutely not," said Ms. Lighthorse. "No one goes back until we figure this out."

At that moment the first- hour warning bell rang.

"You need to get to class," said Ms. Lighthorse.

I rose from my chair but hesitated. This woman, who I had come to care for, was planning on going into the enemy's territory, and she was going to go alone. I glanced over at Devon, his face mirrored my concern. He wanted to say something. I wanted to say something, but her mind was made up. For us, to lose Mother Gina would be a tragedy; an end to a curious friend. But for Ms. Lighthouse, Mother Gina was family; a noble leader who could never be replaced. And what if she was gone? What would we do then? How could I save my father?

"Dan, you need to go," said Ms. Lighthorse.

I turned, noticing the tear rimmed emerald glint of Linda's eyes, and left the room.

*****

The morning crept by like shadows in the early evening. I went through the motions, answering questions when called upon, even kidding around with R.J. on a couple of occasions. But it seemed unreal; robotic and without substance. When the lunch bell finally rang it was as if an alarm in my head had suddenly gone off. I found myself rushing through the hall, not even stopping at my locker to drop off my books. My hope was that Ms. Lighthorse had changed her mind, or had come up with another plan. Had decided to take us with her. But would I go? Yes, if it meant helping her. I wouldn't like it, and I might faint, but I would go.

I crossed the threshold of the lunchroom and felt my feelings of heroism dissipate. Devon sat alone, his hands steepled under his chin. I made my way over, passing a confused looking Holly, and grabbed a seat.

"So she went," I said.

"Yeah, she did,"

"What about Linda and Mike?" I said.

"Mike didn't come in today. Linda went with her."

Of course she would take Linda. Where else would she go?

"They'll be okay," said Devon.

"We don't know that," I said. "You didn't see what I saw, Devon."

"It's him," said Devon.

"Panfilo de Soto?" I said.

"It has to be," said Devon, leaning forward, lowering his voice. "It all fits. Only now he's traded gold for skins."

"But why skins?"

"Maybe gold means nothing to him now. Maybe the wheel allowed his evil to come out. Hell, maybe it magnified it."

It's the devil, Joe had said.

"I can't believe she took Linda."

Devon gave me a smile. I expected some kind of smart ass remark, but instead he said, "Don't underestimate them, Danny. They can take care of themselves."

The image of Devon tossing Kyle into the air ran through my mind. Did Linda possess that kind of power, as well? I could only hope so.

"We'll wait and see if we hear from her tonight," said Devon.

"And if we don't?

"Then I guess we'll have to take a trip."

CHAPTER THIRTY-ONE

Loss

The rest of the day went much like the morning. At one point R.J. asked me if I was feeling okay, to which I said I was.

"I thought it was from all of the guilt you were feeling from holding out on me about Joe."

"I don't know shit!" I snapped at him.

"Hey, I was just kidding," he said.

"I'm sorry," I said. "I've got a lot going on."

"It's cool," he said. "I still love you."

The last ten minutes of my final class ticked away like molasses in December. When the bell finally did ring I rushed out of the school. My car gleamed in the sunlight like a beacon of hand-me-down freedom. I opened the door, throwing my history book onto the back seat. Had I not suddenly remembered that I needed to give Devon a ride home I would have left that parking lot with my wheels spinning. Instead, I sat on the hood and waited. Within moments I saw him clear the front door with his backpack resting on his lap.

*****

"We'll wait for her call," he said, as I turned right onto Main Street.

"If we do go I'll have to tell my dad I'm sick so he can call the school."

"Uh...Dan, you're eighteen. I think you can make the call."

That was something I hadn't considered. Devon and I were both eighteen. The time of parental supervision was at an end. If I hadn't been so panicked by what was going on I might have relished the thought. Now, it kind of freaked me out.

We were just pulling into his driveway when Devon turned to me and said, "Listen Dan, I don't think your mom should go to the wheel, at least not right now."

No shit! I wanted to scream.

"I agree," I said, struggling to keep my voice level.

"I'm sorry," he said, placing his hand on my shoulder.

I sat there for a moment in silence. It was a death sentence for my mom. The one chance to save her was gone, infected by a demon. Devon's father also was gone and not coming back. That misery would soon be shared by his best friend. It was his way of saying that he was there for me and I loved him for it.

*****

There was a pleasant surprise waiting for me once I arrived home: My father was there. The relief was like a wave, rinsing away a mountain of stress. I walked into the kitchen to find him hunkered over a photograph. I plopped down on a chair across the table from him and saw that it was a picture of the three of us from when we had gone to the state fair. I had been nine at the time but I remember it well because I had begged my way onto the Twisted Bullet, just barely making the height requirement, and soon found myself vomiting all over the pleather seat of the compartment. My parents were waiting near the exit. My mother saw my shirt and rushed towards me, her expression nearing terror while my father offered to hose out the cart.

"Just get him out of here," the disgruntled ride operator had said.

I still remember the warmth of my mother's hand holding mine and the low chuckle of my father as I was led away from the ride.

"I miss those days," I said.

"As do I," my father said.

I gazed at his face, his lips were quivering and a single tear rolled down his flushed cheek. He stood and walked over to the cabinet by the sink, placing the picture above it on the wall. He stood there for a moment, his shoulders slumped and his head lowered, much like he did the night of his nightmare.

"The prom is this week," I said, as cheerfully as possible.

"That's exciting," he said, turning towards me with a forced smile. "So you're taking Holly?"

"Yep. She wants to go eat first."

"Sounds like a real date," my dad said, sitting back across from me. "I feel like we should have some kind of talk."

"About?"

"Sex, I guess."

I burst into laughter. My father glared at me for a second and then joined in. A sudden image of Linda in the wheel, her arms and legs wrapped around me acted like an electric shock, shutting me up. My father continued on for another second then reached over and grabbed a napkin out of the container and wiped his eyes.

"I'm serious, though," he said.

"Dad, you know I'm eighteen, right?"

"I know," he said. "You're a regular man of the world. I just want you to know that I'm here for you."

"I know."

We sat there in silence. I won't say that it was awkward but it wasn't exactly soothing, either. But it was a break in the chaos, a momentary reprieve from the schism that was becoming our lives.

Would he take my mother?

Yes. I was sure that he would. I realized that I needed to approach this head-on. Cut it off at the pass, as they say. Mother Gina was gone. Ms. Lighthorse might be gone and with her Linda. Things were moving much too fast and the dangers were coming from everywhere. I decided right then and there to talk to him.

"Any luck on the case?" I said, breaking the silence.

"The case? No. Nothing yet. There's something I need to tell you."

"Is it about mom?"

"What? No."

"How is she?" I said.

"The doctor says that she seems to be doing better."

"I should probably go see her," I said.

"Yes, maybe Sunday," my father said. "Listen, my shift is going to change for a while."

"What do you mean?"

"I'm going to be working overnight. You'll probably be gone before I get home, at least on the schooldays."

"What brought this on?"

"Peterson had too much vacation time saved up and he has to use it or lose it."

"How convenient," I muttered.

"What was that?" he said.

"Nothing. When does this start?"

"Tonight," he said, lifting himself from the chair. "I need to get some sleep. There's cold cuts in the fridge, make a sandwich if you get hungry."

With that, he turned to leave the room.

"Dad," I said. "I need to tell you something."

He paused at the doorway, placing his hand on the frame.

"What is it?" he said, his voice barely above a whisper.

"Don't go— ," I began, but was suddenly interrupted by the blazing sound of classic rock bursting from my jeans.

I pulled the phone out of my pocket.

"Hold on," I said to my father, but he was gone. I pushed the receive button just as the closing of his bedroom door filled the room.

"Are you there?" It was Devon, and he sounded excited.

"I'm here," I said. "Are you okay?"

"She's back," he said, ignoring my question.

"Ms. Lighthorse?"

"Her and Mother Gina," said Devon. "Something happened."

"Do we need to go?" I said.

"Yes," said Devon. "And we need to go today."

The clock above the stove read 4:38P.M. We wouldn't get there until after six.

"Dan," said Devon, "Mother Gina asked for us. I think she's hurt."

"I'll be right over," I said, ending the call.

I left the kitchen and rushed into my room. I grabbed my keys and wallet off of the computer desk and paused only for a moment outside of my dad's closed bedroom door. There was no sound coming from the room and even though the sun was still very much up, only darkness lined the gap between the door and the hallway floor. I ignored the chill creeping down my spine and left the house.

*****

"What else did Ms.Lighthorse say?"

I had pulled onto I-44, struggling to keep the retired cop-car at the speed limit.

"That was it," said Devon. "She found Mother Gina lying next to her chair in the hut. She was bleeding."

"But not really, right?" I said. "I mean this was all in the trance."

"You know better than that, Dan."

Yes, I guess I did.

"Let's just get there," I said.

The sun had just begun to touch the weathered peak of the mountains by the time I made the turn onto the dirt road. There was an eerie motionless feel that covered the terrain. Nothing was moving; no animals or even the leaves on the trees. It was as if the world had decided to hold its breath.

"Something's wrong," said Devon.

"I can't argue with you there," I said.

"No, I mean I can barely move my legs."

I snuck a quick glance down and saw that the lower half of his body still contained a slight twist.

"What the hell is going on?" I said.

"I don't know," said Devon. "This has never happened before."

"It has to be whatever is in the wheel," I said.

By the time we saw Ms. Lighthorse's van parked in front of Mother Gina's shack Devon's leg's had managed to straighten. He opened the passenger door, leaped out, and began to stretch.

"It's better now," he said.

We made our way to the front of the house just as the door opened. Ms. Lighthorse stood in the opening, face flushed, her shirt covered in red dirt.

"Hurry boys," she said. "We don't have much time."

The room was as dark as it had been the first time I was there. A strong odor of cinnamon and pine lingered, covering the faint stench of some unnamed illness. The old woman lay on the tattered sofa, her hands locked over a withered and gasping chest, her eyes closed. Gray hair flowed off the edge of the ripped armrest like a frozen waterfall at midnight.

"What happened?" said Devon, rushing to kneel at her side.

Mother Gina's eyes fluttered open, sparking a raspy cough. A trickle of crimson streamed from one corner of her mouth. Ms. Lighthorse wiped it with a napkin, reminding me very much of Linda. That thought sent a bolt of fear through me. I looked around but didn't see her. A rusted hinge sang out from my left and I saw her stepping out of the rundown kitchen with a bowl of water in her hands. She gave me a quick smile and made her way over to Ms Lighthorse.

"Are they here?" croaked the dry voice of Mother Gina.

"Everyone's here," said Ms. Lighthorse.

"Come closer," said Mother Gina. "I don't have much time."

Trying to argue with her would have done no good. Her frailty left nothing to doubt. The last minutes of her life were well on their way, perhaps even seconds. We moved towards her, forming a semi-circle, crouching so she wouldn't have to strain.

"Listen closely" she began. "I will tell you what I learned."

Her story was horrifying, to say the least. She had passed into the other world, had crept through the thickened brush, astounded by the nothingness that surrounded her. The birds were gone, the deer absent. The air was thick, almost palpable and tension seemed to hover everywhere. She was sure that the wheel was sick, and clutched in her hand was the remedy. The arrow-head looked like something carved out of the ice-age, but that was good. The jagged-edged head came from a wheel much older and much more powerful than the one she was making her way towards. The sharpened stone came from a ring nestled on the hillside of Wyoming that was said to be the creator of all, its rocks laying the foundation for the other wheels that would follow.

She had taken this piece while visiting the ancient ring. Although for her, it wasn't so much a vacation as it was a pilgrimage; equivalent to the Muslims trip to Mecca. Taking one of the stones that made up the ancient wheel could have landed her in jail had she been seen, and stealing one was never her intention, but she had been ordered to; the demand coming from the Wyoming Wheel itself. At first, she declined, sure that what she was hearing was nothing more than her own desire, but the voice persisted. Did it know about the Wichita Wheel? Was that the reason for demanding that she take a part of it? Mother Gina was now sure that it was.

She made her way up the trail, carefully stepping over the fallen sticks and dry leaves. A crawling sensation flitted over her skin and she stopped. There was something watching her. Hunting her. Mother Gina tightened her grip on the arrow and moved silently on. Whatever followed kept its distance, either too afraid to attack or forbidden to. Within minutes she found herself cresting the hill with the wheel laid out before her. The rotted cottonwood stood at its center like a giant skeleton, shrouded in darkness.

Mother Gina glanced back just as a large fur covered creature ducked behind an oak.

"Why do you wait?" she said.

"Because it must," answered a low rolling voice.

Mother Gina turned to the wheel, raising her bow. A sound, like a dozen sails battling a dangerous wind came from above. Mother looked up and saw leathered hides hanging from the bone-like branches of the tree. The shadow at the base of the cottonwood began to swirl, rippling like a polluted pond and then started to rise. Wave after undulating wave stacking upon each other until a human shape towered midway up the rotting trunk. A snap echoed through the woods caused by a breaking branch of the cottonwood, and from it dropped one of the stretched skins. The hide fell onto the mass, encasing it, giving the blob a macabre covering.

"You," said Mother Gina.

"Yes," said the mass. "The one who has tainted your hope and destroyed your holy place just as I destroyed your tribe."

"But why?"

"The fact that you ask shows why your people have faded into a mere shell of what they once were. Pretending to be content with your defeat, taking up the culture of the conquerors and acting like you enjoy it. Still, I should thank you."

A low growl filtered from behind, the creature was coming

closer.

"Thank me for what?"

"If it hadn't been for your kinsman leading me here then I would never have been able to become the god that I am. And to think, he brought me here to end me."

"So the story is true," said Mother Gina.

"Indeed," said the mass. "But don't take my word for it."

A sudden rip formed within the skin covering the mass and from it a postulating boil bubbled out, gaining in weight and sagging until finally breaking away from its producer and falling to the ground. It lay there for a moment wriggling like a worm newly plucked from the ground. Mother Gina ignored the snapping of limbs from behind, her eyes locked onto the abomination that lay writhing just a few feet away. The bubbling gel came to a sudden stop. Its surface rippled, contorting into a face, bland and unrecognizable.

"I'm sorry," it said, and its saturated words were not in English but the stuttered rhythmic language of her people.

"Loshi," whispered Mother Gina.

The jellied face took an expression of anguish and said, "I failed."

The skin covered mass suddenly slammed down onto the horror stricken face, crushing it back into itself.

"Yes, he did fail," the mass said, bringing itself back to its full height. "It's funny actually; by trying to save his people with murder, he created murder. Isn't that ironic?"

"I think it's sad," said Mother Gina. "I'm only sorry that he didn't complete the job."

"But he did and in doing so sealed his own fate."

The creature from behind had moved dangerously near, its breath clearly heard. Mother Gina's theory would have to be tested now. To wait any longer would be risking everything. Would it be enough to destroy the entity? She didn't think so, but it should provide enough to learn whether or not it could work. The stone weighed more than the common arrowhead, its jagged point would throw off the trajectory but at this distance Mother Gina didn't think it would be a problem. What would be a problem was jumping back to the hut before the beast behind cut her down.

The thing within the wheel liked to talk; liked to brag, She would have to use that.

"So what now?" she said, tightening her grip on the notched arrow. "Do you plan on taking over the world?"

"The world? No. I only want to help the world."

"By killing?"

"I only kill those who torture the ones who are unable to defend themselves. I help the helpless."

The answer forced her to pause. Was it possible this thing thought that what it was doing was right?

"Why collect the skins?"

"It is my right as a god. They are offerings."

"Offerings from who?"

"My apostles, of course. My children."

"Who are your children?"

"The ones who can't. The ones who never will. But with me they shall."

Yes, it made sense. The wheel healed the handicapped and ruthlessly punished those who meant them harm while collecting the skins as a morbid trophy.

It was as if a melding had taken place: A blending of the disabled Loshi and the Spaniard mated with the powerful spirit that had first formed the wheel, combining and amplifying their attributes. And it was growing stronger.

"What of my people?" said Mother Gina. "Why destroy them?"

"Because they deserve no better. They are sniveling cowards, content with failure. I will wipe them clean from the face of the earth."

And it wouldn't stop there. This being was sadly no different than the many usurpers and emperors from the past who truly believed in their cause, selling themselves as the only savior from an often fabricated enemy. Each success proof of their benevolence.

"What did my people do to you?"

The skin covered mass began to gyrate as a rumbling, like distant thunder, filled the ring. Had it found the question amusing?

"One of your kind murde–" the mass began.

Mother Gina let the arrow fly. The shaft zipped across the twenty yards, dropping slightly, the ancient stone penetrating the leathered hide right where its chest would have been. A roar, like a wounded bear, ripped through the hilltop, causing Mother Gina to step back.

The beast from behind was suddenly on her, its clawed hand swiping, its savage teeth clamping down on the back of her neck. Mother Gina did the only thing that she could, dropping to the ground and chanting the words for her exit, but even as the world started to fade she felt the beasts parting slice across her throat. Mother Gina, in that world, was dead.

CHAPTER THIRTY-TWO

Farewell

The old woman finished her story. I noticed that sometime during her tale Linda's hand had found mine, our fingers were interlocked as if clinging to each other for support. Ms. Lighthorse wiped away another stream of blood from the corner of Mother Gina's mouth.

"De Soto," said Devon.

"What do we do?" said Linda.

Her hand suddenly tightened, causing me to cry out. She then collapsed to the hardwood floor, her arms shriveling into a broken wing-like position. I fell to her side, lifting her head. Her brilliant green eyes were opened wide, struggling to focus.

"What happened?" said Ms. Lighthorse.

"I think I know," said Devon.

He then told her about our journey and how his legs had at first refused to work.

"I think it knows we're trying to stop it."

"But how could it?" I said.

Linda began to convulse, her jaw clenching, her legs shaking. Within seconds it was over.

"I'm okay," she said, sitting up. "Whatever happened has passed."

"It's the wheel," whispered Mother Gina. "It must be stopped."

"But how?" said Ms. Lighthorse.

"You wounded it," said Devon. "But you didn't kill it."

"No," said Mother Gina. "But I only shot it once."

"Do you think that it can be killed?" said Ms. Lighthorse.

"It can," said Mother Gina. "I heard the pain in its voice."

"Then let's kill it," said Devon.

I looked over at my friend and saw a fierceness that I didn't share. The thought of attacking this thing was terrifying. Mother Gina was a warrior and looked at what had happened to her. And what were we supposed to do, load up a bunch of Wyoming Wheel arrows and attack? What about the murderous servant? Would they work on it?

"Do you have more of the stones from the Wyoming Wheel?" said Devon.

Mother Gina let out a long sigh, and said, "I do not."

"Well, then I guess we're screwed," said Devon.

"Not necessarily," said Ms. Lighthorse.

I looked over at her, she was resting on her knees near Mother Gina's head, her hands wringing the cold rag. "We can get more."

"Wait, are you saying we go to Wyoming and steal more?" said Linda.

"I'm in," said Devon.

"No," said Ms. Lighthorse. "Not you boys."

"Why not?" said Devon. "It could be a class field trip."

"But what about Dan?" said Ms. Lighthorse. "He's going to need you."

"For what?" said Devon. "He's eighteen, he can take care of himself."

"Are you forgetting about his mother?" said Linda. "And the fact that the monster slashed his tire?"

"I'm sure I'll be fine," I said, my voice sounding less than fine.

"No," said Ms. Lighthorse. "You guys stay."

Devon began to open his mouth, and then decided against it.

The death of Mother Gina came in silence. She passed while we knelt beside her, providing what little comfort we could. There was no final farewell, no movie-like speech. Mother Gina simply closed her eyes and let out a last parting exhale. We sat there gazing at her, none of us daring to break the silence. Shadows were crawling across the unfinished floor, winding their way further through the room, swallowing the fading light.

"You need to go," said Ms. Lighthorse, finally.

"But what about her?" I said.

"We will take care of her."

I felt a tinge of jealousy at that, but I understood. Mother Gina was Loshinka and even though I was part Native American I was still an outsider.

"You boys should head back."

To my surprise, Devon didn't try to argue.

"What about tomorrow?" he said.

"I am deputizing you," said Ms. Lighthorse. "You will be my substitute for the little kids until I return. Do you think you can handle that?"

"So you're going to Wyoming?" I said.

"I don't think I have a choice."

"And then what?" I said. "You're going to face this thing alone?"

"She won't be alone," said Devon.

"You're going to fight it?" I said.

"We all will," said Linda. "We have to."

"But why?" I said. "If it stays up here, who will care?"

"Didn't you hear what Mother Gina said?" said Devon. "It won't stay."

"You don't know that," I said.

"Yes, we do, Dan," said Ms. Lighthorse. "Have you forgotten about Joe?"

No, I hadn't forgotten about Joe. He had been murdered ninety miles away and liked to haunt me. They were right, and I knew it, but that didn't do anything for the panic that was now consuming me. Ms. Lighthorse was planning a war-party consisting of the very people that I cared about. I glanced at Devon and could see the smoldering in his eyes. He would have gone that day, if he could. His hatred for this thing burned deep. And I guess I understood. For him, and Linda, this went beyond just stopping something evil: Their very way of life was being threatened. Already the thing in the ring was chipping away at the magic, diluting the healing powers that my friends had shared.

"We don't expect you to help," said Linda.

I looked at her and a pain jabbed at my heart. If I didn't know it before, I certainly knew it then: I loved her. This realization flooded through me like wildfire. Images of her and the others facing this thing alone filled me with a new sensation; one that I wasn't prepared for: Anger. Not towards them, but towards the evil bastard suffocating the gift.

"Oh," I said. "I'm going."

CHAPTER THIRTY-THREE

Devon Gets A Date

The trip back was shrouded in darkness, which didn't help our mood. Devon sat on the passenger seat with his chin resting on his hand gazing out the window at nothing.

"Hey," I said, breaking the silence. "I'm sorry you couldn't go."

"I'm not mad about that," he said. "Ms. Lighthorse is right, you shouldn't be left alone."

"I can't believe Mother Gina is dead," I said, twisting my hands on the wheel.

"It's certainly not the best thing that could have happened," said Devon.

"Do you really think we have a chance?"

"Mother Gina thought we did," Devon answered. "Listen Dan, I think I should stay with you at least until they get back."

"Do you really think something is going to happen?"

Devon tilted his head towards me and said, "I think something already is. It knows we're trying to stop it and I doubt if it's going to give us the chance."

His logic was sound considering the time it took for him to be able to walk once we had arrived at the mountains, not to mention the seizure that had struck Linda. For me the absence of magic meant nothing. There was only one way to deal with me. That thought was chilling.

"I'll call my dad when we get to town," I said.

* * *

*****

He answered after the first ring and agreed without asking a question. We pulled into Devon's empty driveway and I unpacked his chair.

"Should we call your mom?" I said, holding the chair steady as he slid in.

"I'll send her a text and tell her I'm going to stay with you while Ms. Lighthorse is gone. She'll understand once she knows that I'll be teaching her class."

By the time Devon had packed his mother returned with a digital consent.

Just don't get into trouble, was her reply.

We pulled up to my house and sat there for a moment looking at the lightless windows. It was eerie, almost soulless. Devon glanced to the left and then right like some kind of bodyguard.

"You can't be too careful," he said.

I let out a laugh and opened the car door, making my way to the trunk for his chair. A feeling of being watched crept over me like trickling ice water. It was just after ten and my father was gone and would be until morning. I helped Devon through the front door, flipping the light switch. The living room sat empty, the coffee table littered with the various magazines that we rarely touched.

"What time does his shift start?" said Devon.

"Eleven," I said, shutting and locking the door.

Devon wheeled his way into the kitchen, helping himself to a soda from the fridge.

I walked in and planted myself at the table. He took a long drink from the can and made his way over. I glanced up at the window above the sink, staring at the narrow slit of the unclosed curtain, its slender void reminding me that somewhere out there was a killer and I was near the top of its list.

"Are you okay?"

I pulled my eyes away and noticed that my hands were clenched together in a painful grip.

"I don't think so," I said.

"It'll be okay," said Devon.

The absurdity of our situation was hard to accept. Here we both sat, me, a coward, and him, a cripple. What if we were attacked? Could we stop it from adding a couple of freshly stripped drapes to that evil, twisted tree?

"Devon," I began, not knowing how to proceed.

His fight in the schoolyard had been nothing short of superhuman, and his eyes, the way they had burned silver. It was as if he had become the beast.

"What is it?"

"When you threw Kyle, did you know that you could do that?"

Devon leaned back in his chair, placing his hands on the table like a meeting was about to begin.

"Are you asking me if I possess that kind of power now?"

I guess I was. I guess knowing that my best friend was like a superhero helped quell some of the fear.

"Do you?"

"Yes," he said. "At least I did. But the wheel is changing. You saw it for yourself."

"Do you have that power now?"

Devon finished off the soda, crushing the can effortlessly and tossed it into the trash can, which sat eight feet behind him without giving it a look.

"I guess that's a yes?" I said.

"Ms. Lighthorse didn't leave me here just for my looks."

"Good thing, too," I said. "Or we'd really be in trouble."

"You're an asshole."

"And you're the guy that hangs out with me," I said.

*****

Time has a way of making you forget. Monday went to Tuesday without any altercation. Tuesday turned to Wednesday with bright cloudless days and calm, cool evenings. My father even managed to make an appearance between one of his shifts.

"You boys aren't throwing any wild parties with strippers, are you?"

"Can we?" said Devon.

"Devon, how have I not arrested you yet?"

Devon gripped the wheels of his chair and said, "I'm too fast for you, old man."

"I don't doubt it," said my father.

He then looked at me and said, "We should plan on visiting your mother Sunday."

"Let's do it," I said, and a wave of relief rushed over me.

Had he decided against taking her to the wheel? Maybe she was getting better after all, and that had changed his mind.

"So be it," he said, giving my shoulder a squeeze.

With that, he grabbed his keys off of the coffee table and went to work.

By Thursday Devon and I were taking our lunch with Holly and her small circle of friends. All they wanted to talk about was the prom, which left Devon remorseful and quiet. Holly, bless her heart, seemed to notice.

"You know Devon," she said. "Kelly here isn't going with anyone."

Devon gave her a glare that sent ice through my blood, and I reached out a foot and gave him a kick. I could understand his anger. He had suddenly been put on the spot; singled out for pity he didn't want.

Kelly Sheer was a quiet senior who always seemed to be content lagging behind. She was the type of girl who in a race of five was okay with third. I'm not putting her down, in fact, I kind of envy her: She understood the rules of high school very well and refused to play, choosing to survive instead.

"Are you not going with anyone?" she said, sounding surprised.

Devon then did something that I had never seen before; he flushed red and began to fidget in his seat.

"Uh…well…," he said.

"We should go together," said Kelly, her mouth molding into a smile.

And she was pretty. Not beautiful in the millennial I'm both a stripper and singer sense, but in the I could really talk to her sense.

Devon looked at her and I could tell he was running the odds in his head. Was Kelly for real? Was this girl actually asking him out? It occurred to me that my friend and I had fallen into a trap. This meeting of Kelly and Devon was not just by chance. How long had Holly and Kelly been planning this?

"Uh, I guess we can," my flustered friend said, finally.

"Good," said Holly, absolutely bubbling with joy. "You guys can come with me and Dan to Carlito's. We'll make it a double date."

A cloud seemed to pass over Devon's face. The thought of Kelly standing at the side of my car while I retrieved his chair from my trunk, and everything that followed, was playing through his mind like a horror film. Never had he been placed in a situation where an outsider shared in this compromising routine. Then Kelly did something that I will never forget: She leaned over the table, placing her hand on top of his and said, "It will be fun."

*****

What wasn't fun was being stuck in my room and having to listen to my friend for the rest of the day and well into the night. Devon's emotions were like an out of control roller coaster, peaking with the excitement of having a date and then plummeting into the absurdity of having a date.

"It's just the prom," I said, desperately wishing for a mute button.

"Exactly," said Devon. "And I can't dance."

"I'm pretty sure Kelly knows that," I said, my voice low.

"And you don't think that's a problem?" he said. "I should call it off."

"Devon, it's not like this is a contest. We're just going out with a couple of girls to celebrate the end of our senior year."

Devon's eyes narrowed into slits of cruelty and he almost hissed, "Wait until Linda finds out."

My head jolted back as if I had been slapped. Linda knew I was going, Ms. Lighthorse had made that clear. And I'm pretty sure that Linda knew how I felt about her. My friend knew this as well, and was now trying to use those feelings like a weapon. Without a word I stood up and began to leave the room.

"Dan, wait," he said. "I'm sorry, man. I'm just nervous."

I turned back and looked at him. Sweat covered his face, causing his dark hair to stick to his forehead. The sudden sadness I felt quelled the anger. My friend, who had tossed the school bully, who was planning to face whatever evil lingered within the ring in hand to hand combat, was lashing out because he was terrified.

"Forget it," I said. "Everyone knows you're an asshole."

"And you're the guy — " he began, but I cut him off.

"Yeah, yeah, yeah."

CHAPTER THIRTY-FOUR

The Prom

The day that Kyle Bently was attacked began with cooler temperatures and clear skies. I got Devon to school thirty minutes early so he could prepare class for the elementary kids and still have time to grade what papers he had left from the previous day. Because of the dance, the high school would be shutting down after the morning classes, leaving only the volunteer staff to decorate the gym and allowing the hired DJ to do what needed to be done. Excitement charged the air, and at some point the teachers must have given up on anything productive being done. It was as if a group of lawless pirates had replaced their students and against these odds, the educator's stood little chance.

The final bell rang and the doors were flung open, sending explosive echoes up and down the hallways. I expected to find Devon waiting for me by my locker but saw that he was further down the row, actively chatting with Kelly. They were both laughing, and her hand was on his shoulder. I threw in my bag and made my way towards the couple.

"Dan, my man," Devon cried out, holding up his hand.

"You are so weird," I said, swatting his high-five. As if it was her cue, Holly turned the corner, her face lighting up at the sight of Devon and Kelly.

"Look at you two," she said, coming to a stop beside me and it was like a trigger. I found myself thinking about Linda. Why had they not called? Were they safe?

"What time are you boys picking us up?" said Holly.

"Should be early if we're going to eat first," said Devon.

"How about five?" I said.

"Will that be enough time?" said Devon.

"It will leave us plenty of time," said Holly. "You can pick both of us up at my house."

We all agreed and then left the school.

*****

The manic stranger from the night before was gone. Devon was now like a kid going to Disney World for the first time. He spoke with an excitement that I hadn't heard since his phone call about Joe's death.

"Oh shit," he said, suddenly. "I don't have a tuxedo."

We spent the next hour and a half in the south part of the city searching for a suit that would both fit physically, and within our limited budget. Finally, after discovering that all of the tuxedo's were either rented or sold, Devon settled on a three- piece suit with pinstripes. It gave him an old Chicago gangster look that he seemed to like. All I could do was give him a thumbs up and hope for the best. During the trip back we tried calling Ms. Lighthorse but it went straight to voicemail.

"Do you think they're okay?" I said.

"I'm sure they are," said Devon. "Let's not worry about it now."

I understood where he was coming from, for the first time in his life my best friend had a date and it was with someone who seemed to be interested in him, despite the obvious. I pushed down my fear for Ms. Lighthorse and Linda, deciding to enjoy the rest of the day.

I pulled up next to my father's cruiser in the driveway, glancing at the clock on the dashboard. It was a little after three.

"He's probably asleep," I said, getting out of the car.

"I promise to be quiet," said Devon, and I wasn't sure if that was possible.

To my surprise, my father was sitting in his recliner, fully regaled in his uniform and looking about as weary as I had ever seen him.

"Hey boys," he said as we came through the front door. "Ready for the big night?"

"As ready as we'll ever be," I said. "Is everything alright?"

"You bet," he said. "I'm just a little tired. I'm having to pull a double shift."

"Are you going to come by the prom tonight?" said Devon.

"If I get a chance," he said, looking down at his watch. "Well, back to the trenches."

My father then stood, walked over, leaned down and gave Devon a hug.

"I'm proud of you, son," he said.

Devon returned the gesture, his face turning red.

"Thank you sir."

He then released him and made his way over to me. We embraced for a long moment, both of us reliving in an instant the many years, both good and bad, that had led us to this.

"I love you Danny," he said, letting me go.

He gave us a final wave and left. Devon and I waited in silence until we heard the sound of the cruiser's motor fire up. Ten seconds later my father was gone.

"He's a good guy," said Devon.

"I know," I said. "And that's why I'm worried."

*****

We sat at Carlito's enjoying our complimentary chips and salsa, discussing the ups and downs of our senior year. Devon and Kelly kept drifting away into their newly created world, leaving Holly and I adrift and unable to build a bridge. It was okay, I think we both realized that our pairing was really just one of necessity. My mind kept returning to Linda and how instinctively we had sought out each other during Mother Gina's final moment, our hands locking together. I loved her and to sit now with Holly and pretend otherwise seemed unfair. Holly deserved better.

By the time the bill came we had a little less than thirty minutes until the prom began. We loaded into the car with Kelly and Devon sitting in the back, my friend's arm draped over her shoulders. We pulled into the school parking lot just in time to see R.J. and his one true love entering the gym.

"They make a good couple," said Holly, absently.

I was forced to settle for a space near the back of the lot. Devon and Kelly yapped away as I brought the chair around and continued to yap all the way to the door.

The gym had been transformed into a dance room reminding me of one of those high-end cruise ships. A disco ball hung down from the center beam, splashing well placed rays of light off of the dull gray walls. The DJ was working his magic from underneath one of the basketball goals, spilling out the heavy beats of Lizzo. All around us were the jumping children of my age.

"Who wants a drink?" said Devon.

"I'll take one," said Holly.

"I'll go with you," said Kelly.

I watched as they wound their way through the crowd towards the concession stand.

"Are you okay?" said Holly.

"Sorry," I said, offering her a weak smile. "It's just good to see Devon happy."

"Kelly really likes him."

"I can tell," I said. "I don't think they've stopped talking since they decided to come here together."

"Well, at least someone's having a good time."

"Holly-" I began, but she shut me up in true Holly form with a raised palm.

"Listen, Dan," she said. "We're not getting married. We're not even dating, but that doesn't mean we can't have a good time, does it?"

"No," I said, feeling like an admonished fourth grader.

"Okay, then. Let's dance."

So, dance we did, and not just Holly and I, either. Somehow, Kelly had managed to get Devon out onto the floor. He spun his chair, going up on two wheels, even dropping to the hardwood at one point and doing clap-hand push ups. By the time the prom ended I felt as if I had run the most enjoyable marathon possible.

*****

* * *

The parking lot was soaked in silver from a near full moon. We hung out at the front door of the gym talking to RJ as the other members of our class funneled out.

"Devon," said RJ. "That was amazing."

"I'm just a guy trying to get by," said Devon, which caused Kelly to giggle.

She was now sitting on his lap, her legs draped over the side of his chair.

"I need to get home," said Holly.

We all looked at her for a moment in shock.

"I'm not eighteen yet."

"You youngster's and your curfew," said RJ. "Well, until we meet again."

He threw us a wave and made his way to his truck, which sat just a few feet away. I looked out into the moonlight and could just see in the distance the dirty shade of my retired Corsica.

"I can go get the car, if you guys want."

"No way," said Devon. "We'll go with you."

We left the concrete landing, making our way through a mostly empty lot. The few vehicles remaining were from the clean up crew who had been sentenced to late night duty through no fault of their own.

"I had a good time tonight," said Holly, as we drew closer to the retired cruiser.

"Thanks for going with me," I said, reaching for the keys in my pocket.

Kelly had insisted on pushing Devon's chair, saying that it was the least she could do considering she had spent time with the best dancer in the school. She leaned down and gave my friend a kiss on the top of his sweaty head.

"I think we should— " she began.

"Look at this, the cripple got a piece of ass."

Three ghostly shapes moved out from behind my car. It was Kyle Thomas and his two Gestapo guards. The three of them moved to within just a couple of feet from us, blocking our path. It was then that I caught the glint of the Bowie knife that was clutched in Kyle's hand.

"You can't be serious," said Devon.

"Does your dick even work?" said Steve Kemp.

"It won't after I'm done," said Kyle, holding up the six-inch blade. "I told you I was gonna get you back."

"You guys touch us and you'll go to prison," said Holly, her phone in hand.

Kyle gave her a grin straight out of the X-Files and said, "We're going to slice the boys and then we'll see about you."

"You know my dad's the chief of police," I said.

It was all that I could think to say. This caused the three of them to erupt with laughter. Normally, in a situation like that the best thing to do is run screaming. Unfortunately, that would only work for the three of us. I desperately looked around, hoping that someone might see the crime that was about to happen but the place was like a graveyard.

"I'll make you a deal," Kyle continued. "Leave us wheels and you can go."

"Go to hell," said Kelly, her arms now wrapped around Devon like a protective shield.

"You first, bitch," said Kyle, taking a step towards us, the knife rising.

Steve Kemp suddenly made a sound like a kicked dog, then turned and ran past my car, disappearing into the night. Larry Jones let out a small squeal, tripped over his own feet, regained his balance and followed. Kyle stood frozen, the knife held high above his head.

I could smell its stench even before it brushed by me. A mountain of rippling hair, with long gorilla-like arms ending in claws. It stopped inches away from the petrified Kyle, reaching out with its long spear-ended fingers and touched him on his cheek. Kyle let out a long hiss, like an over-inflated tire with a small puncture, and fell to the ground. He lay there motionless, his eyes still filled with the residue of horror.

The creature slowly turned to face us, its maw resembling that of a bear mixed with a wolf. Its eyes a pair of glistening red orbs that seemed to produce a light of their own. It held up the same clawed finger that had dropped Kyle, wagging it in the air.

A low rumbling growl began vibrating from its chest:

"OO...ON... ON THREE."

It then spun with lightning speed, grabbed Kyle by the ankle and bolted into the darkness.

CHAPTER THIRTY-FIVE

Checking Out

Devon and I looked at each other, the shock in his eyes mirroring mine. Everything had happened so fast and I wasn't sure if what I had heard was real or just adrenaline nearing overload.

"Did you hear it?" said Devon.

"I think so," I said.

"You know what that means?"

"Yes," I managed to say.

Mike Henley had wandered into the wheel, lost for hours, until finally returning to the huts. What had he been doing? Of course, Ms. Light Horse had been too relieved at the time that he had come back to question him. But I think that both Devon and I now knew the answer: Mike had made a bargain with the Devil. Joe Clark, Mr. Kemp's goats, Mother Gina. Mike had killed them all, and now he had murdered Kyle Bently.

"I have to get home," said Holly, her phone in hand and tears flowing down her cheeks.

Kelly stood with her arms still wrapped around Devon, her jaw unhinged. They were outsiders, unaware of the truth behind the savagery. I reached out for Holly's shoulder just as spinning red and blue lights turned the corner on Main. Relief swept over me as my father's cruiser pulled into the lot. Holly somehow had managed to keep her composure long enough to dial 911. I began to make my way to the oncoming cruiser. It was time to tell my father the truth. The attack on Kyle could only prove the nature of the thing in the wheel. Surely he would listen. The car came to a stop beside my Corsica. The driver's door was flung open and out stepped Officer Greg Peterson, the guy my father was supposed to be covering for.

Holly broke past me, running to the officer. He let her fall against him and then gently pushed her back

"What's happened?" he said.

All she could do was stutter uncontrollably, her words blending together incoherently.   Officer Peterson placed her into the car, leaving the door open. He noticed me standing there and made his way over.

"Dan, what's going on?"

"Where's my dad?"

"He's on vacation," he said. "Didn't you know?"

"I didn't. Why are you driving his car?"

"He wanted me to take the cruiser while he was gone. Said it looked like someone was still in charge. Now, tell me what happened."

I did, at least most of it. I didn't mention the fact that Mike Henley was now some kind of a were-murderer, nor did I mention the wheel. Officer Peterson, to his credit, wrote everything down without once interrupting.

"So," he began once I had concluded. "Are you saying it was a bear or a wolf?"

"We're not sure,' said Devon.

"But it walked on two legs," said Kelly.

She really was being brave considering a nightmare had suddenly come true.

Officer Peterson scribbled a final note in his pad and then closed it.

"You guys need to go straight home," he said. "I mean it Dan. I'll take Holly and talk to her parents, but you guys get home and call if you see anything."

*****

Devon and I said very little on the way to Kelly's house, nor could we. Kelly was blabbing away break-neck speed.

"It only touched him," she said. "Did you see it?"

"Yes," Devon. "We all saw it."

"How is that possible?" she said, her eyes like saucers.

"Maybe it scared him to death," I said.

"Maybe," Kelly said. "Or maybe it had poisoned claws."

She then went on to tell us about Komodo Dragons and Coral Snakes, and other creatures of the toxic level.

I'm sorry to say, but by the time we pulled into her driveway I was kind of glad to see her go. She leaned over and gave Devon a kiss on the cheek and made him promise to call her when he arrived home. We waited to make sure that she got inside of her front door before backing out.

"That one's a talker," I said, jokingly.

"She's just scared," said Devon. "And so am I."

"How could Mike have done this?" I said.

"I understand," said Devon.

I glanced over at my friend, his dark hair curtained over his eyes. Just two weeks ago I suspected that he might be the beast. Why? Because of the anger buried within him. Because of the torment life had presented him with for just being what he was. But Mike was different. Whereas Devon had been born with his disability, Mike's had been thrust upon him. Mike had gone from the most promising life one could hope for to hopelessness. He had lost everything, including his father, all in one unfortunate night. That thing in the wheel, could feel that. It had pandered that anger with promises of power and vengeance and Mike hadn't hesitated.

"Do you think he's already there?" said Devon.

"Who?"

"Your father," he said.

The murder of Kyle and the relentless words of Devon's new gal had caused me to place that question on the back burner. But the answer seemed obvious.

"We could stop by the center," said Devon.

"It's way past visiting hours," I said. "They'd never let us in."

"We could call," he said. "Surely they'd go check on her."

I reached for my phone and scrolled to the number just as I made a right turn onto my road. It only rang twice before a tired sounding woman's voice picked up the line.

"Hi," I said, trying to sound calm. "This is Dan Lee. I just got back into town and wanted to see how my mother was. Her name is—"

"Hey Dan, this is Rose." The woman's voice suddenly came alive. "I got stuck with a double, which is fine, it pays time and a half."

"It's good to hear your voice," I said. "How's my mom?"

"I should be asking you that," she said.

"What do you mean?"

"She walked out of here four hours ago with your father."

"Walked?" I said, my heart plummeting.

"You mean you haven't heard? I wanted to get the doctor in here, or at least a priest. It was a miracle, but your father wouldn't allow it."

"Did he say where he was taking her?" I said.

"He didn't." she said. "I assumed they were going home."

"No one tried to stop them?"

"He's the chief of police, Dan."

"Did she say anything?" I said.

"No, she just smiled and gave me an odd sort of wave. Dan, what's going on?"

My mind felt as though it had been dipped in ice water, sending hooks down my spine. I vaguely remember telling Rose that I would keep her updated and ended the call. Devon and I sat in silence, staring at the front of my empty house from the inside of my car.

"How could she walk out of there?" he said, at last.

"How does Mike do what he does?" I said.

"Good point."

Images of sheet-like skins flapping from skeletal branches flickered before me. Would there be two more to join them? Or worse, two more creatures out there doing their twisted masters bidding. My father, much like Mike, had taken the deal, had agreed to whatever terms the evil within the wheel had offered. I couldn't allow it.

"I have to go up there," I said, finally.

"You can't," he said. "Not alone."

Five days had gone by since Ms. Lighthorse and Linda had left for Wyoming, and yet we had heard nothing from them. Why hadn't she at least called? As if reading my mind, Devon pulled his phone out of his pocket and said, "Let me try her."

He placed the call on speaker and we both sat fidgeting as the first ring turned into the second and then the third.

"Why won't she answer?" I said, but then she did, and she sounded very far away.

"Devon, what's going on?"

We took turns filling her in on the wave after wave of events.

"Poor Mike," she said, once we had finished. "I should have guessed. I wish I had never taken him."

"You couldn't have known what he would become," said Devon.

"I suppose not," said Ms. Lighthorse. "Where are you now?"

"We're at Dan's," said Devon. "He wants to go up there tonight."

"Absolutely not," she said. "You stay where you are and lock the doors. We have the stones."

"But where are you?" I said.

"We just passed Salina. We'll be there tomorrow morning. Until then I don't want you guys to do anything."

Easier said than done. It wasn't her parents up there in the wheel, possibly transforming into killing machines.

"Okay," said Devon. "But call us as soon as you get to town."

"I will," she said and the phone went dead.

*****

Devon and I sat in my room trying to pass the time with Youtube videos and downloaded games. It was, of course, pointless. My parents were lost in the wheel, becoming God knows what, and I was supposed to sit there, pretending as though everything was fine.

The minutes ticked painfully away, each hour feeling as if it were an era.

"I wonder why he didn't attack us?" said Devon.

"Because he wasn't supposed to," I said.

The creature that was Mike wasn't acting on his own volition. Kyle, much like Joe, had been marked. Perhaps that was part of the deal Mike had made; to serve the thing within the wheel in return for vengeance against those who had done him wrong. It made sense.

Turns out, I was only partly right.

The early morning hours eventually came, and the heaviness of sleep began to weigh on us. Devon scooted himself onto the edge of my bed, his eyes red with exhaustion.

"Ms. Lighthorse will be here soon," he mumbled.

I lay next to him envious of the fact that he could fall right to sleep. My eyes, on the other hand, refused to close. So I resorted to quietly counting off every song from The Beatles White Album and then, when that was done, moved onto Sergeant Pepper's Lonely Hearts Club Band. Eventually, I did finally manage to drop off, and was flung into a nightmare filled with ghostly dancers gyrating within a wheel bordered by laughing skulls and crawling flames. Not exactly a good night's sleep.

CHAPTER THIRTY-SIX

Mrs. Henley

We were awoken by the obnoxious ring of Devon's phone.

"Okay," he said. "We'll be there."

He scooted into his chair, brushing his hair out of his eyes.

"Ms. Lighthorse is back and wants us to meet her at the school in two hours," he said, wheeling himself to the bathroom.

"Do you need help?" I said.

"Dan, it's bad enough that we slept together," he said, shutting the door behind him.

He returned a few minutes later looking somewhat refreshed.

"Does she have a plan?" I said.

"I'm sure she does."

I rushed through my own essentials and we were soon out the door.

*****

The school parking lot was as desolate as a desert. Ms. Lighthorse's van was parked in its usual spot, the only difference being that the fender held heavy chunks of mud. I helped Devon into his chair and we made our way into the school. Funny how just a few hours before we had been having the time of our lives at this place and now it was as if we were entering a courtroom for sentencing.

Ms. Lighthorse was sitting behind her desk, her beautiful face lined with exhaustion. Linda sat to her right. I saw her and it was like some kind of automated device had switched on. I rushed over, throwing my arms around her fragile shoulders, embracing the girl like a soldier returning from war.

"She's missed you," said Ms. Lighthorse with a weak smile.

"You have the stones?" said Devon.

"We managed to grab eight before being run off by the park rangers." she said, pointing at a canvas bag sitting on the floor. "The only reason I wasn't arrested on the spot was because I had Linda with me, but they escorted us out."

"Will it be enough?" I said.

"It will have to be," said Ms. Lighthorse.

"What was the Wyoming Wheel like?" said Devon.

Ms. Lighthorse leaned back in her chair, raising her dark eyes towards the ceiling.

"You could feel it," she said, at last. "The power was everywhere."

"Was it like the one here?" said Devon. "Did it heal Linda?"

"No," said Ms. Lighthorse. "It wasn't that kind of power."

"You mean it's weaker than ours?" I said.

"Just the opposite," said Ms. Lighthorse. "I think the Wyoming Wheel oversees its children."

"It's children?" I said.

"The other wheels of the world," said Ms. Lighthorse. "I think it is the creator of them all. I'm sure it didn't have to let us take the stones from it. But when we were up there it was as if I were being led to the right area, as if it knew its child was sick."

"So what do we do now?" said Devon. "Do we go tonight?"

"Not tonight," she said.

"But what about my parents?" I said.

"It won't do them, or us, any good if we go up there now."

"What do you mean?" I said. "Isn't that what the stones are for?"

"For the virus infecting the ring, yes, but we have someone else to consider."

"Mike," said Devon. "What do we do about him? Do we kill him?"

"Can we kill him?" I said.

The events from the night before caused some doubt.

"I don't know," Ms. Lighthorse. "But I do know I don't want to kill him if we don't have to. This isn't his fault."

"We need to draw him out," said Devon. "Separate him."

"But how do we do that?" I said.

No one seemed to have an answer. The question stood before us like a road block. The monster that was Mike could kill with a touch. Against something like that, what could you do? But was he always in monstrous form? A thought came to me then, and it took all of the courage I could muster to present it to the others. What if I was wrong?

"We could go to his house," I said.

"Yes," said Devon, slapping his knee. "He would have to go back home at some point and surely not as a man-bear."

Ms. Lighthorse nodded her head, her eyes brightening.

"You're right," she said. "It would give us the best chance to confront him."

"We shouldn't go at night," I said.

"I don't think we should waste another second," said Ms. Lighthorse, rising from her chair and grabbing the keys off of her desk.

"We're going there now?" I said.

"Hey," said Devon, throwing a wink my way. "The sooner we deal with him, the sooner we can deal with the wheel."

He said this like it was a good thing; just a casual stepping stone on the way to a sure victory. I let out a fear ridden sigh, grabbed the handles of Linda's chair and together we followed Ms. Lighthorse and Devon back out into the sunlit humidity.

*****

The Henley's house sat in the middle of their fifty acre cattle ranch five miles outside of town. At one point Mike's father had employed twenty hands to run the operation. It certainly wasn't how the family earned their money but I guess it made them feel as though they belonged. Blanchard was a mostly agricultural town, with a feed store and a thriving FFA, so maybe the ranch was a way for two professionals to fit in. Of course, that was before the accident.

Their road was a gravel washboard edged with blooming ivy and thorny thickets. Switchgrass danced in unison from gusts of trespassing wind. The land was vacant, its occupants sold either for slaughter or breeding after the fall of House Henley; a depressing reminder of how quickly things can change.

We crested a hill and saw a chipped mailbox leaning on a rusted post near the bottom of an oncoming valley. Ms. Lighthorse slowed the van and made a sharp turn onto a winding driveway.

"How do we handle this?" said Devon, as the paint-deprived two story house appeared before us.

"You wait with Linda," said Ms. Lighthorse. "Dan and I will go."

"Are you sure that's a good idea?" said Devon.

"We may have to leave in a hurry."

"But what if he's there?" said Devon. "What if he's not himself?"

"That would be hard to explain to his mother," said Ms. Lighthorse, coming to a stop near the front walkway.

She shut the motor off and we sat there for a moment in silence. I reached out and grabbed Linda's disfigured hand. Her silence was torture. I looked at her face, her eyes were filled with tears.

"It'll be okay," I said.

Linda could do little else but offer a soft coo. More than anything I wished that she could speak at that moment, but what would she say? What could she say? We were about to take our first step into the monster's den; about to confront an enemy beyond any of us; one that could kill with a touch. And Linda would be left, unable to run, unable to cry out for help. But to do nothing would be much worse; a sentence of pained immobility coupled with the memory of what might have been. I leaned over and kissed her cheek, grabbed the handle of my door and said, "Let's do it."

*****

Five years had passed since the accident, but the condition of the house made it seem much longer. The screen door hung by one hinge, its frame faded and rotted. The doorbell was missing, leaving two thin wires protruding out of a jagged hole. Paint had crumbled off of the walls, lining the weathered front porch. Ms. Lighthorse reached out and gave the flaked oak panel a quick knock. We stood there looking through the obscure glass. Nothing moved. Ms. Lighthorse gave a harder knock and stepped back as the door slowly opened. A sickening smell rolled out of the house, causing us both to gag.

"What is that?" I managed to say.

"Stay behind me," she said, stepping into the foyer. It was funny, actually, being told to stay behind this woman who stood a head shorter than me and eighty pounds lighter, but I was more than happy to comply. We made our way into the living area. The once immaculate area was now a disaster. An overturned coffee table lay across a ripped leather couch. Pieces of a big screen television littered a stained Persian rug.

We started down a hallway, following the pungent odor. Ms. Lighthorse stopped at a door that was partially opened. The smell was slamming into us in nauseous waves. We looked at each other, neither of us wanting to step into the room.

"Don't," I said as she pushed the panel.

"Wait here," she said, crossing the threshold, but I couldn't.

Mike Henley's mother lay on her bed. The body was bloated, purplish yellow and wearing nothing but a nightgown. Ms Lighthorse crossed the few feet between us and the corpse, stopping at the head of the bed. She reached down and grabbed a scrap of paper that had been placed under an empty bottle of pills on the nightstand.

"It's a note," she said. "I've lost everything."

That was all that had been written. Ms. Lighthorse let the paper fall to the floor.

"He didn't kill her," I said.

"Didn't he?" she said. "Let's go. Mike won't be back."

No, he wouldn't. Mike's transformation into the darkness was now complete. Any ties to his previous life had been erased by his mother's final breath. Mike Henley, the Mike we had known, was now dead, replaced by a one-touch killing machine. It would be up there in its new home, and it would be waiting.

In the van Devon was drumming his hands. I opened my door and slid in as a barrage of questions flew out of his mouth.

"She's dead," I managed to say, and then everything kind of

drifted away.

Mrs. Henley was the first dead person I had ever seen in real time. How long had she been there lying alone and forgotten? I felt a rush of grief threatening to overcome me; a tsunami of sorrow. I closed my eyes and bit down on my lower lip hoping that the despair would end soon.

We drove away from the stricken house in silence. Even Devon seemed to sense the weight. I glanced over at Linda and saw that her eyes were focused on me.

"I'm okay," I said, reaching for her hand.

"What do we do now?" said Devon.

"We go back and pack," said Ms. Lighthorse.

"We're going to the ring?" I said, my heart rate quickening.

"We'll stay at the huts tonight and hope we have a visitor."

"You're thinking Mike will show up?" said Devon.

"I think he will be forced to," said Ms. Lighthorse. "The wheel knows we're coming and will try to stop us any way it can. With any luck we can save Mike and your parents."

CHAPTER THIRTY-SEVEN
Clovis Culture

We exited the town a little over an hour later fully packed, like a small platoon headed for the front line. I sat beside Linda anxiously waiting for the magic boundary to be crossed; that moment when she would be able to speak and be able to reach out for me. I needed her. I needed her strength. I only hoped that the power to bring her back was still there.

"You know," said Devon, suddenly. "We really don't have anything to fight him with."

"We're going to make a stop first," said Ms. Lighthorse. "We'll find everything we need at Mother Gina's."

"She has guns?" I said.

"I don't think guns will work," said Ms. Lighthorse.

"Not even with silver bullets?"

"Mike's not a were-wolf, Dan," she said, stifling a grin.

"Okay," I said. "Then what is he?"

"A creation of the entity within the wheel," she said. "Made by something ancient. I think that he can only be hurt by something just as ancient."

"But you said the stones would have no effect," said Devon.

"They would hurt him, just as if you were to be hit by one, but do little else," said Ms. Lighthorse. "Their power comes from the mother wheel and will only work on its descendants."

That cast a heavy blanket of silence over us. If a gun didn't work, then what would? Were we to face the monster with swords, like dragon slayers out of some fantasy story?

Something landed on my shoulder, causing me to yelp. I turned and saw Linda leaning out of her chair, her face radiating with beauty. I slid over, embracing her, struggling to hold back a sudden onslaught of tears.

"I missed you," I managed to say.

"And I missed you," she said.

"Ah," said Devon. "That's so cute."

"Do you want to talk about Kelly?" I said.

"Point taken," he said, turning his gaze to the window.

"Who's Kelly?" said Linda.

"I'll tell you about it later," I said.

"I can't wait to hear this," she said.

We sat together, each of us grateful for the other's company, trying to ignore the fact that we were going to war. Linda turned towards me, her face taking on a pained expression and I feared that her gift was being stripped away, much like it had when we were at Mother Gina's

"What is it?" I said.

"I was shown something in Wyoming," she said, her voice barely above a whisper.

"What did you see?"

Linda looked at me for a moment longer, her eyes a pair of impending tempests, and then the clouds seemed to lift.

"I'll tell you when this is over."

I thought about pressing the subject, but considering what we were about to face, decided against it. Linda was worried about the coming night, and not just for her. I wasn't one of them, not really, and their strength within the wheel at least gave them a fighting chance. She knew this, I'm sure, and it frightened her. It wasn't until later that I learned just how wrong I was about that. We spent the rest of the trip in silence with our hands interlocked, her head resting on my shoulder.

*****

* * *

Mother Gina's home was like a run down tomb. The cracked cinder block foundation had been lined with wreaths of bright orange Indian Paintbrush interwoven with yellow Sunflower and violet Coneflower. Strung along the ceiling of the front porch were a series of Dream Catchers, much like the ones in her house. Along the walls, half curtained windows stared out at us like unblinking eyes, reminding me of Mrs. Henley.

Our small platoon unloaded with no chairs needed. We made our way to the front door.

"Hey," said a voice from behind.

We turned and walking up the dirt road was an old man with slick gray hair draped past his shoulders. He was wearing a dirty V-neck t-shirt and blue jeans from a past century which were tucked into well-worn leather boots.

"Hi, Carl," said Ms. Lighthorse.

"Are you planning on going in there?" he said, his voice sounding tobacco scarred.

"Mother Gina left me the place," said Ms. Lighthorse. "You know that."

"I'm not talking about the house," he said. "I'm talking about the wheel."

"Why do you ask?" she said.

"It was here," said Carl. "I saw it last night standing where you are now."

"What was here?" said Ms. Lighthorse, taking a step towards him.

"A monster," he said. "It stood there staring at the house like it wanted to go in."

"What did you do?"

Carl let out a gruff laugh and said, "What could I do?"

"Did it go in?" said Devon.

"I don't think it could," said Carl, taking out a cigarette and lighting it. His hands were shaking.

"Thank you for telling us," said Ms. Lighthorse, turning back to the front door.

"You shouldn't go," he said.

"We'll be okay," said Ms. Lighthorse.

"I'm not worried about you," said Carl from a cloud of smoke. "It knows where you're from. It will come for us."

"We have to stop it, Carl."

"And if you can't? What then?"

"If we can't, our community will be the first of many victims."

Carl tossed his cigarette to the ground and stomped it out. He then forced his hands into the pockets of his faded jeans, his mouth contorting into a snarl.

"It's one of yours, isn't it?"

"I don't know what you mean," said Ms. Lighthorse, reaching for the tarnished handle of the door.

"I think you do," he said. "It's one of your messed up kids from school. You and Mother Gina couldn't leave well enough alone, could you? Had to go back to that cursed place and now look at what you've done."

"We've done nothing," said Ms. Lighthorse, pushing open the panel. "But if you are so worried, you're more than welcome to come with us."

The fury that had been decorating Crazy Carl's face seemed to fade. He brought out another smoke, glared at Ms. Light Horse for a moment, then twisted on his heel and trudged off.

"Mike was here?" said Linda.

"That's not surprising," said Ms. Lighthorse, motioning us in. "It's where Mother Gina kept the stone."

"But why didn't he just go in?" said Devon.

"I don't know," said Ms. Lighthorse, closing the door behind us. "Maybe something was stopping him."

"How did Crazy Carl know about us and the wheel?" said Linda.

"Carl may be a little too fond of alcohol, but he's not stupid. And he's not wrong. We are putting them in danger."

"You would think that he would want us to fix the wheel," I said.

"Carl could care less about the wheel," said Ms. Lighthorse. "To him it's an evil place that has brought nothing but ruin down on our people."

"Why does he think that?" said Linda.

"It's not so hard to figure out, really," said Ms. Lighthorse. "If it hadn't been for the wheel we would have followed suit with the other tribes, forming a nation of our own, but instead, our ancestors deemed it more important to protect the secret, leaving us trapped in poverty. And Carl isn't the only one that feels that way."

We followed Ms. Lighthorse into the small dining room. She reached into her bag and pulled out eight jagged pieces of rock.

"That's them?" said Devon.

"Yes," said Ms. Lighthorse, placing them on the dining room table. "Wait here."

We watched her leave the room and then directed our attention back to the stones. They lay in a pile, small black rocks with smooth bodies and sharpened edges. None of them were more than three inches long and looked about as deadly as a water gun.

"I expected something more," said Devon.

I reached my hand out slowly, not sure of what to expect, and grabbed one of the dark rocks. There was no electric charge, no sudden vision. The stone was just a chunk of rough obsidian.

"I guess I did, too," I said, dropping the rock back onto the table.

Ms. Lighthorse returned with a handful of long spears and a small bundle of arrows. She laid them out next to the stones and took a seat.

"Are any of you familiar with Clovis Culture?"

"Doesn't that have something to do with the stone age?" said Linda.

"Very good, sweetheart," said Ms. Lighthorse. "The name comes from Clovis, New Mexico. That is where they found weapons that some estimate to be thirteen thousand years old."

"Is that what you have?" I said.

"Yes," said Ms. Lighthorse. "What you're looking at are Clovis tips, each one of these were brought with us when we left our homeland."

I glanced at the weapons with curiosity. The spear tips seemed to be made from similar stones as the one's from Wyoming. They were black in color but looked scuffed. How many deaths over the millennia had they provided? Hundreds? Thousands? Had one of them belonged to Loshi?

"These are what we will use against Mike," said Ms. Lighthorse. "But only if we have to."

The thought of having to kill him weighed heavy on her mind. He had been her student and it was because of her that he had become what he had become. Of course, if you followed that train of thought, she was the reason Joe and Kyle were dead, and that was heavy, indeed.

"What about the stones?" said Devon.

"That's what the arrows are for," said Ms. Lighthorse. "We need to remove the old heads and replace them with the ones from Wyoming."

The only thing that I could do was help remove the tips and then watch as Ms. Lighthorse chipped away at the obsidian, fashioning them into rudimentary replacements. Linda and Devon then took each one and tied them to the end of the shafts, until eight arrows lay on the table. They looked like something you might see in the Flintstone's movie.

"Oh, man," said Devon, running his hand through his hair.

"It will work," said Ms. Lighthorse, rising from her chair. "Everyone grab a spear. We need to go."

She made her way towards the door, pausing to remove an old compound bow off of the living room wall. I reached for one of the spears, wondering if we would live to see tomorrow.

"We can do this," said Linda. "We have to."

Together, we made our way back to the van, Devon placed himself in the passenger seat as Linda and I sat next to each other in the back. The dirt road was empty with no sign of Crazy Carl. Ms. Lighthorse backed up enough to turn around and then slowly drove us out of the town, leaving nothing but prying eyes and anger.

Ahead of us awaited the wheel.

CHAPTER THIRTY-EIGHT

Mother

We turned the narrow path-like corner and were confronted by trails of smoke lifting towards the afternoon sky. The huts had crumbled into smoldering piles of smoldered ash, all of them reduced to unrecognizable mounds. All of them, except for the one Ms. Lighthorse had stayed in.

"Who could have done this?" I said.

"Do you think Crazy Carl came up here?" said Devon, his face inches away from the windshield.

Ms Lighthorse sat there with both hands throttling the steering wheel, her dark eyes wide and her mouth open. Without answering, she shut the motor off, opened the door and made her way to the remaining hut. Devon followed, leaving Linda and I staring after them.

"We should go," she said, finally, reaching for the handle of the slide door.

We walked towards the domicile, stopping beside Ms. Lighthorse at the opening.

"Something's in there," she said, entering the hut.

The area looked like a campsite: A sleeping bag lay unfolded, placed out like a mattress with another spread over it like a blanket. Two pillows rested at one end. An ice chest sat near the back with a loaf of bread placed on the lid. Next to it were two piles of folded clothes. One pile contained t-shirts and the other, four pairs of jeans. Draped over them was a belt with a holstered gun. I knew those clothes and I knew that gun.

"It's my dad," I said.

"I think you're right," said Ms. Lighthorse. "But how did he get here?"

"He had to have taken a cab," I said.

"Which means he wasn't planning on going back any time soon," said Devon.

"But why would he do this?" said Linda.

"Because it was a part of the deal," I said, dropping to the floor. Ms. Lighthorse came and sat beside me.

"I don't think he's alone," she said, pointing over to where a hospital gown lay crumpled and I felt my heart sink.

Somewhere out there walked my mother, a person who had been confined to a bed for years. My feelings were jumbled, a mesh of excitement and terror.

"I need to find them," I said.

"Do we go to the wheel?" said Devon.

"Not yet," said Ms Lighthorse. "I think it would be better for us to stay here tonight."

"But my parents are out there," I said.

"Yes, but we don't know where," said Ms. Lighthorse. "What we do know is where they are staying."

She was right. My parents could be anywhere; walking the river bank, traipsing the mountainside, or, God forbid, lost within the wheel. It would do us no good to try and cover all of those miles and then take a chance at missing them. It would be evening soon, and all I could do was hope that they might show up. And if they did, what then? What would my father do? I doubted if he would be glad to see us. My gaze drifted over to where his gun sat within its holster, desperately trying to stop the motion picture playing out in my mind.

"Let's get our things," said Ms. Lighthorse.

We unpacked our supplies from the van, all of us forced to set up under one roof. I unrolled my bag, placing my spear close by. Linda set her bag next to mine, offering a sad smile, but saying nothing.

We ate a small meal of peanut butter and jelly sandwiches as the afternoon turned into early evening. Under Ms. Lighthorse's direction we gathered logs and whatever sticks we could find, bringing them back to the burn pit.

"The fire must be big tonight," she said. "I want it to be seen."

It would be a beacon. A challenge to the beast that was Mike. But would he come? And if he did, would he be alone, or would my parents be with him? I focused on the work at hand, trying to keep my imagination in check. Soon the smell of burning oak and pine filled the air, along with the mulch-like leaves and twigs we had used for kindling.   The evenings had warmed up considerably since the last time I had been here, and the fire was less than comfortable, so we sat near the opening of the hut watching the growing flames dance towards a darkening sky. The first star of the night broke through the gloom; a golden light shining down from the west and was soon followed by hundreds more and still nothing came. The minutes slowly trickled into hours, turning nine into midnight. Linda sat beside me with one hand rubbing her stomach and her head resting on my shoulder, her eyelids creeping shut.

"Are you okay?" I said.

"'I'll be fine," she said, planting a kiss on my cheek.

Ms. Lighthorse lifted herself from the ground, walked over to the flame and threw on another log. The flame was by no means a towering inferno, but it was taller than her, plenty big enough to be seen.

"It's getting late," she said.

"Maybe they're not coming," said Devon.

"Or maybe they're not here," I said.

"Perhaps," said Ms. Lighthorse. "But we're already committed."

"I think Linda should go in and get some sleep," I said, lightly squeezing her arm.

"I think all of you should," said Ms. Lighthorse.

"What about you?" said Linda.

"We can do watches," said Devon. "Each of us takes a two hour shift."

"Sounds good to me," I said, lifting myself from the ground and reaching for Linda's hand.

"I'll take the first watch," said Ms Lighthorse.

"I've got second," said Devon, massaging his thighs.

"I'll take third," I said, sounding braver than I felt.

"That leaves me," said Linda.

I looked down at her face illuminated by the flickering orange light and could see the off colored rings lining her cheeks. She was exhausted.

"Let's just see how it goes," I said, gently nudging her into the hut.

*****

Within seconds Linda's breathing had become deep and steady. She didn't seem well and I wondered just how much help she would be if Mike did show up. If possible, Devon and I would solve the problem before I had to find out. I lay beside Linda, hoping that the night might pass undisturbed, but knowing that it wouldn't. Distant crackling and the occasional pop of roasting wood managed to find its way through the silence. I focused on those sounds, desperately trying to fight back the panic that threatened to overwhelm me. It must have worked, because the next thing I remember was looking up at the shade of Devon hovering over me.

"It's your turn," he said, in a low voice.

"Give me a second," I mumbled, reaching for my shoes.

I then grabbed my phone, allowing the low light of the home screen to fall on Linda. She was lost in a deep sleep that I could only envy.

I stepped out of the hut with my weapon in hand to find Devon feeding the fire. The pile of logs was beginning to run low and I hoped there would be enough to carry us through to morning. I glanced at the clock on my phone; it read 4:03 AM. A little over two and a half hours until sunrise. The stars had disappeared, thanks to a western front that had moved in while I had slept. Soundless blue explosions decorated the distant sky, too far away to be heard,

"Wake me if you see anything," said Devon, ducking into the hut.

"You can count on it," I answered, taking a seat on the ground near the fire.

The flames threw cinema light into the darkness, creating a deep orange dome that could only reach so far. Occasional sounds, like hissing snakes, broke through the silence, caused by staggered gusts of wind shaking the treetops. I clutched my spear and hunkered down, wishing that time would take flight. Within this loneliness my mind began to wander, bouncing from one horrific scenario to another like an out of control car. It took all that I had to bring it back into a lane.

Things will never be the same, was the dominant thought.

My father had returned the love of his life to the living and no matter how this played out, there was no way that she could go back. I had to accept that. But what would that mean? How far would he go? Would he be willing to kill? A couple of days ago I would have said no. But now, sitting outside of the remaining hut while the others smoldered around us, I wasn't sure.

Glancing down at my phone, I saw that only forty minutes had passed since I had relieved Devon. That still left an hour and twenty minutes until I was supposed to wake Linda. I wouldn't, though. As much as I hated the idea, I would remain alone at the post until the sun began to rise. Linda wasn't well, that much was clear. What was wrong with her? And what was it that she was going to tell me? What had she been shown by the wheel in Wyoming?

"Dan."

I spun to my right, barely able to contain the squeal that threatened to burst from my throat. A shape stood just beyond the flickering light, a shadow within the coal- black background.

"Dad?"

The shadow stepped forward, revealing my father. He was wearing one of the Sooner football shirts that I had bought him for Christmas. His face was haggard, like a man who had missed more than a couple of nights of sleep. His jeans were caked with dirt at the knees, his boots covered in mud.

"Dan," he said. "I'm glad you're here."

"They said you took mom," I said.

"I didn't take her," he said. "She left with me. Your mother walked out on her own."

"How is that possible?" I said.

My father ignored the question and pointed at where the night seemed to be at its darkest, his aged face breaking into a grin, and said, "She's back there and she wants to see you. Will you come with me?

You can even bring that poker."

My hand tightened on the spear, and I gazed over at the opening. There was no sound coming from the hut. I was sure that at least Devon would hear us, but it was as if we had been placed in another world.

"They'll be fine," said my father. "You won't be gone long."

I hesitated, my heart sending rapid waves of warning throughout my body.

Would he kill?

I didn't want to believe it, but so much had already happened. And why hadn't she just come with him? Were they afraid of what the others might do?

"Dad," I began, but was interrupted by a strained voice that had only existed in my dreams.

"Danny," it said, causing my throat to shut.

The years had chipped away at that melodious sound, tarnishing the truth, replacing ever distancing memories with new images, but there was no mistaking the voice as that of my mother. A pain ignited within my chest, a yearning that must have laid there hidden and dormant for years. I pushed myself off of the ground, dropping the spear, and made my way towards my father. He waited as I left the light, reaching out a hand and lightly squeezing my shoulder.

"She's really back," he said, in an excited whisper.

I followed my father into the ominous shadows, his stride quickening the further from the fire we went. I noticed that we were heading straight for the treeline, the place where the pathway to the wheel began. There is magic in these mountains, this had been made very clear to me, and not all of it was good, as Mike had proved. That thought sent claws scraping down my spine. Was he watching us? Was he waiting within that treeline beside my mother? A light breeze touched the back of my neck, causing me to jump.

My father came to the first tree, an old oak with lurching branches, and stopped. He slowly turned to face me, his expression camouflaged by the starless night.

"You have to be patient, Danny," he said. "She's been gone for a long time."

"Is she— " I began, but was stopped by a sudden movement from behind the oak, and even in the lightless void I knew it was her.

She stepped towards the edge of the treeline, stopping just short of the clearing, wearing nothing more than one of my father's t-shirts which hung down to just above her knees. Even in the low light I could see the results of having spent years confined to a bed. She was thin, her hair hung like mop strings around her shrunken face, her arms skinny and wasted. The ring had healed her, but not completely.

"Mom?" I said.

"Danny, I've missed you so much."

Her words were like a battering ram, releasing frozen moments in time: Images of her sitting beside me as I lay in my bed sick. The funny face she would make when she knew I was nervous, and the gentle way she would hold me if I was hurt. But it wasn't so much the imagery as it was the feeling that hit me the hardest. This was what I had been missing for all those years; the knowing that she was there.

All of the fear that had been holding me captive vanished, and I staggered into her open arms, allowing her warmth to consume me. To overwhelm me.

"Mom," I said, the tears flowing from my eyes.

"You've gotten so big," she said.

"It's really you," I mumbled.

And it was her. The wheel had brought her back. It was then that I truly understood why my father had walked away from everything, forfeited the life he had known. Because it had been incomplete, shattered like a puzzle missing its most valuable piece. We had been a chain once, and our strongest link had been taken, leaving us to rust away in a world that could care less. But here, within an ancient ring, something did care, and as long as you were willing to turn a blind eye to its true purpose you were free to live.

From behind me, I could hear the emotion caused by our embrace overwhelming my father. My mother released me and motioned for him. He stepped to us, and the three of us created our own circle, one built of love, gratitude, and fear. There would be no going back for my mother, it was something that remained unspoken but known to us all. And yet, the truth still hung there, like an awaiting sentence: The wheel killed.

Did they know? My mother seemed to, considering her outburst at the clinic. Did she remember that? I wanted to ask her, but I was afraid to end the moment, to be the one to break the spell. So instead I said, "What happens now?"

"For now, we enjoy what we have," said my father.

"But for how long?" I said.

"For as long as we can," he said.

"But what about the wheel?"

"What about the wheel?" he said.

"It's not well," I said.

"I don't think it's up to us to decide," said my father.

"Mike's killing people," I said. "Don't you care about that?"

"I don't know anything about Mike. But what I do know is that whatever is going on has nothing to do with us."

"Dad, you're the police chief."

"Not anymore," he said, his grip tightening on my hand.

"Danny's right," said my mother.

"Honey, I won't hear this," said my father. "It has given us a gift. I won't risk losing you over something that we don't understand."

"But we do understand," I said. "The Loshinka — "

"I've heard enough," he said, tossing my hand away. "You would really risk losing your mother to save a bunch of assholes, like Joe Clark?"

My mother released my hand and placed both of hers on my father's shoulders. He stood there rigid, his arms shaking. Within seconds, his shoulders slumped, and his hands opened. A long exhale leaked from his half opened mouth.

"It's wrong, Chris," my mother said.

"What's wrong?" my father said. "We're together. How is that wrong?"

"What's wrong is that there are people being murdered," said my mother. "And you know it."

"It's not our concern."

"It is our concern," said my mother. "Just like helping the wheel is our concern."

"Helen, the wheel — "

"The wheel is sick," said my mother, cutting him off. "Loshi needs our help."

"But how are we supposed to help a ghost?" said my father.

A scream suddenly burst through the darkness, followed by an earth trembling roar.

"Linda," I said, turning towards the faint flickering glow of a dying fire.

CHAPTER THIRTY-NINE

Battles And Loss

The screams continued as I stumbled through the field. Another roar ripped through the night and I could hear Devon crying out to Ms. Lighthorse. My foot suddenly became entangled in some unseen vine, causing me to drop to the ground.

"Come on," said my dad.

He was at my side helping me to my feet. Together we cleared the last fifty yards, breaking through the shrunken dome of light.

There was no movement and the only sound was the crackling of burning wood. I made my way around the dying flames and stopped. Ms. Lighthorse lay at the opening of the hut, one arm draped over her chest with a spear laying at her side. I rushed over to her, my stomach tightening into a knot. Her once picturesque face now glistened black in the fire's light. Deep cuts ran from her forehead to her shoulder and one eye had been destroyed.

"No," I managed to whisper, collapsing to my knees.

Her head tilted towards my voice, revealing an open gash across her throat.

"Danny," she said, and it sounded as if she were drowning.

Guilt struck like a train. I had left my post. I reached out and took her hand. It was so cold.

"I'm sorry," I said.

Ms. Lighthorse released a rasping cough. Her remaining eye rolled in its socket until finally stopping on me. Her icy hand tightened on mine, her nails biting into my flesh.

"They've gone after him. Linda's…" she said, and that was it.

Her head dropped to the ground, her lifeless eye gazing into nothing. Our leader, the woman, whose beauty and grace was the inspiration for so many was gone. I placed her hand back across her chest, fighting the urge to scream.

"I'm sorry, Danny."

I looked up to find my father staring down at me.

"Did you know this was going to happen?" I said.

"Of course not," he said.

How I wanted to believe that, and yet it all seemed too perfect: I had been pulled away for the one thing that I had wanted more than anything. Had that been part of my father's deal? My eyes wandered back to where Ms. Lighthorse lay, her lifeless eye reflecting the flames of a fading beacon. That fire would smolder soon, much like the ancient domiciles had done. They, like Ms. Lighthorse, were gone forever. That thought ignited a fire of its own, and I suddenly leapt to my feet and turned towards my father.

"But you did burn their homes," I said.

My father took a step back.

"Yes," he said.

"Why?"

"For your mother," he said. "It seemed harmless enough."

"You still don't see it, do you?" I said, my hands clenched. "The wheel is using you!"

"Using me for what?" said my father.

"To kill," said my mother, stepping into the low light.

Her face was shrouded in shadow, her arms wrapped around her chest. My father walked over to her, placing his arm around her waist, guiding her closer to the fire.

"I don't understand," he said.

"There is a conflict going on," she said, her gaze dropping to where Ms. Lighthorse lay. "The good that is in the wheel has been under attack for centuries and it is beginning to lose."

"But what did I do?" said my father.

"Nothing so bad, yet," said my mother, nodding to where the row of Loshinka homes used to stand. "But this will only be the beginning, Chris. Next time it might have you do something worse, like burn something with someone in it."

"I can't lose you," said my father. "I won't."

I listened to them go back and forth, my mother being the voice of reason, while my father struggled to argue. She was right, of course. The wheel would use him, slowly chipping away at his humanity until the final step was all that would be left. And by then, he would be too far gone to resist. I caught the blackened glint of my Clovis spear lying next to Ms. Lighthorse, and remembered that Devon and Linda had left in pursuit of the beast that was Mike.

"I have to go," I said, interrupting them both.

"Where?" said my father.

"Devon and Linda went after Mike," I said, reaching for the spear. "I have to help them."

"Devon's here?"

I looked at him for a moment in disbelief. Did he really not know? But why should he? The thing within the wheel had no interest in family, its goal was to conquer. The pieces that it used were just that; an expendable means to an horrific goal.

"Yes, dad. Devon is here."

"Just wait a minute," he said, ducking into the hut.

A minute later he returned, his hands buckling the belt around his waist. He pulled out his .38 and checked the cylinder, making sure that it was loaded. It reminded me of something, and I felt my heart grow cold. I rushed by him, using the flashlight of my phone and entered the hut. Ms. Lighthorse's sleeping bag lay to one side. Next to it was the compound bow she had taken from Mother Gina's home and her spear. But the arrows were gone. The wheel had acted first. The link shared between it and the one in Wyoming apparently worked both ways. What else did it know? I placed the compound bow over my shoulder, grabbed the spear and made my way outside.

"He took them," I said.

"What are you talking about?" my mother said, she was shivering.

I explained to them about Ms. Lighthorse's trip and how the arrows that we had made could stop the wheel.

"And you think Mike took them?" my father said.

"I think that's why he came here," I said, handing him Ms. Lighthorse's spear.

"What is this?"

"It's the only thing that can stop Mike," I said, picking up my spear. "Your gun won't work."

"Well, I think I'll bring it anyway."

"We should go," my mother said.

"Not you," my father.

*****

The sky was beginning to brighten in the east, creating a dull light over the clearing. It revealed a face of parchment- like skin stretched over pronounced cheekbones containing sunken eyes.

"It's okay mom," I said. "We're just going to find Devon and Linda."

"But what if — " she began.

"This is non-negotiable," said my father. "You stay here until we get back."

He then turned to me and said, "You don't think Mike will return here, do you?"

"There's no reason for him to," I said, glancing down at Ms. Lighthorse and stifling a chill. "We can't just leave her like this."

"You guys go," said my mother. "I'll cover her with her sleeping bag and we can do what we need to do when you get back."

I hesitated. The thought of Ms. Lighthorse lying on the ground alone didn't sit right, but she was dead and my friends, as far as I knew, were not.

"Okay," I said, finally, forcing myself to look away. "I'm ready."

My father gripped the spear like a Spartan warrior, stabbed at the air a couple of times and said, "Let's go get them."

*****

The sun had cleared the eastern ridge, illuminating the trail. Staggered rows of oak and pine stood like centurions, daring us to enter. Thorn stricken vines weaved from one side of the trail to the other, their newly formed leaves disguising the danger.

"You're sure they went this way?" my father said.

"I'm sure."

Mike's mission had been accomplished; the arrows had been taken. Whatever was infecting the wheel would want them close by, hidden within the safety of its ring. That was where my friends would be, as well. How much time had gone by since the attack? One hour? Two? I wasn't sure. Either way, it was enough time for them to reach the wheel, and plenty enough time for them to run into danger.

The woods remained cemetery quiet, with not even the distant cry of a hawk or crow to break the monotony. It was as if the animals knew that something was about to happen and had retreated to safer ground. My father walked behind me, occasionally stumbling from the outreaching vines. They hadn't been there before when I had found him standing at the cottonwood after fixing my tire. Perhaps it was because it had still been cool, or maybe the wheel was beginning to take charge of the very forest itself. We continued moving, struggling with the slight incline. We rounded an evergreen and stopped. Stuck in the middle of the trail was one of the Clovis spears, its shaft broken in half. My father nudged past me and pulled it out of the ground. He then motioned for me to stay put and began moving in ever growing circles, stopping to crouch here and there. At one point he picked up a ripped piece of cloth and stuck it in his belt. After another couple of minutes of investigating he waved me over.

"A fight took place here," he said, handing me the cloth.

It was a blue strip of cotton and looked very much like it came from Devon's shirt. I gazed around for any other signs, but there was nothing; no other spear, no clawed hand, and, thankfully, no bodies. Whatever had happened had been over for a while.

"It looks like they caught up to Mike," said my father. "We should keep going."

He took the lead, with me following and wondering how he couldn't hear the jackhammering of my heart. We came to a narrow ravine that was hidden by a wall of sumac. My father began forcing the branches away, causing red berries to rain down on us as we struggled through. Once cleared, we found ourselves within a few yards of the ridge. Just beyond that would be the wheel.

"I guess this is it," my father said.

In one hand he held the spear that had belonged to Ms

Lighthorse, and in the other was the broken one he had pulled from the ground. He looked like a gladiator preparing for an assault. We would clear the top, both of us not knowing what we would find, a father and son quite possibly running headlong to their deaths.

He gave me a nod, which I returned, and together we took the final steps.

*****

The ring was enveloped in shade, as if the sun had been forbidden to shine within its area. Shadows rippled across its surface like a wind driven current. Stripped limbs stuck out from the massive skeleton of the cottonwood. At its base were Linda and Devon. They sat on their knees with their arms outstretched and their faces touching the ground. A low moan was coming from them both, an almost alien chant, using words that I could not recognize. Suddenly, Linda rose from the ground and turned to face us. Her emerald eyes flashing silver. She stepped to within a couple of feet from us, stopping at the edge of the outer ring. She then spoke, but her voice sounded like the deep growl of a diseased dog.

"If you want the child to live, then leave."

"What's wrong with her?" said my father.

"It's not her," I said.

"What child?"

"I don't know," I said. "We need to get them out of there."

"How?"

Without thinking, I shot my hand out, grabbing Linda by the arm. I pulled with everything I had. She fell into my arms and then collapsed to the ground. I knelt beside her, my fear for her overshadowing everything else. Her eyes were closed and for a moment I thought that I had failed, but then they slowly opened.

"Dan," she whispered. "What happened?"

I gently caressed her cheek and said, "Stay here."

"What do we do about Devon?" said my dad.

The answer to that was terrifying; one of us would have to charge into the wheel and grab him. Three or four years ago it would have been my dad, but that was before my unfortunate growth spurt, and quite honestly, I was now much faster.

"I guess I'll have to…" but before I could finish I saw the small bundle of arrows leaning against the trunk of the tree.

We couldn't leave them, everything was riding on those weapons, but it would mean running to the center of the lion's den: The very home of evil.

"Do you see them?" I said.

"Get Devon," said my dad. "I'll get the arrows."

Without waiting for my response, my father leapt into the wheel, sprinting for the tree. I laid my spear on the ground, adjusted the bow on my shoulder, and then followed after him, running toward my friend, ignoring the rippling waves of darkness. A sudden shadow moved from behind the giant cottonwood, and even as I was reaching for Devon I realized that we had fallen into a trap: The beast that was Mike had been there, waiting.

"Dad!" I cried out, with my hand locked on Devon's arm.

"Just get him out of here!" he said, reaching for the arrows.

Devon was dead weight, and fell over to his side, forcing me to drag him. The creature that was Mike ignored us, turning its hellish gaze to where my father now stood with the eight arrows in one hand and his two spears in the other. It was the arrows that the being within the wheel feared the most, and Mike would not let them be taken. This thought ignited a panic, and I began to pull at Devon's body nearing hysteria, ignoring the protest coming from my lower back. Something flew by my head, and I looked up to see the Wyoming arrows lying outside of the ring, just a few feet from where Linda now sat propped up on one elbow, watching it all with terror splashed across her face. A roar of blood chilling rage escaped from Mike. I continued to pull Devon, my breath coming in heaves, my muscles weakening.

Mike ignored my father and began to make his way past him. He got to within six feet of the arrows but was then stopped by my father, who had rushed over to block his way.

"Come on," said Linda.

She was suddenly at my side, reaching for one of Devon's arms. I grabbed the other, and together we managed to drag our friend over the rocky outer ring of the wheel. Linda fell beside him, her body spent from the exertion. I grabbed my spear and turned to see Mike and my father facing off. It was a horrifying sight. The beast that was Mike towered over him, like a northern bear, his arms extending into flesh ripping claws. But he didn't need to use them: He could kill with a touch. It occurred to me that my father didn't know this. He stood with the spears pointing out like a man about to skewer a boar, his eyes locked onto Mike's.

"Don't let him touch you," I cried out, grabbing my spear from the ground.

"Take them and go," he said, never turning his gaze from Mike.

I glanced down at the small stack of shafts laying just a few feet away, becoming painfully aware that I had the bow still hanging from my shoulder. What was I supposed to do? Shoot the tree? Should I even try?

"We have to get Devon out of here," said Linda.

My father was slowly backing away from Mike. The monster was matching his steps, but still refusing to attack.

"Grab the arrows and go," my father said.

Linda was helping Devon to his feet. My friend seemed to be coming around, but not fast enough. My father reached the edge of the ring but then stopped.

"Do it, Dan," he said.

By then Linda and Devon had begun to stumble away from the wheel toward the ravine with the sumac.

"Dad, I can't just leave you."

"I'll be right behind you."

I closed the short distance to the arrows and it was then that Mike attacked, rushing toward my father. I grabbed the arrows, turned and sprinted for my friends. A roaring wave of thunder exploded from the wheel. I made it to where the hill started its decline, giving my father one last glimpse. He was using the broken shaft like an old Roman sword, ducking the bear-like swipes of Mike and countering. Another roar cleared the air, causing me to almost fall to the ground. Within moments I had caught up to Linda and Devon. I took one of Devon's arms, and together we continued down the weaving, thorn covered trail.

We broke through the treeline and I handed Linda the arrows. She continued on with Devon at her side. I listened, hoping to hear the sound of breaking branches or crunching leaves, but the woods had fallen back into eerie silence.

I tightened my grip on my spear, cursing myself. I felt like a coward.

The minutes passed by and still I could hear nothing.

He's not coming, said a sinister voice within my mind.

"Shut up," I said.

My vision became blurred, and I realized that I was beginning to cry.

I felt a hand on my shoulder and turned, fighting to see through the prism light. It was my mother. She stood beside me, her haggard face looking even more aged.

"Come back to the hut, Danny," she said.

"He's coming," I said, shrugging her hand off.

"And when he does, he'll know where to find us," she said.

I refused to leave the treeline, to do so would be admitting that he was gone. My mother's arm slid around my shoulders and she gently nudged me until her face was all that I could see.

"We need to go back," she said.

Her hand then slid down and grabbed mine. She gently pulled me away from the treeline, leading me back to the hut. The clearing was basking in the early spring sunlight, creating a fake sense of joy, a false sense of hope. My father was not coming and the late morning sun didn't seem to care. I made it about half way before my knees gave out, dropping me to the ground. A shuddering cry escaped my throat. My mother knelt beside me and I buried my face into her shirt, the shirt that had belonged to my father. She held me as my body began to shake, my breath coming in deep gasps. I struggled to find her strength, reaching for the security that had been stolen from me so long ago. She remained silent, allowing me to cling to her like a buoy in a storm.

"I'm okay," I said, finally, pulling myself from the ground.

We made our way back to the hut, back to where the body of Ms Lighthorse still lay beneath her sleeping bag.

"We need to do something for her," I said.

"We will," said my mother. "But first we need to check on the others."

***

CHAPTER FORTY

One Returns, One Tells A Secret

Linda was leaning over Devon, wiping his forehead with a towel she had pulled from her bag. He didn't look well. Deep scratches ran up both arms, blood blotted his ripped shirt. My mother rushed over to him, kneeling beside Linda, placing her hand on his cheek.

"Mike touched him," said Linda.

"And he lived?" I said.

"He managed to fight him," she continued. "I tried to help, but he was too strong, and I'm…"

She left her sentence unfinished and sat back, placing both of her hands over her face.

"It's not your fault," I said, coming over and sitting beside her.

Devon let out a groan and then rolled over, his eyes fluttering open. He then slowly propped himself up on an elbow, causing his sweat soaked hair to fall over his face.

"That could have gone better," he managed to say.

Linda let out an astonished yelp of joy and reached for him.

"Easy now," said Devon. "You're taken."

"Oh, Devon," said Linda, breaking into tears.

My mother gently moved Linda away from him, patting her back as she did.

"I need to take a look," she said.

"I'm fine," he said, sitting up. "But I wouldn't want to go another round."

"What happened?" I said. "How did you live after he touched you?"

Devon sat there for a moment, his stare becoming far away.

"I'm not sure," he said, finally. "Mike came in while we were sleeping."

Just those words caused my shoulders to slump and my gaze to fall to the floor. Not only had leaving my post cost Ms. Lighthorse her life, it now seemed to have claimed my father, as well.

"No one blames you," said Linda.

I looked up at Devon. His eyes held a tinge of scrutiny, and I wasn't sure that he felt the same way.

"Anyway," he continued. "Ms. Lighthorse screamed. I jumped up, turned on the light on my phone and saw Mike standing over her holding the arrows."

Here he paused, running his hand through his hair. I again found my gaze dropping to the floor.

"Everything happened so fast," Devon said. "Ms. Lighthorse managed to grab her spear and stuck it into his leg. Mike hit her, and I could see the tracks of his claws where they had landed across her face. By then Linda and I had grabbed our spears. But Mike wasn't interested in a fight. He gave Ms. Lighthorse another swipe and then ran out of the hut."

I could see it happening as if I were there. The beast that was Mike had completed his mission, he now possessed the arrows and had even managed to mortally wound the leader and it was all thanks to me leaving my post. A sudden moan filled the hut, and I realized that it was coming from me.

"Dan," said my mother, and again she was there, offering her strength.

But this time it didn't help. The sorrows were mounting up faster than any barrier could be built, like a river swarming a flimsy wall of sand. Win or lose, I knew that I would never be the same.

"Nobody blames you, Danny," Devon said. "The wheel fooled us all."

He then told us about catching Mike on the trail, and the battle that followed.

"He hit me and I suddenly felt sicker than I ever had before," he said. "But I managed to stab him before I blacked out."

"You did," said Linda. "And then you fell and Mike was standing over you so I ran at him and tried to pull him away but he grabbed my arm, and everything went dark. The next thing I remember was sitting next to Dan at the edge of the wheel."

Devon suddenly looked around the hut.

"Where's your dad?"

I felt my throat constrict and the sound that came out was like a choking frog.

"Oh no," said Linda.

"He didn't come back," said my mother.

"Oh shit, Dan," said Devon. "I'm sorry."

We sat there in silence, each of us allowing the pain of that day to run its course. It had been one of utter tragedy, claiming two and leaving the rest of us lost and leaderless.

"What do we do now?" said Linda.

For a moment there was no answer, because none of us truly knew. And then my mother said, "First, we take care of Ms. Lighthorse."

Those words acted like a spell, bringing us out of the depressing fog that had begun to swallow us. Devon rose from where he had been sitting, stretching his arms and revealing a very sliced up shirt. But the wounds were gone. The wheel still managed to do what it could, even though the good within it was waning.

*****

Linda was the only one among us who knew the Loshinka burial tradition. Under her direction we collected enough sandstone to cover the body of Ms. Lighthorse. We then wrapped her in the sleeping bag and placed her near the back edge of the clearing, making sure that her head lay to the east, so that everyday's first sunlight would touch her face first. Linda placed a faded doll decorated with bright blue feathers and red paint across her chest. Next to it Devon set a book about ancient native legends. I contributed a pencil that I had found in the van, ignoring my friends' confused looks.

"What do we do now?" said Devon.

"We cover her," said Linda.

No one moved. No one wanted to be the first to seal in our hero. My mother reached for a stone, picked it up and then placed it by the body. She then reached for another, not saying a word and had we let her, I think she would have completed the entire thing on her own. Devon looked at me and offered a shrug and then began to help. Linda and I followed. Within forty minutes, our teacher lay buried under a pile of Wichita Mountain rocks. The sun was now far in the west, casting creeping shadows closer to where we now stood with sweat and dirt intermingled.

Linda suddenly broke out into a chant, switching octaves like fast forwarded seasons, creating both a warmth and a chill deep inside of me. Devon stood in silence with tears flowing down his cheeks, matching my own. My mother was between us with an arm draped over each of our shoulders. Linda continued to sing in that language that so few now used. It was a dying language, much like so many of the native's tongue. Finally, she stopped and bowed her head, her body beginning to tremble with grief. A realization struck me; Ms. Lighthorse had been with her since Linda's parents had snuck out of the hospital, leaving her alone. And now she was again alone. But was she? I reached out for her hand, and she took it.

"Linda…" I began, but I couldn't finish.

I wanted to tell her that I was there for her, that she could live with me, if she wanted to. But how could I? My father was dead, and I wasn't even sure if I had a home. Hell, I wasn't even sure that any of us would live past tomorrow.

"I know," she said, turning her face toward me and offering a smile.

"We should head back," my mother said.

Together we made our way across the darkened clearing. It would be a cloudless night, offering a bright moon and millions of stars. Plenty of light to see and to be seen by. Would Mike come? Would the wheel enlist its horrific soldier yet again? I was sure that he would. The one thing that could hurt it had been taken.

We reached the hut and Linda tugged on my arm. She waited until Devon and my mother had gone through the opening and then said, "I need to tell you something."

"You can stay with me," I said.

"It's not that," she said, turning toward the pile of ash that now made up our fire pit.

"I was shown something in Wyoming."

"What did it show you?" I said, only I wasn't really sure that I wanted to know.

Was it the future? Were we doomed to fail? My grip tightened on her hand as I tried to brace myself.

Linda lifted her eyes from the ash, locking them onto mine.

"I'm pregnant," she said.

I stood there with my jaw slacked. After a moment I realized that I was holding my breath and a whoosh rushed out of me.

"I'm sorry," she said, turning back to the fire pit.

For a moment, I was unable to speak. My mind had locked up, like a motor. And then I was bombarded by stupid thoughts, like: Are you sure it's mine? And, how could this happen? Thankfully, I said none of those things. I just stood there like a statue receiving a gut punch. Then, an extraordinary thing happened, a warmth spread throughout my body, and I realized that what I was feeling was joy. I loved Linda, and to see her agonized by both fear and sadness broke whatever reservations I might have had. I stepped up behind her, wrapping both of my arms around her, and said, "I'm glad."

She turned in my arms, her eyes shining in the rising moon, and placed her head against my chest. I then remembered what Linda had told me while under the trance of the wheel. If you want the child to live then leave.

The wheel had known that she was pregnant. And why wouldn't it? The conception had taken place within it. Within its sickened embrace. That thought caused my skin to crawl.

"I'm scared," said Linda.

I tightened my arms, pulled her closer and said, "I am, too."

She then looked up and placed her lips on mine. The electricity was immediate and overwhelming. After a moment we separated.

"Do you love me?" she said.

"Completely," I answered. "And we'll figure it out."

But first we would have to live through the night.

The moon was well above the beaten down mountain tops by the time we made our way into the hut. My mother was sitting next to

Devon, their faces ghost-like from an electric lantern that my father had brought. She was holding one of the arrows, listening intently as Devon filled her in about their history and what they were supposed to do. Linda and I sat down beside them. I couldn't help but look at Linda's stomach. There was no sign that she was pregnant. But what would happen as time went on? Would she carry it a full nine months? Or, would the child come early, inspired by the magic of these mountains. And what about the horrible disease that inflicted her? She couldn't very well leave this place with a baby growing inside of her. Linda looked over at me, and I can only imagine the expression on my face. She placed her hand on my thigh.

"Remember what you said," she whispered. "We'll figure it out."

Another hour passed and we found ourselves retreating into silence. Outside the night had begun in full force. We would need to finish what we had come for. But we decided to wait. After all of the battles and the death that this day had brought nothing had really changed. We still needed to separate Mike from the wheel, to take him out, before the real war could begin. We again discussed watches and I made sure to volunteer first. If anything was to be said I wanted it out there as soon as possible.

"Wake me up if something happens," said Devon, and that was it.

*****

The moon's rays painted the clearing, creating a sea of silver that died in a wall of shadow at the distant treeline. I sat near the hut's opening with the last spear placed across my lap. The other three had been lost, along with my father and Ms. Lighthorse. We were now outgunned and leaderless. The wind was coming in soft waves, causing the crab grass to whisper. My mind tried to travel; going from the final moments of my father's life to the body that lay just a hundred yards from where I sat. A shiver gripped me, and I forced my thoughts back to the present. Time crept by like ice beginning to thaw. I glanced up into the sky and was rewarded by thousands of stars looking down at me. My eyes fell back to the treeline and I felt my heart begin to roll. Something was moving: A shade within the shadows had lumbered out into the grass, still too far away to make out.

"Devon," I called out, struggling to keep my voice low. "Devon, get up."

He must not have been sleeping, because a second later he was at my side.

"Do you see it?" I said.

"Yes," he said.

So hard were we focusing on the shape, that we almost didn't notice a second figure burst through the shadow-line. This one seemed to stumble, as if it were drunk, coming forward a few steps and then falling to the ground. The first shape stopped and went back to where the other had dropped.

Devon and I crouched by the opening, neither of us daring to talk. The two forms slowly rose, and again began moving toward the hut. I thought about my mother and Linda laying in there, both oblivious to what was going on. For a moment I considered waking them, but what would be the point? My mother was still frail, and Linda wasn't much better off.

"We need to do something," I said, clutching our only weapon.

"Come on," said Devon.

We began to creep forward, passing the fire pit. We moved silently, and the two figures didn't seem to notice us. Devon and I came to a stop while the two dark shapes moved closer. I could now see that the one that had fallen was leaning on something long and slender, his head lowered. It was then that the one trespasser noticed us and stopped.

"Dan," said a voice and I knew that voice.

"It can't be," I said, taking a couple of steps closer. "Joe? Is that you?"

"It's me," he said. "I have your dad."

The other man lifted his head, and I felt my heart leap. It was my father, and he was leaning on one of the spears.

I rushed forward, ignoring Devon's warning and within seconds I was holding my father. Devon was soon at my side, grabbing the spear off of the ground from where my father had dropped it. My father slumped in my arms, and I gently helped him to the soft grass.

"I'll be okay," he said, in between breaths. "I just need a second."

"I can't believe it," said Devon. "You're really here?"

"Not my first choice," said Joe. "But yeah, I'm here and it's a good thing, too, or the old man would still be bleeding out in the woods."

"Where did you find him?" I said.

"He was lying against a Limber pine about a half a mile away from the trail."

"You just stumbled onto him?" said Devon.

The years of torture were still very much alive in his memory.

Joe turned his skinless face to Devon and said, "Look, I know I was cruel to you, and for what it's worth I apologize, but in case you haven't noticed; I'm paying for it now."

Devon could do little else but look away from the horror.

"I'm sorry," he said, finally.

"No need to be," said Joe.

He then pointed back to the tree line.

"Things are changing," he said.

"What do you mean?" I said.

"I've seen others walking in those woods. They don't seem to notice me, or don't care. They stay close to the wheel, but they won't go in it. It's like they're waiting for something."

"What about Mike?" said Devon. "Have you seen him?"

"Not tonight, I think he's injured. Dan's dad must have done a number on him."

"He's still alive," said my father.

He had managed to climb to one knee. "Help me up Dan."

I reached under his arm and lifted. He was feverishly hot, and there were dark splotches on the back of his shirt.

"Will he come here tonight?" said Devon.

"I doubt it," said my father. "I was able to cut him a couple of times before I ran. But, for some reason, he didn't follow. Although he did manage to hit me in the head with a rock."

My father had been wandering around the forest for most of the day with a concussion, unable to find his way back. He would have died had it not been for Joe. I looked at the gruesome left over that had once been our biggest enemy, and felt an overwhelming flood of both gratitude and sorrow. The kid in life had been an asshole, but now he was a hero. Even Devon seemed to cool off.

"I'm sorry this happened to you, Joe," he said. "You didn't deserve it."

"I think I kind of did," he said. "I only wish that I could leave."

"Why can't you?" said my father. "Is it the wheel?"

"It has to be," said Joe. "It's like it's holding me here for a reason."

"But you're not like Mike," I said.

"No, I'm not," he said. "Maybe it's the other one."

Without another word, Joe turned and began to make his way back to the wall of shadow. My father and Devon started after him, but I held them back. They were not familiar with the mysterious ways of Joe, but I had dealt with him enough to know that this was just how it is.

"Where are you going?" I said.

He reached the tree line and then turned. We could barely make him out within the shadows.

"Back to the darkness," he said.

He then turned and disappeared into the void.

CHAPTER FORTY-ONE

Confusion

We made our way back, with me supporting my father the best that I could. My mother and Linda were standing next to the fire pit. They rushed to us, my mother taking my father's free arm, and together we helped him into the hut. We gently sat him on their spread out sleeping bag. My mother immediately began examining his body for injuries.

"Don't bother," he said, pointing to the back of his head. "I took a shot to the skull. I'll be alright.'

"Just let me take a look," she said, grabbing the lamp.

A knot, the size of a walnut, protruded from a spot just above his neck. A nasty gash ran across it, but the bleeding had stopped. My mother went over to the cooler and returned with a bottle of water and a t-shirt. She poured the water onto the shirt and gently began to clean the wound.

"Mike has one hell of an arm," my father said, through clenched teeth.

My mother then helped remove his blood-caked shirt and brought him a clean one. My father slowly put it on and then lay back, wincing as his head made contact with the pillow. My mother sat beside him, her hand resting on his.

"I thought I had lost you," she said.

"It was close," said my father.

He looked up to see Linda standing close by and managed to

smile.

"Then everyone got out," he said.

"Thanks to you, Mr. Lee," said Devon.

My father closed his eyes and I felt a moment of terror, but then a familiar rumble filled the hut. He had begun to snore.

"Should he sleep if he has a concussion?" said Linda.

"I don't think he has a choice," said my mother. "He's exhausted. I'll sit with him."

The dawn was still hours away, but sleep was an impossibility. So we sat there, with Devon posted by the opening. But I think we all knew that Joe was right; Mike would not be coming, he had been hurt. After a while my mother asked us about Joe. I told her about my late night meetings and how he had shown me his horrific death.

"What did he say tonight?"

Devon took over, and told her about how he had said there were others near the wheel. My mother listened to this with her chin perched on a fist. She waited until Devon had finished, not once interrupting, but I could tell that she seemed to know something, or, at least, had a theory.

"What is it?" I said.

"I'm not sure," she said. "Linda, I need you to do a favor for me."

"Name it," said Linda.

"Watch over Dan's father. The boy's and I are going to take a walk."

"To where?" I said.

"No," said Devon. "You don't think— "

"I don't know," said my mother, grabbing the bow and a couple of arrows from the floor.   "But we should check."

"What's going on?" I said.

Without answering, my mother exited the hut with Devon close behind. I reached for my spear but then realized that Linda's had been lost. I placed the spear next to where she was now sitting with my father.

"Just in case," I said.

"Be careful," she said.

I lowered myself and kissed her and then went out into the darkness.

They hadn't waited for me, so I was forced to jog until I fell in beside them. It didn't take long for me to figure out where we were going. We had made this journey just a few hours before.

"You don't think that Ms. Lighthorse was one of the one's Joe saw, do you?"

"I don't know," said my mother. "Let's keep moving."

A shadow passed over us, streaking through the weak silver glow, a shade of nothingness that fell victim to the lightless line of trees.

"It was just an owl," said Devon.

"I hope so," said my mother.

As we approached the burial site an icy chill was released in my veins, and I stopped. The rocks that we had placed over Ms. Lighthorse now lay strewn about, as if they had been tossed.

"I don't know if I'm ready for this," Devon.

"You boys stay here, but keep your eyes open."

My mother then finished the short distance to the disarrayed pile. Devon stood there shivering, his hand running through his hair. I wanted to say something, but wasn't sure that anything I could say would help. So, instead, I stood staring at the darkness of the treeline, hoping that it would remain still.

A few minutes later, my mother returned and said, "Let's head back."

"What did you see?" said Devon.

"Not here," she said. "We'll talk about it once we're inside."

The anticipation was almost too much, and it made the short journey to the hut seem like a marathon. We finally passed the fire pit and made our way through the opening.

"How is he?" said my mother.

"No change," said Linda. "Where did you go?"

"To Ms. Lighthorse's grave," said Devon, collapsing to the floor.

"Why?" said Linda.

"Everybody take a seat," said my mother. "We need to talk."

*****

We circled around the eerie glow of the electric light, our faces becoming an artist's rendition of spectral fear.

"I think your teacher has gone to the wheel," my mother said.

"How is that possible?" said Linda.

"It's the only thing that makes sense," said my mother.

"She'll be like Mike," said Devon.

"We don't know that," said Linda.

"I don't think she will be," said my mother.

"How do you know?" said Devon.

"You were right, Devon," she said, "The Spaniard has infected it. I have seen it. Loshi has fought him for as long as he could, but he is beginning to lose: Loshi needs our help."

"How have you seen it?" said Devon.

"He has entered my dreams," she said. "Remember, I have slept for years."

"Is he the one who woke you up?" said Linda.

"I think he was," she said. "I hope he was."

"But can we help him?" I said.

She reached for my father's hand, grasping it in hers.

"I don't know," she said, finally. "I do know that we have to try."

"But, how do we help him?" said Linda.

"We have to fight," said Devon. "The evil is in the tree."

"Do we cut it down?" I said.

"We can't know anything for sure." said my mother.

"So what do we do?" I said.

My mother looked over at me, her face wraith-like in the haloed glow.

"We do the only thing we can," she said. "We go to the wheel and face whatever may come."

That was it? Just stumble into the medicine wheel and hope for the best? We had the arrows; the demon within the wheel knew this; it would be planning for this.

"We should try to get some sleep," my mother said. "We'll leave at noon."

*****

* * *

My mind was racing, making sleep an impossibility. If we left at noon then that would put us in the wheel at around one-thirty, which meant that we had only twelve hours to rethink this. I looked over at Linda and saw that her eyes were lost within the lamp. She was thinking the same thing: we all might be dead by tomorrow's sunset. But this was why we were here; to kill the evil that was hiding in the wheel, it's just that we had lost our general. Ms. Lighthorse had been the one who seemed to know what to do, but she was now dead. And not just dead, but gone; wandering off into the treeline-void that had swallowed Joe.

Linda reached over, taking my hand in hers. The future-our future-depended on tomorrow. And not just ours, but our child's, as well. Would it even be born? This marauder that nested within the wheel had created a chaos that had wounded so many. It had disrupted a wonderful thing: A magical thing that had wanted only to help those who were helpless. An image of narrow dark eyes and thin razor lips filled my mind. The Spaniard was a leftover relic of evil, and tomorrow we would have to face him.

We went through the ritual of night watches, with Devon taking the last one, but no one could sleep. My mother sat beside my father, monitoring his breathing and waking him up every thirty minutes to make sure that he wasn't falling into a coma. Linda lay next to me, her arm locked in mine. At one point she turned to face me, her warm breath brushing against my skin.

"I'm sorry," she whispered.

I could feel her body shivering. The terror of what was to come was like a lead weight. Not just because we didn't know if we were going to survive tomorrow, but also the terror of not knowing what she would do if we did.

A weak orange hue began to fill the opening of the hut, and it was only then did I allow the weariness that I had been holding at bay to overwhelm me. My sleep was dreamless, as dark as the wall of trees that had swallowed both Joe and Ms. Lighthorse. It seemed to have lasted only a second, and soon I was being shaken by my mother. I opened my eyes to find that Linda was already up. She and Devon were talking just outside of the hut. My father was sitting, rubbing the back of his very sore head.

"We have less than an hour before we need to go," said my

mother.

Linda saw that I was awake and came back into the hut. Her eyes were rimmed with dark circles, her hair fluffed out like a static conductor. I pulled her away from everyone else and I guess she could see the concern etched across my face, because she said, "What is it?"

"I don't think you should go," I said.

"I'll be fine," she said.

"You don't look fine."

"Is that how you talk to a lady?"

"I'm serious, Linda," I said. "You should stay here, with my father."

"But he's not staying," she said.

I glanced over just as my dad was being helped to his feet by my mother. A sudden rush of anger flooded through me. For him to even consider going another round with the wheel seemed insane.

"What are you doing?" I said.

"I'm getting ready," he said.

"But you're hurt."

"I'll be fine," he said.

I looked at my mother in shock. She continued to help him, securing his belt and checking the gun. She was even bringing him clean socks to wear.

"What are you doing?" I said, glaring at my mother.

"It's okay," said my dad.

"It's not okay," I said. "You have a lump the size of an apple on the back of your head and Linda's... she's not well. Neither one of you should go."

I then fixed my mother with a laser gaze, and said, "I can't believe you're letting this happen."

My mother finished helping my father with his boots and then turned to me. Her face seemed to be even more sunk in then it had been before, like an overripe pear. She came over to me and I was shocked to see tears welling in her eyes.

"I don't want them to," she said. "But we don't have a choice."

She was speaking like some kind of oracle; like a mysterious visionary who had been shown the correct path. She had awoken in the clinic and had spouted off her statement about Loshi, which still gives me the heebie- jeebies to this day, but did that mean she could truly know what we were supposed to do? And then another thought struck me: What if she wasn't trying to help us? What if she were leading us into the very arms of our enemy? My mother placed a hand on my shoulder and then leaned close, placing her lips next to my ear and whispered three words that hit me like a blast from a December storm: "Remember the river."

She then patted the top of my head and turned towards the others.

"It's time," she said.

Before I could say anything else, she grabbed the bow and arrows off of the floor and led the others out of the hut, leaving me alone and very afraid.

CHAPTER FORTY-TWO

A Harrowing Journey

The vines were now intertwined creating a treacherous blanket with thorns sticking out of blackish leaves that gleamed in the high noon sun. The bordering trees were being strangled by runners that had crept up their trunks overnight, creating a trip-line obstacle.

"Where's the path?" said Linda.

"I'll find it," said Devon.

He began beating back the vines with a Clovis spear, until the thin trail became visible.

"This will take forever," said Linda.

"As I'm sure was the plan," said my mother, glancing up at the sky.

It was in this snail-like manner that Devon led us with my father following and my mother close behind. Linda was next, with me bringing up the tail end. The forest was a sea of choked silence, with not even the wind seeming to breach its boundaries. The air that was available hung heavy and hot. It was another obstacle, another defense mechanism designed to deter, and it was beginning to work. Linda soon began to slow down, her gasps becoming louder. The burden of both the uphill journey and the pregnancy was taking its toll. She came to a sudden stop, placing both hands on her stomach, her chest heaving.

"Hold on," I said.

My mother stepped beside us, placing her hand on Linda's arm.

"I have to take her back," I said.

"You can't," said my mother.

"You can't stop me," I said.

"You don't understand," said my mother, pointing back the way we had come. "You can't."

I turned and felt my heart sink. Thorn laden vines had risen just twenty feet from where we now stood. The brambles had stacked upon themselves, creating a six foot tall boundary that had spread out on each side for as far as the eye could see. It had done all of this without making a sound. Or, perhaps, the poisoned air had killed whatever sound it had made. The wheel was forcing us forward. I looked at my mother and felt nothing but anger. Why had she insisted that Linda come with us?

"I can make it," said Linda, stepping away from me.

I could do little else but follow as our small squad slowly continued on. The minutes ticked by, as the hours fell in close behind. Devon had been slicing back the vines until his efforts became swings of exhaustion.

"Let me take over," I said, making my way to the front.

"Please," he said, sweat pouring off of his face.

The vines were tough, but they did eventually break away. On we went, three or four feet at a time until, finally, we reached the sumac covered ravine. It had changed, as well. It stood before us like a prison wall, its limbs interwoven like a net preparing for cast.

"We have to go through," said my mother.

Devon moved up to stand beside me. His face was still glistening from the drying sweat.

"Let's do it," he said.

Together we took the two remaining Clovis spears and began to slice and saw our way through the thicket, ignoring the berries dropping on our heads. My hands blistered, ruptured and then blistered again. Devon's breath was coming in ferocious woofs, his lungs fighting for whatever air they could find. My heart hurt for him, but I wasn't doing much better. Breathing was a struggle, like we were both wearing a mask, made even worse by the sumac enclosure. Even the limbs seemed to be trying to stop us, scratching and stabbing, countering each one of our strokes..

"We have to move faster," said my mother.

I didn't answer. I knew that if I did, it would be a string of angry words that would do nothing but wear me out even more. But I did let that anger fuel me, and it allowed me to focus on something other than the pain blasting my hands. My mother was determined to get to the wheel, determined to have us cross the circumference together, no matter the cost. Regardless of whether or not Linda survived. Or even her husband.

"We're there," said Devon, bringing me out of my depressing train of thought.

Ahead of us was the final twenty yards to the ridge, and beyond that, the wheel. We stepped out of the sumac wall and thankfully were met with nothing more than ankle-high blades of grass. The others soon broke through the ragged tunnel we had created and were standing with us. I noticed the long shadows that we cast and looked up to find that the sun was near the western peaks. How long had we battled our way through the woods? I pulled my phone out of my pocket to check the time and found that the screen was blank. I hadn't been able to charge it, so I wasn't too surprised.

"Mine's dead, too," said Devon.

"They're all dead," said my mother, making her way toward the ridge. "There can be no light."

I glanced over at my father. His eyes were watering and the lump on his head seemed to be getting worse. He lowered himself to the ground, his mouth clenched, his hands shaking.

"Dad," I said.

"I'm okay," he said. "But this is as far as I go."

"You can't just stay here," I said.

"He's not here to fight the wheel," said my mother, without looking back.

"Then why is he here?" I said.

"Contingency," my mother said, topping the ridge. "That's why you and I are here."

"What does that even mean?" I said.

"It'll be okay," said my father, taking the gun from his holster. "Go help her Dan. She needs you."

Did she? I wasn't sure. My mother had become a stranger to me, and not just because of the years that had passed. She had become something more, like Mother Gina, only with Mother Gina there was no question about whose side she was on. But my mother had become withdrawn and mysterious. She knew more than she was willing to tell, and it was the reasoning for keeping her secrets that had me now gripping my spear like a snake preparing to strike.

"Okay," I said, finally. "Then Linda can wait with him."

"No," said my mother, sharply, turning to face me. "She has to come with us."

She then continued on without saying another word. Devon took off after her, leaving me, my father, and Linda gasping near the sumac.

"I don't like this," I said.

"I don't either," said my father, squinting in the setting sun. "But we have to do what she says."

"Why?" I said. "She's not Ms. Lighthorse. She's not even Native American."

"No, but she does love you."

"Are you sure?" I said.

"Dan, I think you know better than that."

My father noticed the doubt on my face and reached over, patting the ground beside him. I lowered myself beside him. Linda gave me a weak smile and turned to follow Devon.

"Wait," I said, but she didn't stop.

"Let her go," said my father.

"Dad, this isn't right."

"That's true," he said. "None of this right."

"Then what are we doing?"

"Trying to make it right."

"By sending a pregnant girl to war?" I said.

My father looked for a moment as if he had been slapped. His face then broke out into the widest grin I had seen from him in years. Of course, he hadn't known, none of them did, but since we were likely marching off to our deaths, I figured now was as good of a time as any to tell him. And, maybe, he might try to change my mother's mind about having her go.

"I'm happy for you," he said, finally.

"Now do you see why I can't let her go?"

"I see why she must go," he said.

It was pointless. My mother had gotten to him. There could be no other explanation for it. I let the spear drop to the ground and placed both hands over my face.

"We have to trust her," he said.

"Coming from the guy who burned down the huts," I said, grabbing the spear and jumping to my feet.

"I was wrong," he said.

"Yeah, well, I wonder if you're still wrong."

I then turned and made my way to the ridge without looking back.

CHAPTER FORTY-THREE

The Wheel

We stood near the edge of the stones, each of us listening intently for any sound. But there was nothing to hear. A shadow crept from the rotting cottonwood at its center, created by the final rays of the sinking sun. At any moment I was sure that Mike would jump from behind the massive tree, like he had the night before, and rush us with his claws extended. But nothing moved.

"What do we do now?" said Linda.

"We wait," said my mother.

"For what?" I said.

"We'll know when it happens," she said.

I glanced over and saw that she was now holding the bow with an arrow notched in its string, her eyes focused on the cottonwood. I couldn't help but wonder, when it all went down, if she would turn her weapon on us.

We stood there, near the edge of the rocks, none of us daring to speak, as the spreading darkness from the tree continued to slink its way towards us.

"Maybe we should try and shoot it," said Devon.

"It would do no good," said my mother. "We are facing a shut door that only opens from the inside."

"Maybe if we hacked at it with one of the spears, it would be forced to open," I said.

"We would only break them," my mother said. "We have to

be–"

It was then that a branch snapped to our left and out from the heavy limbs of a leaning pine stepped the beast Mike. His thick arms hung down, almost dragging the ground like a prehistoric primate. Devon and I stepped in front of the other two, our spears extending out. Mike didn't seem to notice. He made his way slowly into the wheel, lumbering with a stuttered gait. He arrived at the cottonwood and placed a clawed hand upon the scab-like bark of the trunk. Blood oozed from opened wounds along his back and side and trickled down his matted body. The Clovis spears had done their work. The beast slowly turned and leaned against the tree, his teeth laden maw half opened. We watched in silence as he began to slide down the trunk, coming to rest on the ground with his head cocked to one side. He took in a long, shuddering breath and then fell onto his side.

We stood there unsure of what to do. The wheel remained cold, like an ancient forge that had burned out long ago. Devon took a cautious step over the perimeter of stone, his spear pointed at the unmoving monster. He then made his way to where Mike lay motionless, stopping just a few feet away. He reached out with his spear and jabbed his shoulder. The beast didn't move.

"He's really dead," said Devon.

There was no pleasure in hearing this. It was not something to be celebrated. Mike had been thrown into the abyss, had been dealt an earth shattering hand and had paid the price. And yet, even though one of our enemies had fallen, we were still no closer to facing the real threat.

"Now what?" I said.

We didn't have to wait for the answer. A blast of violet light exploded from the cottonwood, knocking Devon back. A blanket of mist began to roll from the base of its trunk, creeping over the ground like an oncoming flood.

"Get out of there," said my mother.

Devon turned and began to sprint, but was tripped and fell into the rolling fog. A sound, like thunder, erupted from underneath as Devon struggled back to his feet, and he was not alone. A shape lifted out of the mist, rising until it towered over Devon.

"It can't be," I said.

Kyle Bently hovered within the wheel, only it wasn't Kyle; not completely. His face still held that sickly pale complexion, his greasy black hair still draped over an acne covered forehead, but his eyes glowed with the raging red ferocity that Mike's had possessed. His fur covered arms ended in the same dagger-like claws, and from his mouth sprouted razor teeth. Devon went to stab the beast but it was faster and moved to the side, connecting with one of its massive hands, sending my friend flying. Kyle then turned towards us, releasing a roar that froze me in place.

"We have to kill it," my mother said, bringing up her bow, but hesitating.

Kyle suddenly leaped for us with both arms extended. I thrust out the Clovis spear just as he cleared the ring, the dark stone slicing into his shoulder. Kyle then struck out, knocking the spear from my hand. I watched in terror as the spear flew end over end, landing ten feet away. Without thinking, I dived forward, brushing past Kyle, my arm stretched out in front of me, like Superman taking flight. Unlike Superman, I had fallen short and quickly began to crawl. A pain erupted in my ankle and I felt myself being dragged back. Kyle had caught me and his claws were cutting through my jeans, piercing the flesh underneath. I let out a scream and tried to pummel his hand, but he only continued to tighten his grip. Out of the corner of my eye I could see my mother, the arrow pulled back next to her ear, and yet she refused to release it. The ground then disappeared, and I was lifted. Another bolt of pain exploded from my shoulder as Kyle's other hand gripped me. He turned me over until his face was just inches away from my own, his eyes glaring. I understood then that Kyle was still in there, was still very much a part of what was happening and loving it.

"I told you that I would get you," he said, in a voice barely human. "I'm going to rip you in half."

I again began to beat against his arms, flailing with my fists, but he wouldn't let go. His claws dug further into my skin and he began to pull. The pain became overwhelming as my muscles and bones began to separate.

"No," someone said, and then Linda was there, my Clovis spear in her hand.

She thrust it at Kyle, sticking him in the side. Blackness was threatening to overcome me, and I barely felt the impact of my body connecting with the ground. A scream went off like a tornado siren, clearing the clouds that were building in my mind. I sat up and saw Kyle holding Linda by the throat. Her feet were off of the ground and she was kicking at the monster, but it was doing no good. I blindly reached out, desperately searching for the spear that she had dropped. My mother was still standing there like a Greek statue, with the arrow pulled back.

"Shoot him," I cried out, rising from the mist infested ground.

"I can't," she said.

Something flew just inches away from me, and it was followed by a horrific roar. Linda was dropped and began to roll away from where Kyle now stood with the shaft of a spear sticking out from between his shoulders. I looked over and saw Devon crouched on one knee, blood pouring from his nose, his chest heaving. Kyle began lashing out, slapping at the spear, his growls turning to moans of agony. I rushed over, grabbed Linda by her arm and dragged her over to where my mother was still frozen.

"Why don't you shoot?" I said.

"They are not meant for him," she said, and I could see tears tracking down her cheeks.

Before I could say anything else Linda was tugging on my arm with one hand while pointing with her other. I followed her direction and felt my blood go cold. Kyle had knocked the spear loose and was now moving toward Devon. The fight was gone from my friend, and he could do little else but watch as this new creation prepared for murder.

"Find the spear," Linda said.

I ran into the fog covered wheel, kicking and groping, desperately searching, all the while watching as the beast moved in on Devon. I wouldn't find it time, and even if I did, I doubted that I could actually hit him if I threw it. There was nothing else for me to do except go to Devon. I cleared the distance just as Kyle was raising his dagger-like hand. My shoulder made an impact just below the gaping wound on his back. Kyle stumbled, letting out a pain filled howl. Devon took my hand, and I helped him to his feet. But there would be no escaping. Where would we go? I think we both realized this at the same time, because together we turned to face Kyle.

"You're such an asshole," I said.

"And you're the guy that hangs out with me," said Devon.

Together we began to laugh. The terror of what was about to happen left us no other options.

Kyle spun around, his expression a snapshot of absolute rage that quickly quelled our humor,

"Stay behind me," said Devon.

I looked at my friend and saw that his eyes were now radiating cold silver. Kyle seemed to have noticed, as well, and paused. The event of his beating was still etched within his fading memory. But it lasted for only a moment. Things had changed since then, and now it was Kyle who possessed a power far beyond the strength of my friend, fueled by an uncaring evil. The monster offered us a soulless grin and attacked. Devon rushed to meet him like a gladiator facing a lion, and for a moment, he was able to stop him, but it was only temporary. Kyle thrust his hand out like a cobra, striking my friend with his extended claws, and sliced open his chest. Devon fell, disappearing into the growing fog. Kyle then turned to me.

Without thinking, I ran at the beast with my hands clenched, and hot tears blurring my vision. This seemed to have startled Kyle, and it allowed me enough time to release a punch that contained everything I had. It connected, and I immediately felt my arm go numb. The strike caused Mike's head to turn, but little else. I stood there clutching my hand, gazing up at him and knowing that I would soon be dead. Kyle glared down at me, his burning eyes becoming brighter, he then spoke with humored malice.

"She looks much better here," he said, motioning to where Linda was now standing with my mother, her face masked in shock. "I think I'll keep her."

I could do little else, but strike out with my other hand. It was a feeble attempt, and Kyle easily caught it. He pulled my arm, forcing me closer, until I could smell his rotting breath.

He then lifted his other arm, his long fingers joining together, creating a horrific saw. It wouldn't be a fast death, of that I was sure. He would first slice my legs, immobilizing me, and then continue to cut away pieces until there was nothing left. I glanced down at the growing mist, hoping that my friend might rise again, like the mythical Phoenix, but nothing moved.

"You know," he said. "I think I'll let them watch me eat you."

My final move was one of utter cowardice: I closed my eyes and waited.

A sound went off like a firecracker and I was suddenly free. I opened my eyes to see Kyle stumbling back, his hands desperately trying to stop the bleeding of a newly formed hole on his chest. Another firecracker went off, and then another, until Kyle fell to the ground. I looked over and saw my father standing at the edge of the wheel with his revolver's barrel smoking in his hand. Linda was suddenly beside me with one of the spears. She lunged at Kyle, who was now writhing in the fog, letting out a scream with every thrust. Within seconds my father joined her with the other spear. I watched them both, unable to move, while they continued to stab and slice. Kyle tried to stand, but was forced back by a jab to the throat by my father. Kyle's growls of anger turned to howls of pain and then went silent. Linda and my father continued their gruesome work. Eventually, they both collapsed near the mutilated body.

******

The fog was thickening, and the violet light became brighter. My father helped Linda to her feet and they made their way back to my mother. A moan came from my right and I dove my hand into the cloud. Devon was struggling to move. I snaked my arms around until I found his shoulders. Just as I was attempting to drag him my father returned and, together, we carried my friend out of the wheel. We cleared the outer ring and fell to the ground. My father reached over and lifted Devon's shirt, letting out a low hiss. The wound was deep, exposing two of his ribs. My father took off his shirt and ripped it in half. He then had me help sit Devon up as he wrapped the cloth around his torso. My father had, once again, saved us from a certain and gruesome death. Had killed his second monster. He was as my mother had said; a contingency. Glancing up I saw that she was still standing there, looking at the tree, reminding me that it wasn't over.

The purplish glow had begun to pulsate, encasing the cottonwood as the mist continued to climb, becoming taller like a storm front.

"It's coming," my mother said.

I grabbed one of the spears and stood, my heart pounding in my ears. My father continued to help Devon, cinching down the shirt.

Linda came to my side, her eyes wide. For a moment I thought that the rocks that made up the wheel were beginning to slowly spin, but realized that it was the mist. It had begun to turn, like a cyclone approaching shore.

"What do we do?" said Linda.

"We wait," said my mother.

The fog continued to swirl with lavender rays bursting through its wall, creating beams of light, turning faster and faster. Its effect was nauseating, like standing on a schooner during high tide. Then it stopped and the mist began to sink back to the ground. The light had narrowed, coming to focus on the lower part of the cottonwoods trunk.

A violent crack rang out and a vertical split appeared in the bark. We watched as it began to spread, opening wider and wider, until a five-foot wide cave-like opening appeared. The violet light could not touch it, and it remained as dark as a starless night. A sudden breeze whipped through the surrounding trees, and we could hear the sound of something large and wet, flapping. I glanced up and let out a startled gasp. The limbs were covered in the shadowy sheets of its victims. I looked back at the void just as a shapeless shade separated from the trunk, gliding a few feet away from its origin and then stopping.

Above it, the skins continued to slap, becoming more rapid, until one dropped from its perch, landing on the shadow. The skin seemed to be held by nothing, hovering above the ground. Slowly, it began to wrap itself, folding over the darkness and taking form. Another skin dropped from the tree, enfolding itself with the first, molding together and growing. And then another fell, and another, until the shape before us stood taller than the beasts it had created. The violet beam spread, creating a haunted hue over the newly formed atrocity. Dried hide intermingled with those that weren't so ancient, and within the form lay telltale remnants of who they once had been: Faded tattoos mixed with age, old scars, and weathered fur. Separate, but now together.

My father stood and reached for a spear. He took a step forward, preparing for yet another battle, but was stopped by mother's voice.

"This fight is for others," she said.

"We have to kill it," I said.

"And we will," said a voice from behind me.

I turned and felt ice sear through my body. Ms Lighthorse was clearing the ridge, her throat leaking drops of blood, her dark hair matted. Behind her walked a young woman regaled in beaded leather with one side of her face unrecognizably shredded. She was the girl who had guided me back from the illness that had almost taken my life: Mother Gina.

"It is our fight," whispered a voice at my side.

I turned to see who had spoken and choked back a scream. The skinless body of Joe Clark stood next to me, eerily reflecting in the violet light. His lidless eyes focused on the small mountain of hides rising from the fog.

"I don't understand," I said.

"Neither did I," he said.

We were soon joined by Ms. Lighthorse and Mother Gina, and it was then that I noticed others stepping out from the darkness. All of them were shadows of what they once had been and it wasn't just people closing in on the wheel, hideless wolves, bison, and skunks intermingled with deer and mountain lions. They made no sound as they stopped near the edge of the wheel, their lidless eyes locking onto the demon near its center.

My mother turned to Mother Gina, her face etched with fear.

"Will he come?" she said.

"He will come," said Mother Gina. "It is time."

A searing howl broke through the night, followed by the whisk of an arrow being released from my mother. It zipped through the shadows and sank deep into the mountain of skins. An horrific scream blasted out of its nothingness, causing me to step back. Another arrow whizzed by, penetrating just inches from the first. It was then that the macabre group of victims leapt forward, charging the mound with a ferocity made for nightmares. Joe plunged forward, racing into the center with nothing more than clenched hands. Another arrow hit its mark just as he made contact. Around him were the fierce beings, each clawing and biting, pummeling with decayed hands and kicking with corroded feet. They swarmed the evil mound, covering it to where only its very top could be seen. My mother stood with another arrow notched, but was unable to get a clear shot. I looked over at Mother Gina and Ms. Lighthorse. They stood stoically watching, neither of them moving.

Suddenly, one of the wolves went flying, landing just outside of the wheel, its leg held in a sickening position. It began to crawl back to the melee, crossing the outer line of rocks. It had only cleared a couple of feet and was then forced to stop. The mist had thickened in front of it, creating a wave-like barrier that began to roll to where the poor creature now lay struggling. Smoke-like tendrils struck out, whipping over it, first restricting and then constricting. The wolf tried snapping at them, but its teeth seemed to pass right through. A final yelp managed to escape from its trapped mouth before the fog spread over the canine like a disease-infested blanket, silencing the animal. The putrid cloud then began to ripple its way to where the others continued to battle, leaving nothing of the wolf.

The mist reached the battle and again struck, encasing first a deer, and then a mountain lion. Within seconds they were gone. It then jumped to one of the men, enveloping him, before moving to another. On the mist went, picking off our soldiers one by one, and there was nothing we could do. It was strange to see this slaughter, and even more unnerving. It was killing those that were already dead, casting them away to some place beyond the beyond.

Mother Gina called Linda and Devon over to her. Devon was still in pain, but at least the flesh over his ribs had knitted back together. They came to stand, one on each side of the young native woman, each of them taking one of Mother Gina's hands.

"Are you ready?" she said.

"For what?" said Linda.

"To help Loshi," said Mother Gina.

"What do we do?" said Devon.

Mother Gina managed a sad smile from her ravaged face, and said, "Just stand here with me."

A scream echoed through the night. I turned back and saw that all but a deer and Joe were left. The fog had climbed, becoming as tall as the mountain of skin. It crashed down onto the deer, disintegrating it. The fog then shot out, striking Joe in the center of his chest, shooting through his body. Joe made no sound, his lidless eyes looked over to where we stood horrified, and then he was gone.

CHAPTER FORTY-FOUR

Contingency

There was no one left. The demon had won, had vanquished, once again, those who it had murdered before. The tower of mist crumbled, spreading across the ground like blood from a newly formed wound, coming to a stop at the perimeter of the wheel.

"It's still confined," said Ms. Lighthorse.

The skin-covered demon began to make its way towards us. Another arrow flew from my mother's bow, disappearing just above a faded tattoo of an eagle feather, producing a scream, filled with both pain and rage.

It had been the third arrow, and still the hide moved closer.

"Why isn't it working?" I said.

"It is," said Mother Gina. "Listen."

At first, the only thing I could hear was the rough scraping of skin, like sandpaper, as the demon dragged itself closer, but then there was something else, distant but becoming louder. A beat was growing, its rhythm steady, and within those heavy thumps was a haunted, wailing voice. The demon paused, stopping just a few feet from where Mother Gina stood with Devon and Linda. The violet haze brightened, changing hues, going from sunset Sangoria to reddish Magenta. At the wheel's center, the giant cottonwood began to shake, causing the remaining skins to drop from the skeletal branches, hitting the fog infested ground. And where they landed, the mist began to bubble like liquid coming to a boil, tossing steam high into the changing light. Sulfur filtered over me, instantly blurring my vision. Then the fog began to thin, until, finally, dissipating.

"Look," said my father, pointing at the cottonwood trunk.

Within its black chasm a yellow pin light had ignited, becoming brighter as the sound of the drums continued to grow.

"Loshi is coming," said Mother Gina.

The demon turned and began to slink its way to the opening.

"We must stop it ," said Mother Gina.

My mother released another arrow, causing the monster to stumble. It hunkered for a moment, shivering within the skins, and then continued for the tree, and again my mother let loose an arrow. The light from the cottonwood intensified, until it seemed as if a star was exploding, filling the void with a yellow radiance. The demon stopped, seemingly unsure if it should go any further. The chasm was emanating from its glare, consuming the pulsating violet light, until only the warmth of its glow remained. The sound of the drums continued to rise, thundering through the wheel and coming to an ear-splitting crescendo before falling silent.

"What's happening?" I said.

"Just wait," said Mother Gina.

The demon was now surrounded by the warmth of this new, conquering hue, and yet it still managed to linger within darkness, as if no warmth could touch it. Its skin cocoon began to ripple, becoming a tide, and from it came a mournful cry. A sudden rip appeared at its top, and the morbid cover fell to the ground, revealing a shapeless shadow underneath.

"It's holding Loshi back," said Mother Gina.

She then looked at Devon and Linda, pulling them closer.

"Will you help him?" she said.

"What do we need to do?" said Linda.

"Agree," said Mother Gina.

"Yes," said Devon. "We want to help him."

A moment later my friends went rigid, their faces contorting into pain-stricken portraits of horror. Their bodies then began to convulse, as if they were receiving a lethal dose of electricity.

"No" I cried out.

I wanted to run to them, wanted to break them out of Mother

Gina's grasp, but my father held me back. A burst of silver shot out of their bodies, like a thin cloud. They floated for a second above where Devon and Linda had collapsed, and then, like beams from a Comanche moon, raced toward the demon, striking it like a pair of lasers, vanishing within its mass.

Linda lay a few feet away from where I was standing dumbfounded, and next to her was Devon. But Mother Gina and Ms. Lighthorse had vanished, as if they were never there. I ran to them, falling to their sides. Linda's eyes were open, gazing up but sightless.

"No," I said, placing her head in my lap.

So lost was I in grief, that it wasn't until my mother spoke did I dare look back into the wheel.

"He's here," she said.

The demon was shuddering in place, its vibrating mass expanding on one side, creating a malignant growth that continued to protrude further and further. I had seen this before, had watched it through the eyes of another. It had been Loshi then, but he had been weak, unable to do little else but cringe before the master that held him captive.

The shadowy blob began to sag. Then with a sound like a wet sack of grain, it dropped to the ground. The yellow light rushed to it, like magnetized steel, wrapping the egg-like sphere. The demon, now freed from its luminous enclosure, began lumbering towards the pulsating orb. My mother released the final arrow, causing the demon to fall back.

The globule continued to grow, feeding from the light, doubling and then tripling in size. A roar split the night as the demon again started for the expanding ball, and I remembered how it had slammed itself down in my vision, crushing Loshi back into itself. A sudden thought filled me with dread: What if Devon and Linda were in there? Would they be crushed, as well?

I had to do something. But before I could move, the sphere leaped from the ground, penetrating the cloud hovering above it. It struck like a bullet, drilling itself deeper and deeper into the demon's body, until vanishing into the gyrating cloud. The demon started to thrash, whipping around like a headless snake.

A battle of storms began. Yellow light burst within the shadowy form, flashing like lightning swelling in a thunder-cloud. The mass started to fluctuate, producing elongated mounds from its side. Within those chaotic blisters were faces frozen in a scream, death masks from ages past. An eruption burst from behind the demon, causing the warring cloud to trip. The cave in the cottonwood had exploded with fire, like flames in a furnace. Another flash flung the mass back to within a couple of feet from where the chasm was now roaring. But the lightning was much weaker than those from before and lasted for only a second.

"It has to go in," my mother said.

"What do we do?" I said, my heart thudding in my chest.

Those that were fighting within the demon were trying to push it into the opening, but were failing: Loshi was losing. Linda and Devon were losing. The burning pit within the trunk stood just a few feet away from the demon, but it might as well have been a mile. The last arrow had been shot, consumed by the evil cloud. They had weakened it, but had done little else. The lightning was now coming in small blips, hardly noticeable. And once they stopped, what then? Would my friends be gone forever?

I could not allow that, so I stepped into the wheel.

"Stop," said my mother.

My father reached out, grabbing the sleeve of my shirt, and pulled me back.

"I have to do something," I said, through grinding teeth.

"There's nothing you can do," said my mother.

She then dropped the bow and turned to my father. I could see tears streaming down her face.

"I can let you do this," said my father, and I noticed that he, too, was crying.

"You have to," said my mother. "It's the only way to be sure."

"But what if you're wrong?" he said.

"Then everything is lost, and it won't matter."

I listened to them both, desperately trying to figure out what they were talking about. A few feet away from us the flashing had become fading pulses, like a weakening heart struggling to survive.

"It's not fair," my father said.

"No," said my mother. "It's not fair, but we've been on that side of the bridge for a long time now."

"What's going on?" I said.

My mother looked at me for a moment, her eyes glistening from the inferno burning in the cottonwood. She then reached out to both of my hands and pulled me close. After a moment, she pushed me back and said, "I'm so proud of you, Dan."

She then released me and turned to my father.

"I love you," she said, and then, without another word, my mother crossed the outer ring and began to make her way to the column of shadow.

"What is she doing?" I said, glancing over at my dad.

He was standing there, his face now sheened with both sweat and tears.

I tried to run to her but was thrown to the ground by my father. He held me down, immobilizing both of my arms..

"We have to let her go," he said.

"Are you crazy?" I said, trying to break free. "It'll kill her."

My mother continued to make her way closer. The shapeless cloud was beginning to spin, as if intending to expel the invaders. She was only three feet away, when a whip-like tendril lashed out, looping around her shoulders. It then began constricting like a python. An odd silence fell over me, as if what I was watching was not real, like a movie or a video. Perhaps it was because of the way my mother seemed to accept what was happening to her, not once crying out, or even trying to fight. It was as if she wanted to die. I glanced up at my father, his face was a mask of utter misery, and yet he still refused to let me go.

The demon continued to tighten its grip, squeezing until the sound of snapping bones filled the putrid air. Finally, the tendril unwrapped, and my mother dropped to the ground.

"Why didn't–," I began, but my voice was overpowered by a thunderous crash.

The ground began to shake. A flare burst from my mother's broken body, consuming her like a threatening supernova. It hovered for only a moment and then shot toward the demon, slicing into the spinning cloud, exploding throughout its ethereal body.

"She was right," my father said.

From the demon came a scream, filled with both pain and fear.

This new attacker had been a surprise, an uncalculated enemy that could tip the scales: A non-Native American, fueled not by the history of her ancestors, or revenge, but by her love for us.   This feeling was as alien to it as was the act of giving. And it was for this reason that the demon's terror grew.

The swirling cloud was now spinning faster, reminding me of a tornado ripping through a field, twisting closer and closer to where the burning chasm waited. It reached the opening and then stopped, the brilliant light within it fading. Another flash, like a giant match being struck, erupted causing the demon to slide to within inches of the fire. But it would not go.

Even now, with all of the sacrifices that had been made, the demon refused to fall. My fathers grip had weakened, allowing me to break free. I leapt to my feet, my eyes darting around in panic. I brushed away the welling tears and then saw it. It lay near where my mother had fallen. A Wyoming arrow.

"What are you doing?" said my father.

I ignored his question and raced for the bow, grabbing it mid-stride, I then leapt into the wheel. The spinning demon continued to hover just outside of the cavern.

"Hold on," I cried out, hoping for anyone to hear.

I ran for the arrow, sliding on my knees the last couple of feet. The base of the demon kicked out at me with a thin tendril, spraying dirt and pebbles over my face. I brushed them away and notched the arrow, drawing it back. I let the shaft go. It was like watching its flight in slow motion; I could see the rippling waves of the slender wood, and could see the fletching bending back as it covered the distance. The arrow disappeared into the column of mist without making a sound, leaving only a small rip in the ethereal skin.

Another rumble rattled the ground. A mournful cry, like a ghost trapped in hell, split the air. The demon was beginning to expand, the light within it swirling with the shadow, creating a hideous candy cane look. I felt myself being dragged back.

"We have to get out of here," said my father, his hands clutching my shirt.

For some reason I tried to resist. Perhaps it was because he was forcing me to flee from a fight that was not over, or maybe it was because he had done nothing while my mother was being murdered. I only knew that at that moment, I hated him. He managed to pull me out of the wheel, before tripping and falling to the ground. Together, we sat watching as the demon continued to grow larger, becoming like a giant shadowy balloon, expanding the diameter of the wheel.

The balloon collapsed, like a dying star, until only a small ball of light remained, hovering just a few feet away from the burning cave. It was them, I was sure of it. It was the alliance of my friends and my mother along with all of those who had become the victim of the demon. They had won. We had won, and now the evil was trapped, imprisoned by the spherical glow. The chasm began belching out tongues of fire. The glowing ball began to move, dancing its way to the cottonwood's opening, the flames licking its surface. I didn't want to be there, didn't want to see the end of them all, but I couldn't turn away. The sphere bolted into the chasm, creating blinding flashes that burst with odors of rot. Screams lit up the wheel, piercing through the dancing inferno and kaleidoscope light. A sudden explosion sent waves of dirt and rocks out from the wheel's center, forcing my father and I to cover our faces. Then there was silence. I lowered my hands and saw only darkness. The chasm within the tree sat like an ancient cave, its hollow opening now a void, black and cold. It had become a tomb.

"They're gone," I said, but was unsure if I had actually spoken.

A sob to my right confirmed that my father had heard me. My mother, Devon, Linda, and the child that she was carrying, were lost to us. I rose from the ground, my eyes locked on the gaping hole within the cottonwood. I stepped into the wheel, wanting to scream, wanting to curse the bastard Loshi for what he had done. To throttle the Spaniard and the evil that he had become, but they, too, were gone.

"Please," I said. "Let them come back."

I continued to gaze into the chasm, hoping that whatever door that had locked them away would again open. Time seemed to have become obsolete and the darkness became deeper, until even the cave became lost in a midnight shroud.

"Danny," said my father. "We should go."

He was standing at the edge of the wheel, not daring to take another step. For him, the wheel had offered nothing but lies and murder; had tricked him with a gift and then took it back. Yes, he had seen enough.

"Not yet," I pleaded, wiping my face.

"They're gone," he said.

I began to turn back, when something appeared. It was faint at first, so much so, that at first I thought that my mind had created it. But it continued to linger, becoming brighter.

"Do you see it?" I said.

"Danny, we really need..." began my father, but then he fell silent.

"I do see it," he said, finally.

The chasm burst with light, and not the fiery hell from before, but with a silver radiance, like a harvest moon. It swirled for a moment, becoming brighter, and then two beams shot out from the chasm, coming to a stop above Devon and Linda. They puddled there, floating above their lifeless bodies, before falling like water from a cliff.

Linda let out a gasp, which was soon followed by a moan from Devon. I stifled a cry and rushed over to them, unable to stop myself from embracing them both.

"Easy, now," said Devon, struggling to sit up. "You're taken."

"It never stops with that one," said Linda, her lips curving into a smile.

I planted a kiss upon her mouth. She returned one in kind, and then I lightly pushed her back.

"Are you okay?" I said.

Linda squeezed my hand and placed her head against my chest.

"I am now."

We sat there for a moment, neither of us daring to speak. Finally, Devon was helped to his feet by my father and I lifted myself from the ground with Linda's hand firmly clutched in mine and together we gazed into the coal-colored remains of the battlefield.

"We should go," said my father.

We turned away from the wheel and stumbled to the path. The wall of brambles was gone, collapsing back into nothingness, much like those who had chosen to fight. My mother had been one of those, and it was only after we began our journey back to the hut did I realize the true sacrifice that she had made. How I would have given anything for one last chance to apologize for ever doubting her. She had become a leader for the leaderless and had chosen her love for family over a life of her own.

We cleared the woods, and finished the last few yards to the hut in silence. We arrived at the opening when Devon stopped.

"We can still walk," he said.

For a moment I didn't understand, but then it hit me. It had been possible that neither he nor Linda would maintain their gift after the battle was over. They could have been left paralyzed within the very structure that had saved them.

"They won," said Linda. "And they did it for us."

"Yes," said my father, looking over at the charred remains of what he had done. "And now we need to figure out what we're going to do."

My father would carry most of the load; confirming that Ms. Lighthorse had gone with Linda to Wyoming, but had not returned. A missing person's report would be filed, but they would never be found and eventually presumed dead.

Linda would have to stay in the hut, but she wouldn't be alone. There was only a couple of weeks left until graduation, and I would commute the drive until the handing out of my diploma. My father had made his own plans. They were based on the anger that he would forever harbor towards the demon that had ruined his life.

CHAPTER FORTY-FIVE

Magic

There is magic within these mountains. For most, it remains unnoticed, or misconstrued as some kind of mysterious breeze; an unexplainable chill. But for us, it is like the air that we breathe; it provides an energy that sustains.

Four months after the war, my father left the Blanchard Police Department, landing a job with the Oklahoma Park Rangers, his jurisdiction being Comanche County; home of the Medicine Wheel. He had become obsessed with watching over the place that had taken my mother, sometimes going as far as camping just beyond its outer ring. I think that he still hoped she might return; that the cave would again open at the cottonwood's base and that she would be there. I didn't think it would happen; she had agreed to become a sentry on her final day, and would forever remain on guard. But I could be wrong.

Devon graduated and then traveled east, much like Ms. Lighthorse had done. He had clawed his way to a degree in teaching, specializing in special education. He then returned to Blanchard and took over the program. And through all of this, Kelly Sheer excitedly waited. She was even more excited when Devon brought her up to the mountains for the first time and rose from his chair. I didn't think she would ever shut up. But they are happy, and Kelly can keep a secret. They were soon married and they are now expecting their first child. But the trips with the kids from school have stopped, at least for now. Maybe that's for the best. What good is freedom when it only comes with confinement?

Because of Linda's heritage, we were allowed to stay on the land where the huts had been. They're all gone except for one. Beside it sits a two-bedroom house. It's not much, but it is big enough for our family. Linda insisted we name our daughter Gina Lighthorse Lee; the reason is obvious.

For me, there was never a need for college. My future had been chiseled the moment that Linda had led me into the wheel, so I followed in my father's footsteps and became a ranger.

I didn't take the job out of fear or anger, just the opposite, really. The wheel had never been the enemy; it was just another victim in a long line of horrific sorrow. And yet, its strength remains, willing to help those who need it most. Many nights I have sat out on the front porch enraptured by its power, with my daughter sitting on my lap, and on some of those occasions, when I look down at her innocent face, I can sometimes see the slightest streak of silver deep within her emerald eyes.

Yes, there is magic within these mountains.

www.ingramcontent.com/pod-product-compliance
Lightning Source LLC
Chambersburg PA
CBHW061228210726
48293CB00003B/699